QUEEN OF MADNESS

THE WICKED WONDERLAND SERIES
LEE JACQUOT

This is a work of fiction. Names, characters, businesses, places, and incidents, as well as resemblance to actual persons, living or dead, is purely coincidental.

Copyright © 2021 by Lee Jacquot

All rights reserved.

No part of this book may be reproduced in any form or by any electronic or mechanical means, including information storage and retrieval systems, without written permission from the author, except for the use of brief quotations in a book review.

Cover Design: Cat at TRC Designs by Cat

Editing & Proofreading: Ellie & Rosa at My Brother's Editor

McKenzie Letson at NiceGirlNaughtyEdits

A Note From The Author

Queen of Madness is the first in the Wicked Wonderland Duet. It will need to be read in its entirety in order to read book two.

This is a dark romance steamy read intended for mature audiences of legal adulthood age.

While it is **NOT** a retelling of Alice in Wonderland, I hope you enjoy the many Easter eggs, and nods to the original story.

The author is not liable for any attachments formed to the MCs or the utter heartbreak one may receive from the cliffhanger.

Reader discretion is advised.

Tasha

What you do for the book community is unparalleled. You are the light, the support and an advocate to both authors and readers.

We see you. We love you. We thank you.

This one is for you.

Onyx
AGE 7
PROLOGUE

"'And who are these?' the Queen of Hearts asked. When she looked at the gardeners and her unfinished roses, her face became red and angry. 'Off with their heads!'" my mother whisper-shouts her best impression of the queen, pointing at the angry puff of a woman on the pages.

The character's mouth is nearly the size of her head, open big and wide, and I vaguely wonder if a bird could fly right in and stoop on her bottom lip.

My mother jabs a playful finger into my side and a surprised squeal mixed with a horrible squawk erupts from my mouth. The pterodactyl sound sends both of us into a fit of laughter, our bodies shaking my white iron bed frame.

As our giggles finally wane, I sigh and look at the toughie woman. "Why is she so angry, Mama? Why not just ask them to fix their mistake."

Her beautiful wide smile fades and I instantly regret making it disappear, letting darkness take over her light. My mama's brows pinch together, and I fight the urge to rub away the deep line running through the middle.

I didn't mean to upset her. But before I can tell her I'm sorry, she shakes her head.

"Sometimes mistakes cannot be rectified, my sweet girl." Her thick patois accent is stronger now as she leaves her bedtime story voice behind. "Sometimes people must pay for them with their lives. That's why we must be diligent in even the smallest of our choices. We must take into account all the ways in which our decisions affect other people and weigh them with care."

I nod, my small mind soaking in her every word. But as I ponder over her explanation, I find myself with more questions as to why the queen was so cruel. "But they only planted the wrong flower."

My mother thinks this over, her soft brown skin glowing under the dim light of my bedside table. "Perhaps she overreacted. But what if those bushes were planted from mere seeds? What if she had to wait years and pay money for them to be tended to and fertilized. Then, finally, as spring comes and the flowers she's waited on for years begin to blossom, they aren't what she wanted. You must agree, she is due some type of penance."

"But to pay with their heads?"

"To each their own. I would assume the gardeners knew the type of woman they chose to work for. They should have known what to expect should they make such a grave mistake."

"Like the people that work for Daddy?"

My mother nods, a small grin curving her lips. "Yes, sweet girl."

I chew into my own little lip, thinking over everything as best I can. For a seven—almost eight—year old, I know more than I have room for. I already speak four languages, one of which is American Sign Language. I'm well versed in what death is and take weekly classes on how to avoid it. At least, that's what it feels like. Mom calls it Krav Maga and brags about my orange belt to her friends during their tea parties. But even with all those things, I can't understand the anger of grown-ups. There are too many things to be happy about.

Fresh chocolate chip cookies.

Coloring with a fresh box of crayons.

Eating cereal with Daddy while watching *Scooby-Doo*.

Or having dance parties with Mama in the middle of the day.

There are so many to choose from to bring the smiles out, yet adults nearly always wear angry scowls and raise their voices when they don't get what they want. Perhaps they all just need a nap. That's what Mama makes me do when I'm upset. It always works.

Lost in thought, I only barely hear the snap of the book in time to see my mother jump, wriggling her fingers into my side with full force. My laughter erupts in the air, the sound bouncing around the walls and wrapping us in a cocoon of happiness, the Queen of Hearts long forgotten.

"Jada." My father's voice cuts through our giggles, soothing them to placid smiles. "Don't keep her up so late tonight. Her tutor says she nearly fell asleep during math."

"It's not Mother's fault he's boring." I let my eyebrows scrunch up as he moves from my door and into my room.

He's still dressed in a suit, the dark fabric sticking close to his body as if made just for him. I once heard him say it means it's tailored, but whatever that means, he looks like the prince out of my fairy tales. He even has the dark inky hair and near-black eyes to match.

Oh, maybe I meant the villain.

But when he smiles, the one he saves for only me and Mama, his face goes through a magical transformation. Those same eyes twinkle as the corners crease, and his body shakes like Santa Claus.

"Math is not boring, baby love. It's fundamental. You must learn it if you plan to take over my money one day."

My heart swells with pride at the unspoken promise. I'd lost a tutor this past winter when she told me I shouldn't work for my father. She'd said he was a bad man and I was too smart to fall into his evil grasp. She said I would end up dead.

I never saw her again.

But I can't say I ever wanted to after hearing her say such a mean thing. I love my father no matter what the rest of the world thinks of him. I love him *despite* it. I see what they don't, and really, I think he's the best there is, even if he does kill a few people. They're bad people anyway.

In fact, I want to be just like him.

I smile, grabbing my father around his neck. The little hairs on his chin scratch my face but I still kiss through them, ignoring the sharp twinge of discomfort. "Alright, Daddy."

"That's my girl. Now get some rest, and we'll see you for breakfast."

With that, my mother kisses my head and pulls up my blanket, tucking in a fluffy white rabbit next to me. "Good night, sweet girl."

After they close my door, I reach for the discarded book on my nightstand. It isn't until the third time I reread the book that I start to think more about the angry queen.

Why is she so mad?

Or maybe I should wonder not why but what *happened* to turn her into the cruel Queen of Hearts that a nap couldn't fix.

EZEKIEL

CHAPTER ONE

Why can't I be lying on the beach off the island of Tahiti, drinking myself into a light coma? I want to feel the annoyingly hot sand digging between my toes, the cool breeze circling around me as I sip a Jack and Coke, watching the waves crash onto the shore. I'd like to fall asleep there. Preferably with my eyes *completely* shut and without a care in the world.

But I guess I really pissed someone off in my past life.

Maybe that isn't the word I'm looking for. Pissed is too merciful of a word for the retribution I'm now paying for those mistakes, and it seems as if the debt will never be paid.

Unless I move my hips an inch forward.

Leaning over, I peer past my dangling boots, down the thirty panes of reflective glass, and at the row of busy people skittering below. All of them are going about their lives completely ignorant to the fact that a man is a sneeze away from ruining their Saturday afternoon.

"Zeke. You know I'm all for living on the edge, but you're beginning to take it too literally."

Blowing out a deep sigh, I glance at one of the two reasons I'd never pay my karmic bill before it's due.

Fiona Kane. One half of my heart. The nineteen-year-old

street artist who has a heart bigger than her head and is far too good for this damn city.

Shadows tint the thin flesh under my kid sister's wide hazel eyes as they scan over my frame, waiting for me to lean back into a safer position. Her dark curls are pulled up in a loose bun, swaying softly with the cool Seattle breeze and I wonder the last time she's gotten more than a few hours of sleep.

It's always the ones with the biggest hearts that worry the most.

And above all else, my sister worries. Hell, if she could figure out a way to profit from it, we'd be loaded, and I wouldn't have to put her in the positions that cause her so much stress.

I grin as I grant her mercy and oblige, shifting my body away from the edge and turning to face her. "What are we doing up here, Fi?"

Her delicate face drops, her telltale sign she got herself into some trouble because of that muscle beating away behind her ribs. It reminds me of the time she managed to sweet-talk me into causing a distraction after a Petco worker bagged her up some saltwater fish and she ran out of the store, delivering them to the nearest port. She dropped them in and waved goodbye, the biggest fucking smile on her face.

Then there was the one time I found her digging in the school's dumpsters after hours, and I had to talk the custodian out of turning her in. Turns out she was getting scraps to feed some puppies that stayed in the alley behind our house every night. I mean, the list goes on with this girl.

Like I said, too good.

"I really messed up, Zeke." Fiona captures my attention as she tries to run a delicate hand through her hair until she realizes it's tied up and sighs, dropping it into her lap.

"Yeah, I figured as much. Tell me and I'll fix it."

It's a recurring thing between us—me cleaning up any trouble she might cause. It's always worth the hassle, though. Almost as if I'm paying a little interest on what I owe to the universe.

She wrings her hands together, her knuckles changing between white and red with her fluctuating force. "Do you remember last week when we went for ice cream? Then you left to grab something from the corner store?"

I nod.

"There... there was this sketchy van at the stop sign."

I remember the creepy van parked a few yards up. It was a Tuesday, and the street was pretty empty considering the time. I'd left her for two minutes so I could grab a bottle of Tylenol for our mom.

What trouble could she have gotten into in two minutes?

"I walked by the van, kinda running an inside joke in my head that it was a kidnapper's. But then—" Her voice cracks and tears spring to her eyes, but when I reach out for her, she shakes her head almost too fast.

Through all the things we've been through, she's never done anything she's felt guilty for or scared of. Mostly because... because they've never affected us. Not in a way that matters, at least. My heart sinks, a viscous realization taking hold.

Fiona's mouth opens but I have to strain to hear her words. "There were women inside, Zeke, and I—"

"Let them out."

A new voice has me up and in front of my sister before I can take my next breath. My eyes narrow, finding the source in a second, and my muscles tense beneath my black Henley.

Leaning in the threshold of the roof exit is a man, half hidden in the long shadows of the setting sun, his head tilted as if he's relaxed. Of course, he's relaxed. Any man eavesdropping on the roof of a thirty-story building has a reason to be at ease, and my guess is, he's the problem I'll have to fix.

He kicks off the exit and stalks toward us, a lazy smirk on his face. He's bald, round and tall, but not quite level with my six-foot-three. He shoves both hands in his pockets as he stops a few yards in front of me, rocking on the balls of his feet. "Ezekiel Kane. Twenty-five years old, graduated high school with a three-point-eight GPA. Something of a tech genius according to your professors at the community college you attended for a couple years, yet you work under-the-table jobs for quick cash. Mostly doing things that involve being the muscle."

I bare my teeth as I scan over the man again, noting the designer watch on his left wrist, and a faint scar that stretches from his right temple and disappears into his days' old stubble. He's a big boy, but I know I'd be able to toss him over the ledge, ruining those poor people's day after all.

Before I can respond, though, he chuckles, glancing past me briefly at the edge of the building as if he can read my thoughts. "Size fourteen shoe, blood type O negative, and currently residing at 3512 Westport Lane with your mother."

"What do you want?" I bite, done with whatever point he's trying to make.

"A few million dollars if you have it. But last I checked, there's only a couple thousand in your account, and you'll need that to pay for your mom's medicine."

As if I can afford it. I clench my teeth, listening to the faint crack of my molar. The pain surges across my jaw, but I keep my expression hard in warning. "I get it. You know a lot about me. You should tell me a little bit about yourself before I throw your ass over the top of this building."

His smirk grows, pissing me off more. I run my tongue over

my teeth and take a step forward, but a soft hand tugs at my pinkie, effectively stopping me.

"You're a smart kid. I'm sure you've put enough pieces together by now to know it wouldn't be in your best interest. Your mom would be dead before my body was cold."

The threat acts as ice water surging through my veins, forcing me to plant my feet into the ground. I swallow roughly, opening and closing my fists. "Your point. Find it."

The man sighs as if threatening my mother's life is boring to him. "The name's Sam. I work for the Murphy family. Your sweet sister here let loose some of our merchandise, and to be frank, she owes us a nice thirteen million."

Murphy family.

Merchandise.

Thirteen million.

What I wouldn't give to take her ass to Petco to steal more fish.

"But as luck would have it, the big man is willing to forgive and forget."

Without having even processed the first bit of information, the second takes me a full minute to digest. First up, it's no secret who the Murphy family is—they own a third of west Washington. It's common knowledge they deal with pretty much everything a typical Irish Mafia would, including women, which Sam here referred to as fucking *merchandise*.

My tooth sends another shot of pain ricocheting through my jaw, forcing me to unclench it. He knows I don't have money, and I'm willing to bet my mom's meds, he's not letting us walk out of here scot-free. But instead of playing into his game and asking, I wait.

Sam checks his watch and I see the moment he loses interest in keeping us in the dark. "Unless you want your sister on our payroll, or your mom in a casket, we need you to come work for us."

A small gasp makes me tighten my hand around Fi's. I want to turn around and reassure her, but I decide taking my eyes off this sleaze bag for even one second isn't a good idea. "And do what?"

He sighs, removing a small handkerchief from his pocket and dabs his shining head. "By working for Onyx Embros."

Onyx Embros. She's nothing more than a ghost, an urban legend, but her trail of dead bodies is proof enough she's alive. She's head of the opposing family that owns the other third of Washington, and no one even knows what she looks like. No one that's alive anyway.

Why the fuck does he want me to work for the opposing family?

My gaze flashes to my sister, whose eyes are wide and red with fresh tears. She didn't deserve the life she was born into. Not the poverty, the glass ceiling, nor the brother who can't get her away from this fucked-up city. I've watched her fire burn through even the darkest of times, her light being the only thing that got us to the other side.

But now, she looks extinguished—a silent beg working through her hazel orbs telling me to find another way. It's because she knows as well as I do that working for Onyx Embros is equivalent to signing my death certificate.

That knowledge doesn't stop me from giving her a small lopsided grin, though. The same one I give her every time she pulls one of her stunts and I have to step in to fix any trouble she may have caused.

My chest aches as she presses her forehead into my shoulder, a sob working through her body. No matter what happens, I'm getting my heart out of this fucked-up place, even if it means my death.

I turn back to Sam, who has a smug smirk curling what little lips he has. For a moment, I entertain the idea of how easy it would be to snap his neck and toss him over anyway.

But the thought passes the more Fiona presses into me, so I give him the answer he's waiting on. "Okay."

EZEKIEL

CHAPTER TWO

Isn't it funny how at first glance, something can appear so charming, so perfect, you take it for face value and trust it for everything it shows you? But as time moves forward, you get a feeling you can't ignore and find yourself brave enough to look closer—just a little deeper. It's then you see the vile, hideous truth just beneath the surface.

That's Sherwood Valley.

To the passersby, we are the gorgeous, picturesque city next to Seattle, full of authentic shops, hidden neighborhoods inside lush forests, and abundant with nature's beauty. Most of my childhood was spent skipping rocks across lakes, chasing after Fi along the side of creeks, and climbing trees with friends until we were too weak to hold on to the limbs.

All the other shit going on in our lives didn't matter when we were out there—only the fresh air riddled with moss, and the stars giving us the light we needed to make it home. Time seemed as if it was slow between the trees. It was almost as though it didn't want to move too fast and force us to grow up, knowing its forests would be void of our laughter.

And for some time, I'd almost go so far as to say things *were* perfect, but when the inevitable happened, I got older, and it became clearer to see what had been blurred in my youthful innocence.

In the center of our paradise was a thick black line, separating ownership of the entire west bank of Washington, continuing its trek right through the middle of our city. And without the veil covering my eyes, it became easier to see when I crossed into either side's territory.

Hell, it would be to anyone who examined us further than face value. But too many people are content with their ignorant bliss, and the local news only polishes our existence by leaving out the brutal reports of murder done by both sides. I assume since citizens never get caught in the mix, they find it unimportant to tell people about the secret blood war taking place throughout the city.

A war that was started from the infamous Onyx Embros not wanting the Murphy's trafficking women. Rumors say she had her people stop any vans that crossed into her region on the way to the ports, and had the drivers butchered in the street. Then the Murphy's coerced new recruits, some as young as high school, to work for them and find ways to sneak girls across.

The whole thing was and is fucked up, but all I had time to worry about was keeping Fiona safe and away from any Murphy fucker.

Looks like I did a bang-up job...

Anger swells in my gut as my thoughts steer toward my mother—another woman I was meant to protect and failed miserably. Now, she's nothing but a shell of her former self thanks to these fucking *families* who decided it was okay to ruin her to make a quick buck.

I couldn't save my mother; I won't make the same mistake with Fi.

I check the car dash for the time as I listen to the GPS

guide me to the bar. I'm doing my best to focus on something other than my deep-set disgust with the fact I'm about to be working for the Murphy family, but the conversation from the roof steeps in my head.

"*So, I'll be working as one of Onyx's bodyguards and reporting back to you with information?*" My mind soaks in everything Sam just told me.

He wasn't lying when he said my sister and I had gotten lucky. Fiona's good deed put our lives in the hands of the Murphy's as soon as she let their shipment of women walk free. But Sam says our only saving grace was the fact I'm "Onyx's type." Whatever the fuck that means. Combine that information with the miracle of not having any priors, and no affiliation to either side, I'm to become a double agent of sorts—working in Embros' territory while giving Onyx's every secret to the Murphys.

No matter how this shit ends, I'm a dead man. I just need to stay alive long enough to make sure my family gets released from the Murphy's clutches.

"*So you want me to just walk into a bar, find a manic looking redhead and ask to work for Onyx? What the fuck kind of a plan is that?*" I throw up my hands. "*I'd be dead the second I said hello.*"

Sam wipes his forehead with the handkerchief I want to choke him with. It'd be so fucking easy. "Well, no shit. You're just going to go to the damn bar, order a drink, and wait."

The light turns green, prompting me to turn my beat-up Chevy on a street that opens into the Embros' territory. Along the main strip are bars, restaurants, sports clubs and other nightlife, all bustling with Saturday night business. Scattered among the people barhopping are bodyguards outside each door. Nothing outside of the ordinary, except the small red heart on the left cuff of their suits.

"The dumbasses are so proud of their affiliation with Embros, they wear a literal heart on their sleeves. Makes them so fucking easy to target and kill." He mutters the last part more to himself than to me before clearing his throat. "Now, just remember, no one is going to know you. You're just another guy. You act like it, and no one will be the wiser. You start looking skittish and shit, they'll know something's up," Sam reiterates for the third time for me to just act cool. The more he spouts off, the more I'm coming to realize he's more nervous than me. Almost as if he's depending on this.

"In twenty feet, your destination is on the right." The feminine robotic voice directs me straight to the bar. It's a corner spot, tucked behind tall, skinny trees lining the sidewalk. The deep red brick runs along either side of the massive black doors, with two massive knockers in the middle.

There're no windows, no line to get inside, and the only streetlight right outside is flickering. Strange, considering the whole strip is upscale, and is illuminated under not only the lamps but string lights that run across both sides of the street.

Since the moment I met Sam, till I left the roof, never once was I afraid or had nerves find me. But now, as Rabbit Hole Bar draws closer, reality sets in.

I can't fuck this up. If I do, it's not just me who pays the price. A grim type of seriousness weighs heavy on my shoulders, ripping the delicate edges of my calm exterior. My knuckles bloom white as I grip the steering wheel, pulling into the parking garage behind the building.

When I get out of my car, the door leaves my slick hands too quickly, and the resounding slam echoes through the stillness. My steps are cumbersome, almost as if they're stilted by the consequences of failure.

Each few feet I tread takes longer than it should, and by the time I reach the entrance, no air I pull in is enough.

I picture my sister fawning over the puppies in the alley, her wide hazel eyes full of that hope she's always carrying. She only saw the good deed, the happiness in the little tails wagging as they consumed their dinner. Her light is all that matters now, and I use it to force my final steps toward the door.

After a deep breath, I'm able to clutch one of the cold metal handles and pull open the black door.

Down the rabbit hole I go.

Maddy
CHAPTER THREE

"Hmmmm, I like this, Shi. It's like a sweet apple but with poison. That bite at the end tells you you'll die before you finish, but it's so good you just can't help yourself!"

My raven-haired companion blinks slowly, grinning wide as she circles her finger around her martini glass. "What an idiotic way to die."

I roll my eyes as she draws her words out slowly, popping a hand on my hip. "You're no fun, no fun at all. What better way to go than sipping on something delicious and feeling a little mad in the head?"

She doesn't hesitate. "From an orgasm so strong my heart stops."

I can't argue with that. In fact, I'd give anything to find an iota of what she's found in the twins she falls under every night. How they're able to love so fiercely and unapologetically is something I can only dream of.

Which reminds me...

Another look around the bar, and I come up just as empty as I did the first time. Not a single man, or woman, is calling to my soul tonight, which means I'll leave with second best—and definitely won't get a heart-stopping orgasm.

It's becoming a drag to come here every week.

I'm always hopeful and am always disappointed—a vicious cycle of cat, no mouse.

Out of all the places on this strip, though, the Rabbit Hole is my favorite. The people here are older, local, and every one of them knows this entire place belongs to the Embros family, which usually means they know who I am. There's none of the awkward introductions or having to tell them I run narcotics for the largest supplier on the West Coast.

It also means there's no confusion on whether or not I'll kill them if I find out they have any involvement with the scum across the way. No Murphys allowed on this side of the city, and damn sure nowhere near this bar.

I flop down on my stool and drum my fingers on the edge of the counter. Even though it doesn't seem like I'll get the pleasure of taking anyone home, being with Shi outside of the estate is nice. She's always laid back and calm—the total opposite of me—but when we're here, she's funnier, and not so fucking cryptic.

Shi bats a thick lock of hair over her shoulder, revealing the pink-and-purple strands hidden beneath all the black. "The look of defeat on your face is heartbreaking, Maddy. Would you like to call it a night? The boys and I can keep you warm tonight if you wish."

I sigh before taking back the rest of my appletini. "Thanks, but you know I'm in search of my own all-consuming love. There are a couple men I need to kill tomorrow, and I assume I'll need rest. You know how Boss doesn't like for me to be too jittery when I'm working."

"You mean, high out of your mind?" Shi's words come out so dang slowly, I feel a dribble of drool pool on the edge of my lips.

Waving her away, I motion for the cute waitress. "Tomato, tomáto."

The girl walks over briskly, and when she stops and beams down at me, I find myself lost in her chocolate depths. They are smooth, and layered in various shades, like the center of a tree, and I wonder how I didn't notice it before.

"Can I get you ladies anything else?" Her voice is sugar sweet, dripping with something I'd love to lick up.

What was I going to ask her?

"I—y-you." I swallow in a gulp of air and re-form my statement. "You are breathtaking, my dear. What is your name? Wait, let me guess!" I shake my head, leaning back so I can soak her in.

Her long coffee-colored hair lies in waves down her curvy frame, a cute black sparkly headband pulling it away from her face. Her skin is so flawless and pale, I can do nothing but picture her twirling beneath my silk sheets.

"It begins with the letter M," I declare, perking up at the way a smile slides across her pink lips. "Melony? Margaret? Molly?"

"Harlow, Harly to my friends."

"Harlow," I repeat, loving the way it tastes on my tongue and wondering what it would take for her to consider *me* a friend.

My eyes track the slow blush creeping up her neck.

Such a responsive little thing.

"When? No. I mean, how long have you worked for the Hole?" My own flesh begins warming at my cheeks. Normally, when I flounder, it's because of my wandering thoughts, and not being able to grasp one, but right now, it feels as though I have none at all.

"Just last week, actually." Harlow runs a hand along her arm, unsuccessfully taming the goose bumps decorating them.

Her voice is so delicate, I can't help but wonder if her skin is as delicate.

Catching her soft hand in mine, a spark lights up my fingertips, but when I open my mouth to tell her just how luxurious she feels, a new visitor entering the bar in the door directly behind her steals my attention. At the same moment, Shi chuckles from across the table. "Duty calls."

I drop the girl's hand, an apologetic smile tilting my mouth. "The bill please, Harlow."

Her shoulders drop slightly, but she does well to keep her face customer friendly. "Of course, be right back."

"Leave your number on the tip receipt." Shi smirks.

Though partially reluctant, I nod before focusing on what distracted me in the first place. He's well over six feet, suntanned skin, a strip of black ink creeping onto his neck from under a tight ass long-sleeve shirt, and muscles I could hang from. He's not too big, though. He could definitely still scratch his back without the bulk stopping him, but he's stacked with just enough mass, my mouth waters. His jaw is sharp lines and perfectly structured, leaving me to wonder how the fuck I've never seen him before.

No way we'd get this lucky with a tourist wandering inside this bar.

He takes a heavy step toward the bar, his dark brown boots slamming into the wood floor beneath him. I note how his dark-green eyes flicker around, almost as if he's searching for someone. That makes more sense.

Shi purrs beside me. "He's perfect."

I nod again, running my tongue along my top lip. He is, quite literally, everything that embodies what Onyx prefers in her guards. Well, not the regular kind, but her personal ones, the ones that she calls in the middle of the night. "If he's meeting someone here, we should get to him first."

"Agreed," Shi murmurs, before her lazy gaze slides to me.

"How do I look?" I purse my lips, fluffing up my wild curls. My torn AC/DC shirt slouching off my shoulders hides my breasts, but I have a strange inkling tickling my ear that I won't need to seduce him. No...

There's something different about this one. He's got a darkness slithering around him, waiting for the opportunity to claim him, and I can tell he's becoming tired of keeping it at bay.

Curious.

"Go on. Before you lose him."

"When have I ever—you know what? Don't answer that." I hop up and elaborately sashay toward the bar, flopping down next to him. I somehow manage to bump into the person on the other side of me who silently curses at his now spilled drink. Silly me.

Somehow, over the scent of liquor and stale peanuts, I catch a whiff of his cedar scent. It's as if he's bottled up a piece of the woods with a slice of the sun and put it in his aftershave.

I perch one elbow on the bar top, wincing when it makes contact with the sticky surface. He doesn't turn his head, but his eyes flash in my direction and I see the flecks of gold hidden inside his dark-jade eyes. It's as if spotting treasure in the depths of Lago di Carezza.

Oh, she's going to like this one. "Why is a raven like a writing desk?"

The corners of his lips twitch, but he doesn't commit to the grin playing there and instead keeps his gaze trained at the bartender. Still, he entertains me. "Why?"

His voice is rugged, almost as if he has a frog in his throat, but when he thanks the bartender for his drink, I realize it's natural. I wonder vaguely if he's a growler.

"You wouldn't happen to be waiting on someone, would you?"

21

He sighs heavily through his nose, his shoulders dropping an inch before he takes a quick sip of his drink. "I was supposed to. Ran a little late, and I guess she didn't want to wait."

She. *Hmm.*

I push the stray hair from my shoulder, twirling to put my back at the bar. "Well, it's rude to keep a woman waiting, don't you know?"

From my periphery, I see him down the rest of his drink. "Don't I. But I had an interview. It took a little longer than I thought."

"An interview for what? Construction?" I twirl around, giving his outfit a once-over as if it's the first time I've noticed it.

Up close, it's easy to see the black ink peeking from the top of his Henley. It's something of the leaf variety, perhaps a part of a tree. The muscles I saw from my end of the bar are much more defined than I initially thought, and his jaw is much sharper. The darkness is easier to see too. It creeps around the edges of his eyes, taking whatever softness was once there and turning them hard, impenetrable even.

He runs a hand through his thick dark hair. "Nah. Just some bouncer gig."

How perfect. "Ah. Well, did you at least get the job?"

The stranger grins, lifting his empty glass toward the bartender. "They said the girls working inside might become too distracted."

My mind takes only a few seconds to catch on before my lips form a perfect O in understanding. A strip club.

A mischievous smile takes over my face as I send a quiet thanks to whoever wove my web of fate for the night. "I may have something you're interested in, if you're still looking."

He arches a dark brow, taking a tentative sip of his new drink. "Oh yeah?"

My smile grows, but I let my voice take on a more serious edge. "Sure do. My friend is looking for a... bodyguard."

With the recent tension rising with the scum across the way, our guys are getting harder and harder to keep alive. More so, the ones that worked on the estate. Those fuckers are difficult to find, and after being vetted and trained for months on end, it was a pain in the ass for the twins to replace them. After the fourth one, Onyx made them move into the estate and upped the security all the way to the edge of the property line.

After a little digging, we found out they were somehow being watched as they left to go home and some of them made the mistake of letting their guard down when they crossed over territory lines. We still can't figure how someone is watching our every move without us knowing, and it churns my stomach into horrific knots. The knowledge I'm not completely in control of protecting the woman who saved us all eats at my conscience when I let it, reminding me how much I owe her. How I need to do more to protect her so she can save others.

"I'm not sure if I should be intrigued or intimidated, but that wide, far-off gaze of yours tells me the latter."

His rough voice pulls me from the brink, and I shake my head to rid it of the lingering worries. "Accurate assumption. But the money's good and the woman of the house will more than likely add a little extra for any after-hours extracurriculars."

No point in lying. Onyx has a type, and our guy here checks all the boxes. She'll probably fuck him before his background check comes through. "What's your name?"

"Ezekiel Kane."

"Hmmm. I like Z better. So what do you say?" I tug a bill from the side of my boot and drop it on the bar to pay his bill.

His dark eyes track the movement before snapping to me as I hop off the stool. "I didn't get your name."

"You didn't ask."

Z smirks, a dimple I hadn't noticed popping on his left cheek. "What's your name?"

Shi slides up beside me, handing me a folded piece of paper. I look down briefly, my heart fluttering in my chest when I see the curl of a y and a heart sticking out. Harlow's number. When I return my focus to Z, he's up, his hands in his pockets as he watches us.

"Madeline. But you can call me Maddy. And I think I can get you in for an interview, if you're interested." Shi hands me a card, which I flip through my fingers twice before holding it out for him.

It's a tattered queen of hearts card, just the remnants of the queen's face still visible under the thick black Sharpie with my contact information.

Z takes it and examines it briefly before I see the moment recognition flashes in his green orbs. His pupils dilate slightly, and his shoulders lift inward, but a second later, he schools himself and stands up straight. He looks back at the fifty-dollar bill I left on a twenty-dollar tab and nods. "Thank you. Can I take a couple days to think about it?"

"Of course." I run my tongue along my bottom lip, my eyes flashing to a fan of brown hair at the corner of the bar. My heart thumps at the same time my cunt squeezes as I watch Harlow take a tray of drinks away from the counter.

"Thanks again, I'll be talking to you soon."

I let my gaze travel back to Z, my smile widening. "Splendid."

EZEKIEL

CHAPTER FOUR

A lot can happen in forty-eight hours.

The annoying to the unthinkable. The triumphant to life changing. All of it can go from nothing to tragic in the blink of an eye.

One wrong decision.

One bad choice.

Even the smallest of catalysts can set an entire forest on fire. And right now, I feel as though everything around me is burning to the fucking ground.

After meeting with Maddy, I decided to take a couple of days before reaching out. It was more of a strategic move on my end at the time. I didn't want to seem too eager to go with them, especially after the confirmation of the heart card telling exactly who I'd be working for. I already knew, but to look down at the worn edges of a trinket Onyx is known to leave on her *victims* was something else entirely. Also, I just wanted a fucking minute to digest everything that had happened in such a short time. Besides, I hadn't gotten to say much to Fi before Sam was cramming directions into my GPS, and I needed to talk to her.

But when I got home, she wasn't there.

Turns out, she was taken the second I got into my car, and

the realization was like a freight train barreling into my body and knocking me on my ass.

This is *real*, and not only that, but I have no fucking clue where she is, how to reach her, or what they could be doing to her. That notion alone curdles in my stomach, forcing hot bile in my throat when I close my eyes for too long.

Fuck, if it wasn't for the fact that I needed to take care of my mother, I might have succumbed to the dread and rage swirling in my mind, threatening to shred it to nothing but bad decisions—ones that would have gotten us both killed.

My mother was passed out on the couch, an episode of *The Price is Right* playing at low volume on the TV. Her prepackaged dinner I'd left for her was half eaten and hanging partially off the edge of the coffee table. After having her move to her bed, I double-checked if she had enough medicine to last her a few weeks, and then made myself so damn busy, I had no time to think. Between cleaning and meal prepping for my mom, I was finally able to breathe.

But it wasn't enough work to keep me busy for long, and with nothing left to do but surrender to the pressure driving me into the ground, I researched. *Hours* of research. I needed to know more, and fast.

On public fronts, I was able to discover that the Embros family isn't really a family. There seems to be just Onyx and her uncle, and they actually *do* own a very large part of the real estate in Washington. All rental houses are under an LLC of Embros Hearts, and some are designated for low-income families. She also owns a foundation for victims of abuse, specializing in those involved in kidnapping and human trafficking. Insane amounts of her real estate profits are poured into her foundation and others like it along the West Coast. I'd almost say it's a noble thing if I didn't find private forums with rumors as to the truth behind Embros estate.

It's home to some of the most dangerous people in America. Each associate of Onyx is known for various things, but most notable is the amount of blood on their hands. They don't give a single fuck about taking anyone's life, and from what I can tell, they are far more dangerous than their counterparts—the Murphys.

In every aspect, they are opposites. The Murphys own shipping containers and warehouses rather than homes. Instead of the underground gambling club they run, they have more than a handful of strip clubs. Strip clubs that all guarantee happy endings to the highest payers, whether the dancer wants it or not.

The sleazy ass family is also different. All the leaders are blood related, and it's rare for them to get their hands dirty. Instead, it seems like they pay their lackeys to take care of the messier tasks.

Though I'm sure I've only barely scratched the surface, it's enough to give me a good idea of what my sister is enduring and what I'm walking into.

"I am so fucked."

"Oh. I can give you another minute to decide."

My eyes flash up to the pretty brown-haired waitress. Her face is flushed pink, and I wonder what else I may have muttered aloud. "Sorry about that. Just another beer is fine."

She nods and hurries off to another table as I sink back into my thoughts.

I have everything to lose and absolutely nothing to gain from this. It makes me feel reckless and obligated at the same time. Both possibilities are pulling me from either side, and I'm unsure which one will win in the end. Which is shitty as hell, but I'm also able to admit that I've been unraveling at the seams for a long time, and there's no telling what it will take to finally break the thin thread.

"They say *I'm* mad." A high-pitched, singsong voice steals my attention.

Across from me, Maddy's sitting comfortably at my booth, leaning on one elbow, while drumming her finger across the wooden top. She's dressed differently today, and I realize quickly this must be her work attire. Her wild red hair from Saturday is tamer, the curls tighter, brushing against the padded shoulders of her green blazer.

Seeing her makes my pulse thrum, and I rub against the thin skin on my wrist to calm the violent pounding. I'm not anxious or scared, though, just ready to get this started so I can get my sister back.

Maddy's eyes shift briefly to my hands before she grins. "It's quite normal to be neurotic, but you have me a tad concerned with your far-off gazes. We both can't have our heads in the clouds, Z."

Z. The nickname feels so personal, yet for some reason it doesn't bother me when she uses it. Almost as if she's an old friend. "I'm good."

"Hmm..." Maddy's lips pull into a tight line as if she's sincerely considering my two-word sentence. After another pause, she sighs. "Why wasn't the almond allowed to join the club?"

Unlike her riddle from the other night, this one I know. "Because he's nuts."

A loud cackle rings out at the same time her delicate hand smacks against the table, jostling my beer. I catch it just before it tips and witness her pupils dilating so wide, they nearly push out the color, giving her a manic expression. But really, I'd expect nothing less.

My research into the dark web told me the five-foot-three tornado in heels is one deadly ass woman. Though I'm not one-hundred-percent sure, it's said she's in charge of the narcotics and has had to put a few people six feet under when they cross her with tainted drugs.

Looking at her now, I wouldn't doubt it for a second.

"I like you, Z. I hope you last."

Rather than read for the clarity in her words, I simply nod. "That wasn't my interview question by any chance, was it?"

She hums, wagging a finger at me, and I notice three of her nails have dirt beneath them. "Don't you wish. You want to ride in my chariot, or do you want to follow behind in that old hoopty?"

"I'll follow."

Maddy nods and taps the table twice before standing and brushing her hands over her dark-green slacks. Her eyes bounce around the bar, but when they don't land on anything, she huffs from her nose and heads for the front door.

I trail behind her, observing the stray midday patrons who sneak glances as we walk past. When we get outside, she pops both hands on her hips, and inhales a large breath, poking out her petite chest. Even in the overcast, the spatter of freckles along her nose and cheeks seems to glow against her pale skin.

She's such a peculiar woman, and I find myself more intrigued than wary. Which is probably not a good thing.

"I'm in the black SUV right over there." She smirks, stepping off the curb before adding, "And if you lose a hubcap or something, just honk twice."

* * *

Twenty minutes later, Maddy's SUV slows to a near stop before turning on a road hidden between massive oak trees. After a quarter mile, the street widens and the trees become sparser, only leaving the ones lining either side of a cobblestone path. We wind around a small curve and stop outside an equally impressive gate. Thick iron bars stretch into the distance, disappearing into the woods. Maddy sticks her hand out of her window and curses as she swipes some type of badge against a small box on a metal post.

"Stop it, Trick. I know you're fucking with the button," Maddy booms at a camera glinting in the top corner of the gate.

A long clank resonates in the air, and she flips the camera off before driving through the now open road, allowing the massive Embros estate to slide into my view.

Massive is probably an understatement for what I'm looking at, though. Behind a ten-foot-high fountain is what looks to be a small mansion with a coldness looming overhead despite the vast hedges of rose bushes circling around the property. About a half dozen gardeners are tending to the soft white flowers, and not one of them turns to the sound of us approaching.

Three stories of natural stone and brick encompass the front with black iron framing the windows. The same dark theme continues in the shingles atop the roof and front double doors. The metal has a matte finish, matching the lanterns posted on either side of the steps leading into the mouth of the estate.

I pull my car in behind Maddy's, and it's only after I get out that everything begins to settle and my heart accelerates with new possibilities. What I haven't considered until this moment is that this isn't a sure thing. Just because I'm here doesn't mean Onyx will hire me. Or hell, she'll know I'm working for the Murphys and just kill me on the spot.

Running my hands down the front of my jeans, I replay Sam's advice in my head. He's the last fucking person I want to be thinking about, but there isn't much of a choice when my thoughts are beginning to dwindle, and I need to be reminded what's at stake.

"Be quiet. Let her talk. We don't know much about her, besides she kills first, asks questions later, so you have to just be cool. Don't give her a reason to off you. You die, there's no one left to save your baby sister's cunt from being our newest moneymaker."

My stomach churns, and even the thick swallows I take do little to push back the vomit tempting an appearance.

"You alright there?" Maddy's already at the top of the steps. Her gaze is more pointed now, her brows furrowed as though she's gauging my reactions.

I decide to be honest in hopes it makes me appear a little less sketchy. "Haven't slept much the past couple nights."

"Nervous?"

Shrugging, I climb the half dozen steps to meet her. "I wouldn't say nervous. Cautious, maybe."

A genuine grin tilts her mouth and I feel more relaxed. "Onyx has a type, so I think you'll be fine. Besides, the queen is little fun without a jester to play with."

My eyebrows lift at her insinuation, but she merely twirls and opens the door. An older gentleman nods his head at Maddy before peering up at me. His black suit hangs heavily on his frail body, but he stands taller when I step forward. "You've brought a guest, Lady Madeline."

She bounces on her heels, a look of pride crossing her features. "I have. Boss in her office?"

The butler gives me another once-over before blinking away whatever thoughts he has, then backs away, opening the door wide enough for us to enter. "She is."

"Wonderful."

A tightness pulls across my chest as I follow her inside, stepping into the grand foyer. As I expected, it's large—the ceiling alone is about twenty feet high. White marble tile covers the floor, and two black wrought iron staircases appear at either side of me, leading to the crossway right above. Dark sconces line the walls, providing the only dim light, while the massive chandelier dangling above the center glass table seems more for show. Behind the table, with a fresh vase of white roses, are two dark French doors.

Maddy tips her head toward them before leading the way and entering without stopping. "Boss! I got a surprise for you!"

Unlike my arrival, or stepping into the estate, I have no time to examine the office I've just walked into. No time to notice much about the white-haired man or the two massive bodies standing next to a large oak desk. Nor do I get to over examine or worry about the many eyes trained on me, with everyone's right hands positioned over guns at their sides.

No. I don't notice much of anything else besides *her*.

A woman with smooth amber skin leans against the desk, her feet crossed at the ankles as her dark eyes scan over a document in her hand. At least a half dozen rings wrap around her long fingers, and the sharp tip of her black nail slides back and forth over the paper as she reads.

She nods to herself once, causing her long sleek ponytail to sway to the front of her tailored suit, and it's then I notice she has nothing on under the jacket. A delicate chain rests between her breasts, where my eyes linger longer than they should.

There's no way this is her. One of the most dangerous women in the fucking world, who is nothing more than a ghost to the public eye. A woman who can't be more than twenty-five years old. There's no way...

"Boss, this is Ezekiel Kane. Z, this is Onyx Embros."

Fucking hell.

"To what do I owe this pleasure?" Her eyes never leave the paper but the two big figures next to her move, shifting to the corner of the office as if their conversation is over. I take a second to let my eyes drift with them and notice they are a set of twins. Both tall, about my height, but packing a good twenty extra pounds of muscle. With these two, I'm a little confused why she needs to add to her security detail at all.

The man next to Onyx jerks his face and my gaze flashes to him. He's not much more than pale skin sticking to bones, with long legs. His eyebrows and lashes are near invisible against his face, and the wavy hair lying mussed on his head is paper white. The only color on him besides his clothes are the gray orbs that are bouncing from the paper in Onyx's hand, to Maddy, to me, and back to Onyx.

He does this three times, all within a few seconds, before stopping on me. His eyebrows draw together and his head twitches to the side as he considers me. The notion almost seems as if he recognizes me, and I have to lean my weight on my heels to keep from shifting under the uncomfortable scrutiny. Thankfully, Maddy bounces farther into the room, and he breaks his dazed trance and peers back at Onyx, swiping a hand under his nose.

"I found him down at the Rabbit Hole. Thought you might like him." Maddy pivots on her heels and gestures to me like a proud child showing off artwork. "And he likes my riddles."

Before I can respond, Onyx finally glances up at me, her near-black eyes connecting with mine, and making my pulse twitch. I shouldn't find this woman even the slightest bit attractive, but my body fails to get the memo and begins humming as blood rushes through me.

She's fucking gorgeous, there's no denying that, and her microscopic check down my frame pushes my nerves into a small frenzy.

Handing the paper to the jittery man next to her without removing her gaze from me, she takes a few slow steps forward, her heels clacking against the marble causing an echo.

"Does he?" She speaks to Maddy as her dark eyes remain

on me, traveling slowly over the features of my face, before dipping down to my arms and hands and back up again. She's looking at me as one would look at a new car they're considering taking for a test drive.

I clench my jaw and tilt my head back as I feign a look of indifference.

"Why would you want to work for me?" Onyx's voice is smooth, sultry even. Her words come out much slower than her employee here, and I assume it's because she spends a lot more time considering her words before speaking.

I shrug. "I hear the pay is good and college is a lot of money."

"You want to go to school?" Maddy squeaks, but still, I don't break the standoff I seem to be having with Onyx.

"I'm pretty skilled with computers. Thought it'd be a good idea to go back and actually learn a thing or two that YouTube can't teach me."

Maddy twirls one of her curls. "Well, Shi can teach you more than one of those fancy schools can, that's for sure. Right, boys?"

A unified hum of agreement sounds from the back of the office, but I pull down the corner of my lips.

Onyx erases the remaining space between us, stopping less than a foot away from me. She reaches just below my nose in her six-inch heels, but the power radiating off of her suggests she's the tallest one in the room.

Her scent surprises me, the faint smell of lemons wafting over me and seemingly drowning out everyone else. There's only she and I, stuck under the heavy air, an unexplainable tension swirling in the small space between us. Her focus remains fixed, and being the ass I am, I can't help the small smirk that twitches the edges of my lips.

Onyx's eyes flare briefly as they flicker to my mouth, but

whatever veil she wears moves back into place, and a dull expression takes over her features. "There are other jobs that pay well. Other *families* that pay well."

My eyebrows furrow slightly but I lift my chin, my voice made of nothing but resolve. There was a very real possibility this would come up, and that's what we planned for. "It's not as if *I* sought *you* out. Your girl approached me and offered me an interview. Who am I to—"

A tender hand with a strong grip forces my chin back down, her cold rings sending shivers through my jaw. "And who are you exactly?"

My heart hammers into my chest as I make her wait for my response. It's a small thing—the brief pause—but it feels as though I'm playing a dangerous game with fire, and I can't seem to help myself. Another second passes before she loses her focus on my eyes, and her hand slips, gliding with her gaze down the column of my throat. A sharp sting of pain follows her path and I realize she's using her nail to cause it.

I swallow when she reaches my collarbone, my blood surging through my body. Her dark eyes flash back to mine, and it's then I notice the small flecks of caramel hidden in the black irises.

She really is stunning.

"Ezekiel Kane." My reply is flat, but my insides are fucking whirling. There's something so intoxicating about her, and I can't fight the tickling in the back of my head that would kill to dominate someone so... powerful.

"Hmm," is all she says before the nail in my skin is replaced with a cold metal crescent.

I react before I can properly think, knocking the gun from her hand and holding in the internal wince when it clatters against the tile, sliding toward a nearby bookshelf. My breath increases, the realization that I probably just fucked up everything wrapping around my throat.

But then Maddy's cackle rings out, reminding me we aren't alone. "See, Boss? He's going to be so much fun!"

Onyx doesn't respond and moves to pass me, but pauses at my shoulder. I may be out of my fucking mind, but I swear she inhales deeply before continuing toward the door. Odd as it may be, the calmness in her stance flushes through me like cold water, soothing my temporary apprehension.

"Run a check. If he passes, get him suited." Her voice is level, perhaps even a little bored, as she directs her errand to one of the twins.

In a room full of killers, you'd think I'd be more cautious, especially after knocking a fucking gun from Onyx's hand, but in all honesty, the atmosphere feels more familiar to me than I'd care to admit. It's the only explanation I have for why I smirk and peer at her from over my shoulder. "And if I fail?"

There's a long pause and I almost take the bait and turn to face her, but I steel my feet and keep only my profile toward her. A moment later, she huffs from her nose.

"I'd hate to kill something so pretty."

Onyx
AGE 10
CHAPTER FIVE

"**B**uoyancy and density are not the same thing. Related but not identical."

For the seventh time, I repeat the words of my latest science tutor. Unlike math—the class I cherish the most because of my future place in the family business—science is difficult. With math, things are easy. There're formulas that don't change, algorithms with concrete steps, cut and dry answers, as my dad likes to say. But science? It's all vocabulary. It's memorizing terms that all seem like they mean the same thing but have a single word that makes them completely different. And for a ten-year-old, I'm *already* a walking dictionary for my dialect. I don't have much more room for scientific terms I'll probably never use again when I'm done with school.

My only saving grace is that by being two grade levels ahead, I only have a couple more years of basic science until I'm introduced to anatomy. I've watched plenty of videos about the fun dissections I'll get to do on frogs and have already started to get a head start on the human skeletal system. Now that's when things will get interesting.

Dad even said he'll sit in on some of my classes and give me tidbits about the muscular and nervous system. He claims there're things I'll need to know that my teachers and martial arts instructors won't tell me. Above their paygrade, he says.

But until then, though...

Buoyancy and density are not—

Ouch!

A sharp pinch on my thumb forces me to jerk my hand away from the bush I was pruning, watching a bright strip of red blood fall onto a white rose.

Stupid freaking flower. Ugh. If I knew mother wouldn't be furious, I'd kill all her pretty roses. I'd cut them off at the base and spill some of Father's acid straight into the roots for good measure.

I've been pricked a few good times since we've been out here pruning the dang things, but a fat thorn just sliced through my thumb and the burning in my hand brings tears to my eyes.

"Who could love a flower that rewards all the hard work by cutting your finger open?" I nurse my stinging thumb, staring daggers into the offending thorn's petals stained with my blood.

My mother's smile is soft as she wipes a stray curl from her face, standing from her crouched spot. Her warm brown skin glows under the midday sun, and a light seems to radiate around her. "So because it's hard to take care of, you detest it?"

Her voice is mellow and free from judgment. She's asking for a genuine response, and I don't bother lying. "Yes."

She nods, stripping off her gloves and resting them next to the basket we bring out when tending to the garden. After plucking out two bottles of water, she pulls out a small first aid kit. "Come, let me have a look."

I do as I'm told and give her my hand. She turns it to either side, quiet in her inspection, before nodding and grabbing one of the bottles of water. "I want you to think in the perspective of the rose, Onyx."

My eyes begin to roll, but as if on cue, she pours a bit of the cold water over my tender thumb, forcing a hiss as I suck in a breath. "Fine."

My mother rubs the small cut with a miniature cloth from the first aid kit before washing it again. She doesn't take her gaze off my wound when she speaks. "Though it's merely an opinion, the rose is arguably one of the most sought-after flowers in the world. It takes lots of care and patience to grow something so beautiful."

She tears the top off a single-use ointment and squeezes the smallest amount over my thumb. The cool jelly soothes the burning and my frustration ebbs with the receding pain. "As you know, once a flower is taken from its bush, death is imminent. Imagine if the flower didn't have those thorns to protect it. Do you think there would be many roses left?"

I shake my head, trying to understand the underlying lesson my mother always seems to weave into her logic. "No, ma'am."

A fresh bandage is wrapped around my finger before she kisses her own index and touches it against the sealed wound. "All people see is a pretty flower they want to cut away from its natural place and put on display until it withers and dies. After it's no use to them anymore, they toss it in the trash. I think it's only fitting that such a beautiful and delicate flower has a way to deter anyone from cutting its life short."

"Just like you, baby love." My father appears from behind one of the bushes. His suit jacket is missing, but he looks dapper nonetheless—his long sleeves rolled up, the bottom still tucked into his slacks. He runs a hand through his dark messy hair before kissing my mother and leaning over to take my hand. "You not only have us to protect you, but your skills in combat will help you should you ever be in a bad situation."

He gingerly rotates my wrist, inspecting my mom's nursing abilities. Once satisfied, he kisses me on the forehead and picks up our discarded basket of pruned branches. "My love. A word?"

Ugh. I hate when they do that.

Depending on what it is, they spoon-feed me things in tiny bite-sized pieces as if too much at once may break my brain. It's as though I don't have the best homeschool teachers money can buy and they're pushing me way harder academically than I think my parents realize. It's time I use all the skills I'm learning and show him I can handle it and need to start being included more.

Decision made; I turn toward my father.

"I'd like to know too." I straighten my spine, pushing away the slight waver in my voice. Daughter of the don doesn't mean I'm exempt from fear. My father is intimidating through and through, but I try my best not to show it. He taught me that a long time ago.

His eyebrows pinch together, the skin between them creating a deep crease. My nerves begin to shake the longer he retains my gaze and I have to hold my breath to keep from showing how quickly I'd be breathing otherwise.

Finally, his gaze flashes to my mother, who I see nod slightly in my periphery. He sets down the basket and folds his big arms across his chest. "Alright, Onyx. I have a slight problem."

I swallow behind the ball of unease suddenly lodged in my throat. "Okay."

"Too many of the women we *relieve* from the Murphys are falling back into their clutches. Whether it's because of their addiction or their family's rejections, we lose over half of the ones we rescue."

The Murphys. The crappiest people in the world. They are the family on the other side of the city, and while I don't know too much about them, I know enough to appreciate I wasn't born on that side. For one, they make a lot of money selling women, which is one of the main reasons both my mom and I are both black belts.

My father has our ports monitored and is able to stop any shipments from passing through our side, but it seems as if the Murphys are getting some of them back anyway. It makes sense considering they get the women addicted to some type of drug and promise them more after they do their *duties*.

Hot nausea roars in my tummy, and I wince at the thought.

Imagine if the flower didn't have those thorns to protect it.

These women don't have a family like mine. Some are left for dead. They need to be helped in more than just saving them from a van. They need... "What's that place Uncle Antonio went to a few years ago?"

"Rehab?" My mother speaks up, moving beside me. "We already send them there."

"But do we ever check up on them and make sure they're going?"

My mother's angelic smile fades. "It's not our main priority, honey. We have other things that take precedent."

Ugh.

My shoulders deflate, the death of my idea before it's even formed weighing heavy in my chest. I get what she's saying. I mean, heck, the first van my father blocked was him making a point to the Murphys that they weren't allowed to run through our territory. But then my mother urged him to save the girls inside. Now, the soldiers at the port, and even in neutral areas, keep a lookout for their vans.

I like to think of us as a twisted type of vigilantes. It helps me compartmentalize—my vocab word of the week used in a sentence, check—but in the end, it's not enough to me. There has to be something more we could do.

"What about a place they can check into full time? And

they don't get out until they're able to take care of themselves. Oh, and therapy. Uncle Antonio used to tell me how much he loved it. Do they have a place like that?"

My father sighs, pinching the bridge of his nose. "Baby love. Please don't misunderstand what I'm about to say, but I'm not Batman. I am the leader of a very large and lucrative crime family. We supply drugs and weapons to thousands of people while also running various other businesses. You know this."

That I do. I don't touch the money, but once a week, I sit with some of the accountants that go over money drops and things. I've picked up a few terms here and there, but there's still so much to learn.

He places a soft hand on my shoulder. "It is not within my moral compass to waste any more manpower to check these women into facilities they can't afford for the long term."

I think over one of the few finance lessons I received. There was something we talked about... something about why we use real estate. It was called... "What about if we opened our *own* place. Use it for taxes, maybe?"

He chuckles at this, but I know I got the term right. "We use our real estate properties for that."

"Yes, but..." My mother perks up, her eyes bouncing between mine. "Perhaps if we had a private rehab center where they live part time, we'd save them, while also not wasting our time by having them run back to the Murphys. It would be an additional tax incentive and may put us in more favor with the right side of the law."

I nod, pride swelling in my chest at the smile on my father's face. He likes the idea. I love when I'm able to help them with the business. It gives me a feeling of purpose I can't quite describe, and the happiness streaming from my pores is pure glee.

My father looks at my mother, who pulls me into a hug. "This is a perfect idea, Onyx."

He nods, rubbing his chin thoughtfully. "That could work. But since it was your idea, you have to draft up some plans. Get with Floren and Winston in finance and work up a budget. It will be your first real project, baby love, so take your time and do it right."

My heart quickens, the sudden need to run into the house and get started right away, making my arms shake with jitters.

Mother must notice and runs her hand along my arm, her voice calm when she speaks. "What will you name it?"

I gaze past the bush that broke through my skin, to the red heart roses lining the hedge just outside the kitchen windows. They are my mother's favorites and my least, since their prickles are the worst. But they are her most prized possession, and I'd almost bet my life she'd pull a Queen of Hearts if anything happened to them.

These women need to be protected just as fiercely. Mind made up, I uncoil myself from my mother's embrace and peer up at my father.

"Embros Hearts."

Kilo
CHAPTER SIX

Three shipments on First Street. So busy there this week. I'll have to talk to Maddy and get some more pick-me-ups to get me through. There's just so much to do this week. There's so much. I won't stay awake if I don't have something. There are some drop offs in neutral territory too. I wonder why.

But Onyx approved the list. She said it'd be fine.

Onyx.

She has a new toy. He looks like a good time. Her perfect type, with that dark messy hair and that broody look she likes. I've never seen anyone disarm Onyx that fast. He must know his way around a gun. I'm sure he does. I can tell. I can always tell. There's a familiarness I can't quite place. Something about him.

Oh! It's his eyes. Yes. Those eyes.

I've seen them somewhere before. But where? Where have I seen them?

I don't know.

Fiddling with the silver watch in my pocket, I listen as the seconds tick by. So much time has passed since this morning. How? Where did the time go? No, I'm late. I'm late. I must go.

I have no time to do anything. I'll remember another time, but I can't right now.

I'm late, and time is of the essence.

EZEKIEL
CHAPTER SEVEN

I've been sitting in Onyx's office for the better part of an hour now. After she'd taken her leave, the twin men and Maddy left me inside, promising to return when my background check came through.

None of them seemed to have much emotion with regard to me slapping a gun from their Boss's hand, which has led me to a few different assumptions. Either it's a common thing she does at interviews, or they knew if I'd inadvertently hit *her*, I wouldn't be able to... well, live.

I'm not going to lie, the latter intrigues me more. Which is one of the many things I've felt today that says something about my psyche. But instead of thinking about it like I probably should, I stand, running a hand through my hair as I wander to one of the bookshelves to busy my mind.

Deep mahogany shelves line both sides of the walls, and like everything else, are pristine. The marble floors have a soft sheen, indicating they are regularly waxed. Everything seems to be precisely placed, with nothing cluttered together, and no space between the books has a speck of dust. The dark color seems to be a continuous theme throughout, with black accents and dim lighting coming from the wall sconces.

A quick look over some of the titles has me realizing they're sorted into specific categories.

Unsolved mysteries.

Forensic files.

Dozens of leather-bound law books.

Human anatomy and chemical makeup of every illegal drug I've ever heard of, as well as a few for natural remedies. Each one gives me more insight into the type of people in this estate.

I grab one of the human anatomy books. It's an older textbook—thick, heavy, and worn around the edges. When I hold the spine in my palm and let the pages fall naturally, it opens to a page bookmarked with a queen of hearts card similar to the one Maddy gave me.

The fine hairs on the nape of my neck stand at attention, an odd type of shiver racking down my spine as I scan the pages. It's a familiar diagram of the muscular system, only unlike one you'd see in a science course, this one is riddled with notes over certain areas. Areas marked with information stating how much blood the victims would lose, meaning they are prime for slicing into and causing the most pain—filleting without killing.

Makes sense. Best method of torture, if you think about it. But also, Onyx doesn't seem like the type to want to prolong death. I'd imagine she's a *get to the point* type of woman. Then again, I know nothing about her, and even the slivers I read online were speculations at best.

Why am I curious about her at all? That's not why I'm here.

Get the information. Get my sister. And get the fuck out of this city.

I snap the book shut, replacing it on the shelf just as the office doors open. Taking a deep breath and attempting my best bored expression, I turn to take in a bouncing Maddy. "So, did I pass?"

She pauses so abruptly, her wild curls fly in front of her face, a soft laugh filling the space. "Hate to break it to ya, Z, but if you didn't, you'd already be dead."

Blowing out a truly relieved breath of air, I shove my hands into my pockets. The burn blazing through my nerves begins to recede, and I suck in my first full breath in three days. "Well, that's oddly comforting."

A smirk curls her lips as she rocks on her heels. "We do need to go over a few things before you formally accept the gig though, big guy."

This gives me pause. *That's right.* I was only told she needed a guard, which could mean plenty of things, and if it's outside of the estate or away from Onyx in general, this is all for nothing.

She gestures to the desk, and I nod, sitting in the oversized wingback chair while she hops on top of the sturdy wood, swinging her feet. "So basically, you'd be a live-in bodyguard, six days a week. You'll follow her around the grounds and monitor the area with other guards walking the property. Pay is two hundred thousand Scooby snacks a year, and you'd also have to moonlight as Boss's escort."

Maddy pauses, twirling a stray curl around her finger, as if giving me time to digest what she just said. I'm sure she's seen from my background check that not only am I used to getting my hands dirty, but none of the under-the-table cash jobs I've worked ever paid me even a fraction of what she's offering. A small shard of regret digs into my chest, burrowing just behind my heart. To think I could have worked for this woman and gotten my family out long ago...

Before I can dwell on shit I can't change, something in the way Maddy's jaw tightens makes my muscles twitch. I quickly realize she's waiting for me to accept, but I focus on the mention of escorting Onyx. "As in when she leaves?"

She shrugs, letting the strand she was toying with go and coil back in place. "That too, but she doesn't leave much. We have some issues with the men on the other side of the city. But what *I'm* referring to is helping escort her to an orgasm now and again."

Ah.

I can't stop the very real surprise that forces my eyebrows into my hairline. Maddy lets out her high-strung giggle, kicking her legs in short bursts before flopping down. "I feel as if I already implied that part at the bar."

"I guess I thought you were joking."

She sobers quickly, her head tilting to the side as though I've stumped her. "I don't mess around when it comes to Boss, Z. None of us do."

Her tone isn't threatening but more informative. I nod in understanding. "Got it. Anything else I need to know?"

A smile brightens her face, and she strides to the office doors, pausing at the entrance as she waits for me to catch up. "With time. So am I wrong in assuming you're accepting?"

"Not wrong at all."

"Wonderful." She beams, pushing open the French doors. "Wonderful indeed."

We exit the office and enter the large foyer. Maddy gestures to the right. "Kitchen, laundry room, and study down there. To the other side is the theater room, a small library, a gym, and a conference room."

A sudden dryness appears in my throat as I scratch at the back of my neck, following her up the stairs. "When is my day off?"

"Tuesday."

"That's tomorrow," I point out.

She releases the banister as we reach the top landing, twirling around so that her curls fall into her face. "And today is

Monday. This is up while that is down. I wonder how long it will be before you take Boss to town."

I narrow my gaze, an unwelcome feeling of ease trying to work through my tight muscles. "Should I expect a lot of those?"

"When she isn't around? Absolutely. Even I like my head attached to my neck, so you'll get a reprieve when she's around."

Good to know.

Again, she points to the right. "Down here are Onyx's quarters. They're massive and basically include a living room, bar, and a big ass bed you'll likely be warming later this week. Right here in front of us is your room. And down that way are all of our rooms. It also wraps around to another part that overlooks the pool in the back. There's a lab, another office, a few guest rooms, and a sunroom."

She opens the door to what appears to be my room, and the pesky feeling of guilt bleeds into my stomach, making me nauseous. I shouldn't be here, standing in the middle of a room half the size of my childhood house, surrounded by expensive linens and hardwood furniture. I shouldn't be enjoying the fact that my window overlooks the back portion of the estate, where the high sun is shining over an immaculate pool. Nor should I fucking like the vast view of the woods lining the edge of the perfectly cut grass.

My kid sister could be enduring the fucking worst possible fate and I refuse to have one iota of my being fall victim to enjoying this. A tightness pulls across my sternum as I walk inside.

Before I can say anything, one of the twins fills the doorway. He leans down, dropping four bags near the bed.

Maddy smiles, jumping the small distance and searching in the bags. "You work quickly, Trigger."

He nods, grunting as he motions to me. "He's a hair bigger than me and Trick so it wasn't hard to find something."

Trick. Trigger. Maddy must see the pieces working through my gaze and she answers my unasked question. "Trick and Trigger. They are in charge of security and weapons distribution. They also specialize in making inconspicuous weapons that look like your everyday jewelry or office supplies."

She begins pulling articles of clothing from the bag, acting as though this is the most casual conversation she's had all day. "Shi, my companion from the night we met, is something like Onyx's right hand, while me and the white-haired man from the office earlier take care of narcotics."

Her small tidbit gives me a good insight into what I'd sort of already deduced, but at the same time, does something to solidify my new position. Just as easy as it was to be invited into her home and given the job of an associate, I'm sure it's equally as easy to have me killed should I open my mouth in the slightest.

That knowledge would make anyone nervous, but instead, I feel something else, something dangerously close to anticipation. It pumps alongside the adrenaline already soaring in my veins and too much of this feels... natural.

Maddy finally decides on a pair of black slacks and a button-down, tossing them at me. "Get changed really quick and then we'll take your measurements."

For what seems like the millionth time, I merely nod and disappear through the door in the corner of my large room, clutching the clothes in my hand. I didn't expect anything less, but seeing the large claw-foot tub, dark fixtures, marble floors, and gold accents makes my stomach drop.

Luxury is not something I've ever needed or even really desired in my life and being suddenly dropped into it has left me overwhelmed. No matter how comfortable I may feel here, this isn't where I belong. This isn't what I should be surrounded by. And like the view in my room, I damn sure shouldn't enjoy it.

It's in this moment I force a hard swallow and steel my nerves, locking my wayward thoughts down. I'll bodyguard the woman, fuck her, and stay focused on what matters rather than the materialistic crap floating around me.

I've already gotten in, now all that's left is to get the information I need and get out.

* * *

After getting dressed and measured by Maddy, the other twin showed up with a map of the state. His breath wafts in front of me, the telling smell of vodka coasting under my nose.

"This red line here is our side. These stickers signify our rental properties, but you don't need to worry about that." Trick points to a different side of the map, just outside the forest near my house. "This is Murphy territory. After running your search, we saw you live here in neutral territory. But based on your debit card usage, you sometimes go to bars or markets on their side. You can't do that anymore. As an associate for Onyx, you now have a target on your back."

Though the only people I should fear are under the same roof as me currently, I feign concern, drawing my eyebrows together. "Should I worry about my mother?"

Maddy speaks now, her voice giddy as though she has a joke she's just waiting to tell. "Nope. They are killing Onyx's boys to prove a point. They don't bother threatening them or targeting their families."

"Am I bait?" I'm not sure where the question came from, but the moment I say it, it all starts to make more sense. I got in too easy. And sure, I don't know how the Mafia works, but I don't think a simple background check and having muscles immediately gets you in the damn club."

The twins stiffen at my side but don't say anything. Instead, Maddy leans off the bed, a far-off gaze making her eyes widen. "Yes, and no. You *are* Onyx's type. She likes burly guys, you know, the whole tall, dark, and handsome thing. Plus, you fit our normal profile with good qualifications when we look for new recruits. Little family, no known group of friends, only work cash jobs. I mean, the list goes on. You really are a magical fit. Hell, the only thing that could make you perfect is if you had military or combat training."

She hops off the bed, a small hand finding my chest, a sincere look of concern pulling down the corner of her lips. "But also, Onyx is so close to achieving something we've wanted for a very long time, and with her men being knocked off so easily, it forces us to postpone our plans. If we can figure out how they are finding them and killing them, we can get back on track."

I sigh and shake my head, a slight burn itching the back of my throat. I'm positive all the people working for the Murphys know I'm not to be killed, considering I'm a fucking rat. But also, that means without me being a target, the Embros will catch on and become privy to that information too.

I'm going to have to work fast.

Shi

CHAPTER EIGHT

I suppose I should have smoked a bit more before coming down here, but the twins wanted a few more minutes wrapped between my limbs and my time was cut short. In truth, I hadn't wanted to leave their warmth at this hour either, but alas, duty calls.

Biting back a yawn, I lean into the cool concrete wall, drawing my sweater closer around my shoulders. Onyx always keeps it so cold down here, it's a wonder I can't see my breath billowing from my mouth.

Goose bumps prickle along my arms as my low gaze flits to the goddess herself, standing near the basement stairs. As always, she's donning an elegant black outfit, and an abundance of jewelry that keeps them so distracted they don't see her when she makes a move. Tonight, though, there is something different, a very thick metal bracelet that Trigger has been working on for months. It's about five inches in width, matte gold, and has pretty little intricate roses burned into the material. There's also a small chain that hangs from underneath, attached to a ring resting on the upper part of her middle finger.

The realization settles over me, and I nod to myself. Whether I'm here for ten minutes or six hours, tonight will end with death.

I look around the basement to find our guest. Unlike the modern estate just above us, this place is nothing more than stained concrete, a pair of metal chains hanging from the ceiling, and the usual lone foldable chair in the middle of the room.

In the chair is a battered blond male with his hands bound behind his back. His head is slumped almost to his chest as he continues to sleep. Judging by the blood stuck to his temples like '90s hair gel and stained into his tattered jeans, I'd say he's been unconscious for a few hours.

I know she didn't take either twin to go get him, and I'm more than positive she didn't take the new guard. Anger swells in my limbs, locking them in place to prevent me from doing anything that will get me scolded. My voice remains calm. "Where did you find this man?"

"You think too little of me, Shire." Onyx takes a step forward, and the single dome of light on the ceiling spills over her, casting her face in an ominous shadow. "Becker found him on our side. Seems as though he tried to take one of my guards. I'm beginning to think it's a sport of some kind."

I blink a few times, embarrassment briefly sweeping through me. Of course, she wouldn't leave without us. She knows the importance of her life, especially since we are so close now.

A wide smile takes my lips as I bow my head. "My apologies. And I agree. A game to see who can catch the most of your soldiers. The rewards must be big."

"It must. But I'm growing tired of losing them. Perhaps it's the greed in me speaking but those men are mine. And I don't like my things being broken."

She moves in front of the man and lifts one sharp heel, pressing it into his chest. It's always mystified me how she can wear heels meant to be kitchen knives, while I creep the estate barefoot and pout when I must leave because I have to put on shoes.

A quick hiss of air informs us our guest is awake. Unlike most, he doesn't lift his head and look around frantically, or ask who we are, or what we want.

Good.

"Good." Onyx says it the same time I think it, as she shoots me a wink. "Now, let's get some answers, shall we?"

He peers up, and though we both know he's well aware of where he is, no one is ever ready for when they first lay eyes on Onyx. She's been a ghost in the public eye since she was fourteen, and when an entire decade passes, you can only imagine how much someone can change.

For starters, she's got the figure of Athena—strong, yet curved, feminine, yet toned. She's an hourglass thanks to her Jamaican side and the perfect shade of amber because of her father's Italian blood. Now her face? It would bring Aphrodite to her knees. Large, round eyes under a forest of thick lashes, and perfectly set cheekbones with the cutest freckle under her pillowy lips.

Onyx is not cocky by any means, but she uses her beauty to her advantage, and anyone with eyes falls victim to the tactics. Like now. The fool in the chair is so focused on the barbells on her nipples poking through the sheerness of her blouse, he doesn't notice me walking to his back.

"Do you know who I am?"

"A slut with her foot in my chest." He peers down at where her heel is still between his ribs, but my hand quickly threads through his hair and forces his head back to look at her.

"Slut. Such an outdated insult." She drops her leg, the resounding clink echoing in the space. "I'm not sure if you've watched the news or read a book lately, but a woman being comfortable with her body, *her sexuality,* does not define her as anything other than free. Free from the constraints you pathetic people try to place on them based on what they do with their own fucking bodies. Their own cunts."

Onyx lets out a humorless chuckle before bending to his eye level. "Without the portal between our legs, your feeble existence wouldn't be. So remember that every time you open that vile mouth tonight to address me."

She lifts, backing away as I let my hand drop from his nape. "As I was saying. Do you know who I am?"

"Onyx Embros," he mutters.

"Wonderful. And you work for the Murphys, I assume." It's not a question, and she doesn't wait for a response. "Tell me, what do you get from taking my guards on their days off? It's becoming quite the inconvenience to find more."

"For someone who's said to be smart, you're really fucking stu—"

A loud pop rings out, and I have to quickly grab the chair to keep the entire thing from tipping over due to the force of Onyx's right hook. "I just told you, merely ten seconds ago, to watch how you speak to me. You must know you're not making it from my home alive. But it'd be wise to consider that *how* you respond will determine how *painfully* you meet the man beneath our feet."

He scoffs, spitting a cluster of blood on the cement before peering up at her. "And you, whore, should know you'll get nothing from me."

"Hmm. I see you have a complex." Onyx peers up at me, her dark eyes narrowed. "Would you mind grabbing a toy from Maddy? Tell her I'll buy her another."

I give a curt nod, whisking around the man whose face is scrunched in confusion. Before my foot connects with the first step, her voice stops me. "The biggest one she has."

"Yes, ma'am," I purr and disappear upstairs.

Moving through the quiet house, I travel up the long marble steps and through the west wing to Maddy's room. Inside, naked above the sheets, is her pale body, tangled with tan limbs. Long brown waves fan across the woman's back and over the pillow, while various shades of Maddy's paints streak in random strokes around her delicate places.

The girl stirs as Maddy's eyes peel open, her gaze connecting with mine. I slip next to her, a hand held up to show she shouldn't move. I keep my voice low and let myself glance over.

Ah, the waitress. "Onyx has a guy. We need him to choke on his words."

She takes only a moment to digest my words before pursing her lips and loosely waves her hand toward the front of her room. "You're both lucky I don't think I'll need it anymore. Bottom drawer in the dresser over there."

Smiling, I nod, grabbing the absurdly large silicone penis from its place, then travel back through the estate. On the way, a light that wasn't on before steals my attention.

It's the new guard's room. A shadow beneath his door slips back and forth, forcing my curiosity to get the best of me. I stop just at the edge of the threshold of his door, and the movement stops instantly. Oddly enough, as quiet as I've been, and as out of sight as I've kept, he knows I'm here.

Interesting.

We both stay still, and the strong urge to gauge his reaction should I step in front of the door plays heavy on my nerves, but the cold toy in my hand reminds me of my Boss awaiting my arrival downstairs.

I shove the thought in the back of my mind with a reminder to look more into that later. Within another minute, the guard is forgotten and I'm back in the near-freezing-cold basement.

When the man's eyes fall to the dildo in my hand, his eyes

widen, the pupils dilating so vastly, they nearly erase his muted-blue color. I smirk, handing the toy over to Onyx, who doesn't even waste a second grabbing the man's chin and forcing his head back.

"To be a woman is to be strong in more ways than you could possibly understand. And one of our many talents is to take something as large as this into our throats without suffocating. I do wonder if the same can be said for you."

The fool shakes his head and stupidly opens his mouth to say something, but she shoves the silicone straight through his teeth. His muffled cry sounds like singing to my ears as I take my place behind him, gripping his shoulders so he isn't able to thrash loose.

"Now, isn't this silly? I can only ask you yes or no questions now." Onyx huffs, moving her face sharply so her long ponytail flips behind her. "Do you have an inside informant? Someone on my payroll, giving you information about my men?"

The guy's jaw tightens, and I realize he's biting down on the dildo to prevent it from going farther. This only makes her tsk, and she uses the hand holding him to dig her sharp stiletto nails into his flesh. With her strength, they break the skin quite easily and blood beads before trailing through his five o'clock scruff. It does the job, and when he opens his jaw to yell in pain, she shoves it in deeper, coercing a horrific gag from him.

"Come now, us women must learn to hold our gag reflexes, and you have a much larger mouth than I do." Her voice is so serene, it's as if it's something he should already know. "Tell me. Do you have someone working for you inside my home?"

This time he shakes his head furiously, and though it's invisible to anyone else, I see Onyx's features relax. It's always been a worry of us all, that with running through so many guards, we were bound to get a mole of some sort. It's too late in the game now to be taken out by something like a trojan horse.

"Do you have people watching my home?"

He stills at this, and though muffled, I make out a few choice words he tries to spew.

Onyx rolls her eyes before shoving the toy farther. This time, the gag he produces is wet and we both take a quick step backward to let him empty his stomach onto the floor, along with Maddy's dildo.

After he's thoroughly done, rage overcomes his now disgusting features as snot runs from his nose and into his soiled mouth. "You are nothing more than one of the sluts who warms my cock every night. I have worked for the Murphys for ten years. If you don't return me, they will skin you alive, you stupid bitch."

Onyx's head tilts to the side, a genuine look of confusion drawing her eyebrows together. I, too, find myself baffled at his misstep. Does he not realize where he is? That no one is coming, and he has probably already been replaced?

"I never said I didn't plan to return you," she coos. "I fully intend to. And as it stands right now, I think it will be in four different pieces. What do you think, Shire?"

Moving around, I join her side, looking over the mess of a man in front of me. Visions of my own mother's face pierce through me. Her knees soiled and bloody. Vomit clinging to every inch of her clothes. Her promises of being able to come home soon falling on deaf ears. It wouldn't be till long after her death, and two months after my sixteenth birthday, that I found the same image looking back at me in the mirror—swearing to myself I'd be able to escape them soon.

A gentle squeeze of my bicep brings me back, and I force two slow draws of air before I'm able to hear her over the frantic beat of my heart. I shake my head and decide to ask him something to better answer my Boss's question. "What do you do for the Murphys?"

"Fuck you." The guy spits in my direction, and before I have a chance to respond, Onyx moves, hitting him with such force his lips split open. Anger and frustration swirl in his irises and he tries to jerk himself free of his restraints.

Onyx kicks her leg up and digs her heel into his upper thigh, the dark fabric instantly growing darker. His screeches of pain echo in the room, and I can't help but laugh at how easy he is to hurt. Though the Murphys don't do any of their own heavy lifting, the members that have worked with them the longest have much higher pain tolerances.

His face falls to me, his chest rising and falling as he tries to control the sobs working through him. "You're fucking crazy in the head, bitch. Completely fucking bonkers."

"I'll tell you a secret, friend." I move to the edge of the room, knowing his time is near. He hasn't been useful in the slightest and Onyx doesn't like to waste her time. "I like to think all the best people are. It was lovely meeting you."

His head whips back to Onyx, who is still watching him, boredom playing on her features. "Sure you don't want to answer her?"

"Phineas will find you just like he found your whore of a mother. Only this time, he's going to fuck you until you beg for death, like he should have done to her in front of your shit fath—"

He didn't see that Onyx made a fist with the hand attached to the bracelet. He didn't see that the ring being pulled caused a blade to slide out from the top, stopping just five inches past her knuckles. And his arrogance, or perhaps stupidity, stopped him from seeing her move. But he *did* feel the moment her knife pierced through his windpipe, just before slicing it open vertically.

Blood splatters, his garbled cough causing it to spray out, and land across her chest.

Unable to grab at his now filleted throat, his face morphs into pure horror as an unfazed Onyx dips her clean hand into her sheer bra and pulls out her queen of hearts card. She kisses the back before shoving the shiny card inside his gaped-open mouth.

"Apologize to the boys for the late hour but have them deliver this lovely specimen of a man to the front gate of his Boss's." She wipes the blade on her slacks before letting her fist go and withdrawing the knife. "Have them cut his tongue out and have one of my gardeners grind it up and put it in the dirt for my roses. As much shit that comes from his mouth, I just know it will make good fertilizer."

EZEKIEL

CHAPTER NINE

It's three a.m., and to say I'm exhausted is a fucking understatement.

Little sleep isn't new to me. Stress isn't either. But I've also never been a double agent working against two opposing sides of the Mafia while racing a clock. And while I'd literally kill to quiet my mind for just a few minutes and attain a fragment of rest, I know it'd be pointless. I've sunk into the soft bed—my bed—more than once, but instead of sleeping, I only replay my conversation with Maddy.

Shortly after fitting me for a concealed weapon belt, she and the twins left. She informed me on her way out that I was free to rest or roam around until my shift ended at six, mentioning she knew it was a lot of information to absorb. But even without already knowing what I did, I caught up fairly quickly.

Besides, no matter who these people are, what they do, what my job is, how much I get paid, or where I'm allowed to shop—all of it... *none* of it actually matters. The only thing I need to understand is that I'm nothing more than a pawn on the board being moved by both sides. It's not prevalent information, and it damn sure doesn't surprise me to learn I'm bait here as well, but still, my mind is restless. Every thought I could ever have are tangling with each other, fighting over what I should worry about more.

Whether it be my mom and her inability to eat the fucking food we make and leave for her in the fridge.

My sister and where she is or what she's having to go through right now.

My life and the bill due to some imaginary force that won't accept anything I've paid thus far.

Or maybe the fact that I'm content under a roof full of killers, like the one currently stopped in front of my door.

It's a female, based on her light and hurried steps, and she's positioned herself to the right, just out of my limited view, keeping her shadow away from the bottom of my door.

Initially, I almost think they've figured out who I am, after all, and a sick sort of peace creeps into my muscles. It calms the swell of anxiety over everything else, promising a swift end to the shit hand I'm holding. But the thought washes away when I think of what that would mean for my sister.

With a brief look around the room, I find four objects I could use to kill whoever's on the other side. I don't move, though, and instead wait, mirroring her stillness.

The moment only lasts another breath before her presence vanishes and she rushes down the stairs as quickly as she'd come up.

The anxious veil returns, forcing my mind back into a frenzy. My hands fist at my sides, my short nails biting into the flesh of my palm to the brink of breaking through, until I release my tight grasp. Over and over, I do the same thing until small crescent bruises form in the skin. I'll go insane if I continue to stand here for the few remaining hours of my shift.

The small bedside table shines in the dim room, the red

digits casting an eerie glow against the wood, showing me how long I'll have to wait.

One hundred and eighty minutes.

Such a small portion of time in the grand scheme of a day. But like anyone watching the clock, the seconds drag by, threatening to stop altogether if I don't refrain from staring at the slow-moving changes in the numbers. I can't help it though, because when my shift ends, I'll go back home to some type of message left from Sam, proving my sister is okay. He said all I have to do is get in and survive long enough to get back and receive it.

My eyes drift to my exit. There's no point in staying here when I could be touring the house. And without an eye over my shoulder, it gives me longer to explore. To memorize.

Decision made, I open my door to a dim, quiet hall and glance to my left, toward Onyx's room. Like all the others in the estate, her door is black, stark against the gray walls. But unlike everyone else's, hers has a keypad where the handle should be. With no light coming from the sliver of space beneath the wood, I wonder if perhaps it was her who just passed my room.

An unwelcome spike in my blood pressure forces my gaze away at the thought of her. It doesn't seem real that someone can be so damn breathtakingly beautiful while commanding a near army of men. But even more than the bout of temptation that drains into my thoughts, I can see through the veil and know exactly what she is. She's half succubus, half death, and if I'm not careful, I'm likely to sell my soul after I'd fall into her.

I mentally add the space between Onyx's legs to the long list of things that are bound to kill me as I round the hall and quietly walk down the stairs. My feet coast across each step, feeling for any loose boards or screws in the banister that may make a noise. When I reach the foyer, I glance back and forth, trying to remember what's where from Maddy's quick spiel.

The offices need to be looked at first, and then perhaps the labs. But when I turn toward what I think is the right direction, the smell of sweet waffles forces my feet the opposite way, my stomach tightening around the acid sloshing inside.

How long has it been since I've eaten?

I don't dwell on the thought long before a heated conversation stalls my steps.

"Why are you slicing the berries so thin? He won't be able to pick them up with a fork." An older woman's voice spills from the kitchen, a tightness in her lazy tone.

But only a scoffing grunt is her answer.

I roll my thumb across the pads of my fingers, debating whether to venture to the labs instead of down here where I may get caught, or inside, where two more unfamiliars seem to be in a standoff while cooking breakfast. I do need to know all I can, as quickly as I can, and perhaps I can get some of that information from the people living here.

Decision made, I round the wide entry and into the open kitchen. As expected, marble floors continue through the space, and nothing but sleek black cabinets line the walls. Not a thing is out of place, and if there weren't two people currently standing in front of the massive island, I wouldn't think anyone even cooks in here.

My gaze finds the owner of the hostile grunt first. He's a heavyset man, wearing a classic crisp chef's hat and an apron, sweat glistening across his forehead as he works over the gas stove. He doesn't seem to notice my presence, but the woman does.

She's older, perhaps in her late fifties, with short gray hair. At least, I assume it's gray, but the low lighting and the angle in which she leans into the countertop make it look blue. She appears impassive, almost annoyed at my presence.

Her face tilts as she examines me, and after her eyes trail

back to my face, she sticks a long, thin cigarette holder between her lips and takes a lengthy pull.

"A new guard." Not a question, but an introduction. The large man peers up between bushy brows to glance at me momentarily before grunting again.

I take a few steps forward, taking a seat at one of the barstools, despite their current squabble. "Yeah, I'm the—"

"Who... are you?" she interrupts, dragging out her words as she pushes off the counter and blows a stream of smoke from the side of her pursed lips.

I rub the nape of my neck, shifting in my seat. "Ezekiel Kane."

"The very same one you were just going on about, you ol' bat." The chef huffs, plating up what I'd imagine is a five-star breakfast. A short stack of thick waffles, topped with fresh berries, and a side of syrup. Two over-easy eggs, and three strips of perfectly browned bacon.

My stomach rolls loudly, forcing the woman to stop whatever retort she had ready for the cook and look back at me. Her eyes crinkle in the corners as if she can see that it's been almost three days since the last time I ate.

As if she's made some sort of deduction, she squares her small shoulders and tucks a loose, indeed blue, hair back into her low bun. "I'll take this to Antonio. Make the stray pet here a plate."

I raise a hand to oppose her offer, but another contorted sound echoes from my stomach.

The man nods, waving the woman away. "Go on, Caterina. You've got me up an hour early for his breakfast today, so make yourself useful and take it to him. I'll make me and the kid some food."

Kid?

Again, I open my mouth to make a remark, to demand they

acknowledge I'm sitting a mere few inches from their faces, but then I quickly snap it shut. I don't know these people, and I'm smart enough to know not to show my hand too soon and damn sure not to bite the hand that offers to feed me. At least for now. I urge the sharp prick of agitation to ebb back in the shadows and stare at the two.

The woman, Caterina, rolls her eyes, practically shoving her shoulder into the man's bicep to grab the tray. She dangles the cigarette in her mouth and disappears into the hall, leaving me with the cook.

"A big guy like you must have the appetite of a horse." He chuckles more to himself than to me. "But you're all muscles. I bet you don't even know what sugar is."

I shrug. "Studies suggest sugar is as addictive as cocaine."

The large man guffaws, his long, droopy handlebar mustache flopping around with his belly laugh. "I can attest to that. I've done both and am still only addicted to one."

He cracks three eggs on the hot skillet, flipping his spatula around before scraping the translucent edges. "So. New guard, huh?"

I nod, moistening the corner of my lips to hide the sudden drool pooling there. Hungry isn't even the word for the way my gut is contorting at the sight. "And you're the cook?"

"Private chef," he corrects, but doesn't seem overly offended. "Russ."

"Worked here long?"

"Fifteen years."

My brows lift. "So you've worked here since before Onyx took over."

I internally wince after I say it, not sure how much I'm supposed to know. I'd assume it's common knowledge, but also, I have no fucking idea.

But Russ lifts the bubbling edges of an egg, boredom in his tone. "A few years prior, yeah. How do you like your eggs?"

"Over medium."

His muddied-brown eyes flash to mine before he nods, flipping the three eggs over before I can blink. "Same as Boss."

I'm not sure why it interests me how she takes her eggs, but now I find myself curious if she likes her bacon crispy or slightly charred. "Orange juice or coffee?"

"That should be obvious, should it not?" The sultry voice from yesterday flows into the kitchen, wrapping around my cock.

Dammit.

I narrow my eyes at the offending extremity before slowly turning, watching as Onyx enters the kitchen. My breath catches in my throat as I take her in, and for a moment, I'm grateful her eyes are pinned on the cook rather than at me ogling her.

But it isn't the snug black slacks hugging her curves, or the way she saunters in her heels as if she isn't wearing them at all that garner my attention. No, it's the splatter of bright red blood staining her bronzed skin. Flecks of still-glistening droplets decorate the bridge of her nose down to the dip in her satin top, highlighting the tops of her breasts.

My nerves coil, a desire I've never felt before taking hold of my mind, draining out everything else. The invasive thought of stripping the soiled fabric from her body and adding my cum to the masterpiece on her chest overwhelms me and it isn't until the sharp underside of the counter bites into my palm that I realize I'm gripping it so tightly.

Fuck.

I reel in the darkness that's been flirted with enough for the day and catch Onyx's eyes watching me. My jaw clenches as she stares at me, the notion that she can read my thoughts making me shift in my seat.

The air thickens, her gaze growing darker the longer she examines my face, her eyes flicking to my lips I'm currently licking. I swallow hard, suppressing the strong urges tearing at the edges of my sanity, willing my mask to remain intact.

And just when I think she may never relent, one side of her supple lips draw up. "Coffee. Black."

EZEKIEL
CHAPTER TEN

Just when I didn't think she could possibly be any more enticing... more *tempting*, she grins.

This time I know that if what Maddy said was for real, I'm already dead.

I internally move Onyx's cunt to the top of that list, since it seems to be the thing that will get me in trouble the quickest. Still, even with my body vibrating at the thought of being on top of hers, I calm my features. "Too bitter."

"Says the one who claims sugar is as addictive as cocaine," she counters, her dark eyes now trailing down my jaw.

"Because he's never had ours." Caterina reenters the kitchen, and her snarky words are quickly replaced with genuine concern, her tone dousing me in cold water. "Onyx!"

She rushes in front of the island, shooting both myself and the chef a warning glance as if we had something to do with the blood covering her Boss. Russ does a decent job of ignoring her before sliding a stone plate across the high bar and wiping his hand on his apron. "Usual?"

"Yes, thank you." Onyx's voice is still low, but the allure is replaced by something softer. More delicate. Her eyes flash to me as if she can hear me reading her before brushing aside Caterina's hands currently fretting over her chest. "It's not mine, Cat. You should know as much."

The woman sighs, grabbing a dish towel, but Onyx shakes her head and waves her away gently. "Really. I'm going to head up and take a shower now. I just heard talking and wondered who was up so early."

Cat purses her lips. "Your uncle woke from a dream. He didn't sleep well, so I asked Russ to make his breakfast."

Onyx nods. "I'm sure he'll recover after some rest. Get some things from Maddy if you need it."

"Will do. But you need to eat."

"And I will." Onyx looks at Russ before motioning toward me. "Have him bring it up, will you?"

"Yes, ma'am."

She gives me one last pass, her low eyes coaxing the inner beast I work so hard to keep locked away. It's almost as if she's looking past me and straight at him, and that shit makes me as uncomfortable as it turns me on.

Even though it may seem like I'm submitting to her, I force my attention to the food in front of me. It's been less than twenty-four hours and this damn place is already fucking with me.

I am not these people. I shouldn't feel comfortable here. I shouldn't be turned on by the obvious aftermath of a murder. It's nothing new to me. I've seen blood, been covered in it myself on a number of occasions. This is no different. *Onyx* is no different.

Even as I think it, I taste the bitterness in my lie. Like myself, there is so much more to her than what she's showing me, and while I fucking loathe the foundation from which she profits, I can't help but find myself wondering what she's hiding. From me. From her people.

...From herself.

"Who are you?" Cat's slow words pull me to the now Onyx-less kitchen.

"I've answered that. Who are you?"

Russ grunts, a smile barely visible under his thick mustache.

Cat scoffs, folding her arms across her small chest. "I know who I am. But since you so foolishly don't, let me educate you. I am Caterina Mostoff. Estate manager and nurse. One of the first women saved by the Embros family. I—"

"Saved?" I cut in before shoving a forkful of eggs in my mouth. The flavors explode on my tongue and within seconds, the three eggs are digesting in my stomach.

"Animal," she hisses, gesturing to me with her chin. "Make the street rat another serving, Russel."

"Already did."

Sure enough, the chef replaces my empty plate with another, this one with four strips of bacon that are browned perfectly around the edges. I mutter a quick thanks before devouring the meal, not giving myself even a moment to feel guilty. It may be only breakfast but it's by far the best thing I've had in my life.

I'm owed a good meal, at the very least.

It's then I realize, should I die here, my last meal will be five stars.

"First he interrupts me, and now he's smiling to himself like a goon."

"He fits right in." Russ shrugs, going back to what I assume is Onyx's usual meal.

"As I was saying." Cat pulls a cigarette from nowhere like Houdini and lights the end over the stove, ignoring Russ's pinched brows. "I was a nurse, had been for ten years before a night out at the bar ended with me in a musty white van. The scum who took me forced me to care for the other women they took. Fixing them up and getting them ready for sale."

Her face contorts as the memories wash over her. She swallows thickly as if she's fighting back bile, then pushes a stray hair from her face. "One night, I rode with the deliveries, taking care of a few who weren't quite ready. Onyx's father saved us. Slaughtered the vermin in the streets and took the women. When he learned of my skill, he asked me to work at the Embros estate. With the ongoing war running wild in the streets, I would prove to be very useful. So you see. I know who *I* am, boy. The very one who may save you one day, should you go and get yourself shot. Now, who. Are. You?"

She blows a plume of smoke in my direction, which I inhale, forcing the pungent herbs down my throat and out through my nose. "I am no one."

"Here. Take the Boss her food. Lunch is at eleven."

I accept the plate, not bothering to tell him I won't be around in a few hours, and I do my best to quell my raging stomach to the fact. Without another glance at either of them, I disappear into the hall and up the stairs.

Is it valiant what the Embroses do? Yes. But that doesn't matter. They are still guilty of their own sins, such as using people for their own gain. Hell, they think I'm willingly acting as a target just for them to find out how their men are being taken. This isn't done of goodwill. They are merely protecting their assets so they can continue whatever fucked-up shit they're running. Besides, no matter how many women they save, the amount of blood they've spilled will never be able to purge their wrongdoings.

I focus on that thought as I round the hallway and find Onyx's door slightly ajar. Stopping at the threshold, I mistakenly take in a lungful of air and am immediately filled with what I assume is her body wash.

Lemons. Just the faintest smell, with something else reminding me of the moment just before it rains.

Fuck. The fragrance embeds in my nostrils, and I know it will be too damn long before I forget her scent.

I open my mouth to call out to her, but my jaw audibly slams shut at the sight of her naked frame emerging from the bathroom. Steam billows around her, sticking to her curves as if it wishes to stay attached to her smooth skin. Her pert breasts, now clean of the blood, glisten under the warm light of the bed lamps, her dusty pink nipples drawn tight between barbells.

My eyes drop of their own will to her toned stomach, noting the faint scars barely visible above her navel.

Onyx turns, grabbing a black silk robe from the bed, giving me a full view of her back, and *holy fuck.* Her bottom half is far thicker than her dark wardrobe gives her credit for, and my mouth waters as it follows the round globes of her ass to the small divots just above.

The perfect spot for my thumbs to rest as I bury everything inside her.

"Are you just going to watch me?"

Her sultry tone has returned, beckoning me to enter like a siren out at sea. And just as the sailor drives his crew to their death, I too move into the room.

She threads an arm through the robe, covering just enough to allow me a second to fend off the drunken haze clouding my logic.

I'm not here for this. Give her the food and le—

When she turns, I see she's kept the front open, and while it covers her pebbled nipples, it leaves a small patch open that my eyes flicker to.

I've had my fair share of women, enough to satisfy even the hungriest of men, but fuck if Onyx doesn't call to something so much deeper. To something even I haven't fed in fear I'll never be able to satiate its appetite.

Every muscle tightens as she nears me, erasing the space between us until only the plate's few inches separates us. Without heels, she's about a foot shorter, but even having to peer up at me takes nothing away from her powerful aura. No, she's in control here.

Naked but not vulnerable.

Small but not powerless.

I wonder if any of her demeanor changes when she's overcome with lust and on the brink of exploding. If she ever finds herself so lost in the euphoria, she sheds her armor for a brief moment to merely *feel*.

"Are you going to hand me my food or shall we let it get cold?"

"I'm standing here with your plate in front of me. Why won't you take it?"

Her head tilts back, a bored look leveling her features. "Because I want you to hand it to me."

"And I want you to take it," I challenge. I'm not sure why I'm playing on the dangerously thin line with a woman I don't know, but what better way to find out more about her?

Though she doesn't seem amused, she no longer looks bored. Her blinks slow, and her heavy-lidded gaze falls to my mouth, then to my neck. She runs her pink tongue along the seam of her lips, making my cock twitch.

"Give me what I asked for." Not a request, a command.

A test.

Something I need to desperately pass if anything I'm doing here is going to work out in my favor. But Onyx has stirred something I can no longer ignore. I lower my head, and it doesn't surprise me when she doesn't flinch away.

"If you want it, take it." My breath coasts across her earlobe as I whisper, "Boss."

A sharp pinch in my side forces me to slowly back up, rising to my full height. My eyes follow the source of pain to see the point of a small blade pressing into my shirt right above my kidney. A smirk ghosts across her lips before she holds out her free hand.

"Why take it when I know you will give it to me willingly?"

My now fully hardened dick presses uncomfortably into the zipper of my jeans, but I manage to return her grin and press the plate into her hand. Her gaze drifts to my dimples as she takes both the blade and breakfast from me. "Good boy."

This gets a chuckle from me. "I'll see you tomorrow, ma'am."

But instead of waiting for a response, or lack thereof, I turn and return to my room, where I wait out the remainder of my shift. Only now, all my worries have been replaced with long black hair and even darker eyes.

* * *

I hate this house. Have since I was thirteen.

Staring at the weathered porch, barely held up by the wood posts and concrete, anxiety wraps around my throat, as memories I work every day to suppress surface. The day that changed everything.

It was around eight o'clock, a little after the streetlights turned on. I had to carry Fi home because she rolled her ankle, trying to skateboard with the new kid down the block. The moment the door opened, I knew something was wrong. I knew it before I put Fiona in her bed and told her to stay still while I got her an ice pack. I even knew it before I saw my mom's feet shaking from the aftermath of her seizure as she lay nearly comatose on the kitchen floor.

A pot of spaghetti sat idle on the stove, and three placemats were perfectly aligned on the table, waiting for us to find our rightful places. After making quick work of the ice pack, I promised Fi I'd be back shortly.

When the neighbor saw my mother's brittle limbs strewn across the weathered linoleum, it took a shit ton of convincing for her to help me take her to the hospital. We were already going to be in debt with the visit alone, and I knew we couldn't add the cost of the ambulance too.

Later that night, I'd find out that my years-long suspicion of a possible addiction was accurate.

At first, I blamed the pieces of shit that sold her the drugs, the off-brand Adderall that promised to give her all the energy she needed to work eighty hours a week. I confronted a few of the well-known sellers in the area. Even at thirteen, I was big as shit, already pushing six feet and tipping the scales close to one fifty. Scrawny, but lean, with enough muscle to knock some of the grown men to the floor before they did what the weak always do and pull a gun. It was the only way I'd relent, because with each punch, with each crack of their jaws, I'd feel better.

Why?

Because it wasn't really them I was hitting. It was me.

The real person who let my mother almost die.

I'd agree with her every time she asked me to take care of Fi. To feed my sister dinner and get her ready for school or bed. I made Mom feel content with leaving us at home while she picked up extra shifts and side jobs. I allowed her to think that it was okay for her to run herself ragged as long as our homework was done and the house stayed as clean as it possibly could. I thought by doing that I was relieving her stress. Helping her see that we were okay while she busted her ass to make ends meet and put what she could on our table.

But all along it should have been me who was picking up the side gigs. Not only that, but I should have told her about the little things Fi was starting to do. Her small cries for attention. The fact that there were things I couldn't teach her that Mom needed to.

A week after our mother came back, everything changed. She was forced to stay home, to learn to cope and live with her new symptoms, and with barely a trickle of money from our absent sperm donor, I was allowed to pick up the slack.

That's when the darkness I'd been born with started to grow. When I was younger, it'd been shoved into the furthest corners of my mind, too busy with all my focus on helping raise Fi to feed it. But when I started picking up the jobs, it was like feeding it a protein shake.

I've done well keeping it in line, but now that I'm in the belly of a beast much bigger than my own, it wants to come out to play. To compete.

Shoving the dangerously idiotic idea back down, I close my hand over the worn metal handle. As expected, the door is unlocked, but inside, my mother isn't there.

I quickly walk through the small house, my boots echoing against the faux wood sticky tile. My sister's and my shared room remains empty and untouched as it was when I left it yesterday. Our two beds are pressed against opposite ends as if an invisible line runs down the middle, either side completely different. Fiona's side is nothing but green pothos and cream bedding, while mine is as bare as can be with only posters of local bands on the wall.

Traveling back through the hall, I find my mother's room is empty as well, along with the shared bathroom and living area.

My nerves begin to wind, a sickening sensation curdling the amazing breakfast in my gut.

What if—

Thankfully, I don't have to finish that thought as a single piece of paper and a small box on the dining table catch the corner of my eye.

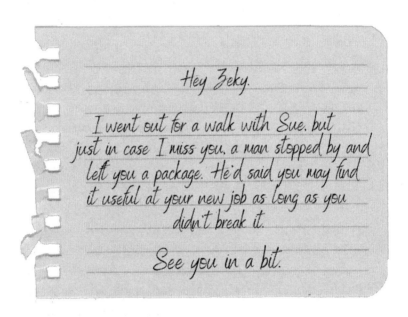

Hey Zeky,

I went out for a walk with Sue, but just in case I miss you, a man stopped by and left you a package. He'd said you may find it useful at your new job as long as you didn't break it.

See you in a bit.

I can't help but sigh a bit of relief that not only is she okay, but out in the fresh air. Most days she's a recluse, staring at old reruns or griping over her latest soap opera. Slowly, our neighbor has begun coaxing her out of the house, and I think it's helped with quite a few side effects of the drugs.

Grabbing the small box, I rip off the single strip of tape holding it together. Inside is a single item, something I didn't even know they made anymore.

Is this a fucking Nokia?

I take the ancient piece of technology and power it up. On the microscopic screen, a text pops up from a number already programmed.

SM: Call me when you get this.

After clicking the number, it only takes half a ring.

"So you're alive. That's good."

"Where's my sister?" I cut to the chase, invoking as much poison in my words as possible.

He tsks, and I hear the phone's plastics squeak as it gives way to my tight grasp. "All I have is a map right now. I'm sure it's the same one you have."

"Perhaps. Got any codes or anything?" His voice is as sleazy as it was the day on the roof, and it begins to boil my blood in how laid back it is. Like this is a casual conversation, and he doesn't have my kid sister locked away in some fucking basement or some shit.

"No! I just fucking started. All I know so far is who is in charge of what and how far their property lines go."

Sam scoffs. "Fine. Call your sister so you can feel better. Also, for common sense reasons, she'll be the one you tell information to just in case your dumb ass gets caught on the phone. And if by next week you don't have shit to tell me, her current living arrangements will get a lot less comfortable."

The phone clicks as he ends the call and I have to fight the urge not to chuck the phone across the room. Because it may be the only way to contact my sister, I flop onto the old green couch and quell my anger while I dial Fi's number.

She answers on the first ring. "Hey, you."

My back jolts from the couch, a calmness I haven't felt in years washing over me at the sound of her voice. "Fiona. Are you okay? Are they hurting you? How do you have your phone? I swear to God, Fi, when I come for you, I'm going to slice every one of those fuckers—"

"Zek. It's okay. *I'm* okay. I promise."

My sister has always been soft spoken, but the firmness in her words gives me an ounce of relief. "What? Be specific. Now."

"I'm in some type of mansion, fifth floor, if I had to guess from all the stairs they had me climb. I'm locked in a guest room with a private bathroom and a guard standing at my door twenty-four seven. They're rude as shit, and when they give me food, half of it spills from them slamming it across the table. Last night, one of the younger ones ate half of it and said he couldn't wait till my brother fucked up so they could treat me how prisoners are meant to be treated."

My anger returns, swelling in my sternum until the surrounding organs burn. "Have they touched you, Fi?"

I squeeze my eyes as I await his answer. "No, they haven't touched me or anything. Besides their misogynistic arrogance, the only thing that sucks is the loneliness. I mean, they gave me Netflix, and even let me keep my phone."

Confusion has my brows nearly melded together, but the relief she hasn't been abused physically is damn near tangible. "Yeah, why the fuck did they let you keep your phone? How do they know you won't call for help?"

She actually laughs at this. "Because I don't want to die. I'm not an idiot, Zek. If I called for help, I'd be dead before the police even exited their cars. The Murphys also know I have a little social circle and don't want people getting suspicious, calling attention to the fact that both you and I all of a sudden disappeared, so they let me chat with my friends. I couldn't keep up with all the excuses on why I couldn't hang out, so I told them I was on a Habitat for Humanity tour."

What in the actual fuck?

She sighs. "Really, I'm good for now. I just think there's a contingency on how I'm treated, but I do know they are really banking on you coming through."

"Correct. Their hospitality won't last."

"I know. But for now, I'll milk what little they give me while I can. Also, any information you get on the Embros family is supposed to be given to me."

"Yeah, Sam said something about that."

"I think it's because if they find your phone or trace your calls or whatever, it won't seem weird that you're talking to your sister."

I'm not sure if that's true, or if Onyx would even think to watch my calls. As powerful as she is, I'm sure she doesn't think anyone is stupid enough to cross her. Not if they wanted to keep their balls attached, at least.

"Are you okay?"

I run a hand through my hair and realize the heaviness in my chest has significantly decreased. "Better now."

"Good, and don't worry about me. It's not like I can die from boredom and bad manners. Just get what you need and get us the hell out of here. I'll be fine. You just better stay alive."

I nod, even though she can't see me. Part of me wonders if they're doing more things that she isn't telling me. But also, I need to believe they aren't. I'd go insane and wouldn't do anything but get the both of us killed.

As if she can feel my reservations slipping, my sister yawns, like this is just a normal conversation. "I adore you, big brother."

"Ditto."

When we hang up, I close my eyes, pressing my head back into the lumpy couch. Within seconds, sleep finds me.

Kilo
CHAPTER ELEVEN

That drop was quick. Neutral territory has to be quick. I know. But they seemed to want to disappear before my hand was even pulled away from the bag.

That was rude.

So unkind.

I don't even think they said thank you. Nope, they didn't. I don't recall. Now, let me see. Next stop. Next stop. They wanted three. Why so much? They are a weekly drop. How could they possibly run through so much?

Shaking my head, I rid my thoughts. Onyx says it was fine. I trust her. She—

Oh! That's the new guard. Ezekiel. What is he... oh, that's right. I remember Trick saying he lives in the neutral. I must say hi. He seems kind. I bet he would say thank you.

But I'm late. I have to go.

Just as I blink, the big man disappears inside the tiny little house, taking his long, dark shadows with him. It's a wonder he fits in such a small thing.

KANE.

The old sign by the window shakes even though he closed the tattered door with a gentle hand. Kane. Kane. I know that name. How do I know that name? I knew it before today, right?

Lee Jacquot

I'm not sure, but I have no time to ponder how. I'm late. And time is of the essence.

Onyx
AGE 12
CHAPTER TWELVE

"I like that, Onyx." Trick points one of his long, pale fingers to the logo I've been doodling all afternoon. "It looks like Kilo's birthmark."

Before I can respond, Kilo appears from seemingly nowhere, bouncing in the middle of where we're sprawled out with art supplies on the Persian rug. "Where?"

A high-pitched giggle slips past my lips as I push him up and over onto an unsuspecting Trigger. "Hey, watch it!"

The boys spend the next few seconds wrestling as I lean against the edge of the couch and spectate. Limbs flail, tangle, and thrash while they all grunt hushed obscenities. Being such newbies in the world of defense and fighting, their skills are still very much lacking, and it's entertaining to watch. Kind of like watching three fish in a shallow bucket of water, all trying to suck in the last droplets of water.

I've known the three newest additions to the family for a year now. The blond Swedish twins, Trick and Trigger, and the albino, Kilo, were all kids to single women who my parents weren't able to save during a trafficking deal. With no other family and their... medical conditions, my mom knew they'd get lost in the system and suggested they be brought home with us. And I've been so grateful for it.

It's been amazing having friends at the house to suffer the same tutors and lessons, to fight and play with. To sneak around the estate at three in the morning and smuggle glasses of cookies and bowls of milk back upstairs. And yes. I said it right. Bowls of milk. And glasses of cookies.

Being with the three of them has reminded me that while I may be more mature and educated than ninety-percent of other twelve-year-olds in the country, I'm still a kid.

My mother seems to notice it too and has stopped fussing when we sometimes become distracted while gardening and play hide-and-seek instead. My father doesn't grumble when we come in long after the sun's rays have faded into the horizon and we have mud staining the bottom of our soles to the tips of our noses.

But also, they probably don't care because the boys deserve any moments they can get that're full of light when all they ever knew is darkness. And not just any darkness. What they experienced was the kind that seemed everlasting. The kind that sucked the air from the room, from your skin and lungs until your body was on fire and you were begging for death.

"Kill me, please. *Jag ber dig.*" *I beg you.*

"No, you are going to make it through this." I try my best to soothe him, brushing his matted hair from his moist forehead.

Trigger's head shakes so violently, I think it's going to break. Hot tears stream down his face, mixing with the snot as tremors shake through his frail body. "Please, Onyx."

"You can't leave your brother. He needs you, Trigger." I know it's probably not kind to hold something like that over his head, but I want him to fight it as hard as he can. He only has to make it a little longer. Cat says if they can make it through the four days, they will live.

It's been two. They're already halfway there. "Just a little longer. Stay with me, Trig. Please."

I force my eyes away from my new friend, shielding him from my own traitorous tears burning around the edges. On the opposite side of the room, his twin brother, Trick, has puked himself to sleep, while my mother and father are currently restraining Kilo from banging his head through the wall again.

Out of them all, Kilo is hurting the most, and I think it's because he was addicted the longest. From what my mother tried to explain, even as a baby, he had drugs in his system from his mother, so she knew his fight was going to be the hardest.

His thrashes and screams echo through the estate, and when he begs for his mother... It's all I can do not to ask my father to send an army to kill every last one of the Murphys. But I know better. He'd say it's not our job. That we do the same thing every time we sell a drug to someone not knowing who's going to use it. That while these boys' stories are sad, they are not the only ones.

Between the pure hatred that coils my insides to the physical ache in my heart, I feel... powerless. There's absolutely nothing I can do more than sit with them when all I want to do is take their pain away. But to them, I'm asking them to fight a battle I can only see but not feel. I'm asking them to allow this agony to rip them apart, making the seconds feel like hours, and the hours feel like days.

I make a promise to myself as I watch Trigger finally succumb to his cramping stomach and retch over the side of the bed into his bucket.

When they make it out of this, and years later, when I'm in charge of everything, we will kill them all. Every last one.

Visions of sweat-covered beds and vomit-filled toilets flash through my mind. The first week of their stay here was the worst. All of them had a heroin addiction that stemmed from before they were even ten. Sniffed in their little noses when their mothers had fallen asleep.

I still very much intend to kill every last Murphy there is, but for now, designing the Embros Hearts logo with my boys is a step. We finally got the majority of the foundation set up and now we need to make a logo of sorts.

Mine resembles Kilo's *birthmark*. He once told me in secret it was a scar but one he's proud of, so I decided to incorporate it. It's shaped like a sad tree—tall, thin, with fans of long stringy branches.

A weeping willow that never got to grow to its fullest potential, but beautiful, nonetheless.

"Through here." My father's booming voice forces the boys to scramble away from each other, their backs suddenly upright as our eyes shift to the foyer where a shuffle of feet skirt across the freshly waxed floors.

Three of his men struggle with another who has a black sack over his head. He jerks his shoulder away from my father's soldiers and muffled words spew from under the cotton hiding his face.

This does nothing but annoy my father who merely moves to the thin door under the right side of the stairs. He nearly yanks the door from its hinges before grabbing the hooded man by his neck. His fingers dig so fiercely into the sides, the man's veins bulge out, and his body stills.

My father edges closer, his words calm but so commanding that goose bumps prickle along my arms. "You're going to show some fucking dignity and walk down these stairs. If not, I have no problem breaking your knees and dragging you down. You have one second to comply."

The man's shoulders drop as my father's hand leaves his throat, and he makes no move to shove away the soldiers when they grip him again. One of the guys stays at the door as Father disappears, shutting the door behind him.

"No, Onyx. I see that look in your eye. Don't even think about it."

My eyes narrow as I whip my head around to look at Trigger. "Did you just tell your future Boss what to do?"

He sighs, rolling his eyes. "My job will be to protect you one day. I'm trying to keep you from doing anything that may get you hurt."

"But that's no fun," Trick chimes in.

"Yes, no fun at all." Kilo bounces on his butt, his eyes wide as they skirt between the boys and me. "Onyx needs to watch her father if she wants to rule like him."

"If she was ready to watch his interrogations, he'd have invited her down." Trigger shifts back to his logo, ignoring the daggers I'm throwing with my gaze.

He's right. Father and Mother alike say there's still some time before they want me to watch that, but really, if I was a boy, I'd have been down there years ago. I mean, the twins and Kilo have already started going through something called torture training, and when I asked to join, my father nearly blew a fuse.

"No *princessa* of mine will endure such barbaric things. That's why we have men that will protect you with their lives," he all but shouted across the dinner table.

"You're doing her a disservice, brother. I know we wish only for the best but, we need to prepare her for the worst. You've given her the brains and the brawn but not the resilience." My uncle Antonio pushes away his empty plate, his thin lips drawn into a tight line.

"We agreed when she's sixteen." My mother's soft voice does little to calm the fire radiating from my father. But the moment she places a tender hand across his, he blinks, dismissing his anger and staring at her. "We have plenty of time to worry about *it. But for now, let us enjoy that the boys made it through three months of sobriety."*

He nods before kissing her hand, his dark, disheveled strands falling over his forehead. "Yes. Let this be a celebration."

That was almost ten months ago, and anytime either myself or my uncle brought it up, he merely referred to my sixteenth birthday and refused to waste another breath on the matter. Well, if he doesn't want to subject me to the same treatment as the boys, I can at least learn how to get answers from my enemies.

Besides, I know he'll forgive me... if I get caught.

I shoot a wink at the boys before venturing around to my father's vacant office. Behind the third bookshelf is a hidden door leading to the basement. It acts as a second entrance, but also a hidden observation area for when my father wants to watch prisoners who are kept for longer times.

The cold tile is a shock to my bare feet, shooting little waves of chills up my calves. But before I can dwell on the frigid temperature, voices and a scuffle capture my attention.

"Now that you're all set up, let's get started, shall we?" My father sounds calm, bored even.

"Fuck yo—"

A sharp pop rings out, followed by what sounds like spit hitting the concrete. It forces my feet down another few steps until I can peer over the side just enough to see them.

The two soldiers who came down with him are positioned against the far side of the gray room, near the wooden steps. My father is positioned in front of the now bound man, his arms strung above his head with ropes that are tied far too tight, rubbing his arms raw already as he struggles uncomfortably.

His cover has been taken off, and under the thick blood sticking to the side of his face, there's a vague familiarness to him that has me wondering where I've seen him.

"I shouldn't have to advise you to watch how you speak to me. But because I'd rather get answers than your screams when I slice your fucking thighs down the center, I will. Tread carefully, Mario."

Mario. Mario. *Where do I know that name?*

"Let's try again. How long?"

The man's light-blue eyes fall to the floor before he swallows thickly. It almost reminds me of someone who's done something they feel guilty for. But why would a Murphy feel bad?

"How fucking long?" My father's hiss cuts through the air, the don in full effect.

Whatever feelings of guilt he had dissolved, replaced by a smug snarl. "The entire time."

"Good." Mario's head pops up at Father's comment, his pupils going wide before he recovers himself. "I love feeding rats to my dogs."

Rats. Mario. He's a *soldier*. One of my father's. He... he's one of the guards that goes with my mother when she goes to Protestant liturgy.

He's a mole.

"Tell me. What was your grand plan? Find a way to kill your partner guard and my driver, and deliver my wife to your Boss? Or perhaps you thought you'd turn and kill her and face a quick death? Do you not understand I have eyes *everywhere*? That the moment you walked into their territory, I was informed within a minute?"

"Lies." Mario spits on the floor, the mucus a nasty shade of brown and red.

"I am many things, but a liar I am not. Tell me what I want to know."

Mario smiles, but it's anything but happy, and it sends a chill down my skin, making it feel as though bugs are trailing over my flesh. "Sure. I'll tell you this. They are coming, *Boss*. You'll watch her be slit from throat to cunt and be fucked while they bleed her dry."

Mother. My lungs constrict, my heart squeezing in my chest. There's no way he would ever let anyone hurt her, but the mere thought of anything happening to her makes bile burn my throat.

Father doesn't respond, but even from my perch, I see the vein in the side of his neck throbbing. He strips his jacket from his shoulders, hanging it from a hook on a nearby column before slowly and methodically rolling up his crisp black sleeves.

Both Mario and I's gaze flit to the silver knife one of the soldiers hands him. He twirls it between his fingers, his blinks slow and lazy. "Ah, but you first, Mario. You first."

Then come the screams. Screams of anger from my father and wails of agony from the man he slices from limb to limb. He spills his blood with every last secret Mario tells, and after each one, he begs for death.

The same death my boys begged me for. The very same they had to fight against. And as I watch the skin be stripped from the rat piece by piece, I find myself hoping he has to fight as long as they did before my father finally grants his wish.

Shi

CHAPTER THIRTEEN

A vibration is what wakes me. My phone rattles against the wooden nightstand with a picture of a heart filling the screen.

"Two nights in a row?" Trigger's sleepy words warm my neck he's nuzzling.

That is odd. But also, Onyx is more stressed than she's letting on.

Stretching my arm out, I grab the phone, tapping the small green circle before pressing the phone to my ear. "Another late rendezvous, Boss?"

I'm met with silence.

Shit.

"I'm coming."

Normally, when I'm tangled in the bed with the twins, it takes a lot of willpower to force myself away. They are the anchors keeping me from drifting out to sea and becoming lost in the raging waters of my mind, and I'm so grateful to have them. But I also know that Onyx *doesn't* have that.

There is nothing to keep her company in the night except death and memories of death.

I turn my face, kissing a sleepy Trigger before slipping my naked body away and leaning over to sneak a quick peck from

Trick, who's lying on the other side of the large bed. He grabs my wrist, pulling me closer and turning a chaste kiss into a make-out session. My core aches as I force myself to slow him down, running my thumb along his jaw before he finally releases me.

"I won't be long tonight," I promise.

"It's okay. Take care of her."

I grant him a solemn smile, grabbing my discarded gown from the floor and slipping it over my head.

It only takes half a minute to reach Onyx's room, where I punch in my code to open the door. Quiet music plays on her bedside speaker, a half-empty bottle of Jack Daniels resting next to her phone.

I climb into her bed, the cool silk sheets falling over my frame as I find her and curl up in front of her. In the years that I've known Onyx, I've never seen her upset or distraught, and for once, I wish that when she had one of her nightmares that she would give herself a second to be sad. To cry. To mourn. To hate. To be angry. To *feel*.

But I understand why she doesn't. It could be the thing that tears her apart. Keeps her from finishing what we all so desperately want.

Revenge.

Justice.

Peace.

Onyx takes a steadying breath and moves a wayward strand of hair behind my ear. "Your pink is fading."

"Would you like to help me color it again?"

She nods, pressing the side of her face deeper into the pillow. "After my meeting tomorrow."

My chest draws tight. She leaves the house only once a week, but every time, I get nervous. With her guards being killed so often, it's only a matter of time before they step up their game and go for who they're really after. "Are you sure I shouldn't go instead?"

"Stop worrying yourself. I'll be fine. I always am."

The distinct smell of whiskey coasts across the silk pillow, and I find myself impressed she's coherent.

"Besides," she continues, tracing my jawline, "Maddy got me a new shield."

"He is big. And handsome."

Her blinks slow, her gaze becoming unfocused as I assume she pictures him. "He's different."

"I know."

"Do you think Maddy told him the lie she tells them all?"

This makes me smile. "Yes."

Maddy is as desperate as I am to have Onyx feel something, even if it means the pleasure of an orgasm, and tends to tell the new guards sleeping with her is a part of their job. Onyx never actually sleeps with any of them, but watching the men walk around waiting to be beckoned is one of my favorite pastimes now.

The unfortunate truth, though, is Onyx probably *would* fuck them, but deep down, I think she knows their inevitable deaths will only upset her more if she has any attachments to them. This new guard, however... he is very different from the others.

I don't know enough to be able to see how, but the dangerous aura surrounding him is almost as dark as Onyx's herself, and he does just as good a job as she does keeping it hidden.

The twins and I have eyes on him though and tomorrow will be a test of his character, considering we are suspicious of the man she's meeting with—a new vendor for slot machines.

Nothing out of the ordinary, but he refused to deal with me, and insisted he meet with Onyx. Money is money, regardless of who works the deal, and him demanding to work with her is a red flag. But Onyx fears nothing and sees warning signs as an invitation to kill with no questions, so I'm letting her take the lead.

"Trick told me the new guard will be stationed in the building tomorrow. Is that okay?"

"And who will be at my side?"

"Williams and Thorn." Two longtime estate guards who I trust to stop a bullet with their heads should the need arise.

She nods, tucking her hand under the pillow. I want to ask her about the reason she called me up. I know it was a nightmare—it always is—but I wonder how bad it was. The times she doesn't tell me, I think they are the ones that tempt her sanity to crumble.

But she's too fucking strong for her own good and a quick thirty-minute conversation is enough to distract her—enough to allow her time to cram the agony that haunts her back into its locked chest.

It's not healthy, and damn sure isn't going to work forever.

"How bad?"

"Bad enough."

I sigh, watching as she turns on her back, her dark eyes finding a spot on the ceiling to lock on to. "Want me to grab something from Cat or Maddy? Something to put you to sleep?"

"In the top drawer on the right." She points a stiletto nail toward her dresser, holding a TV I've never seen turned on.

My brows snap up. "You were prepared?"

"The guard." She takes a greedy breath before blowing it out slowly. "He's different."

Maybe she's drunker than I thought. "You said that, O—"

"He reminds me of my father. Not in the *daddy issues* type of way. But in his resolve. I can already tell he's stubborn.

Smart, but never given the chance to show it. And a nurturer. A man who takes care of people. But also..."

She trails off, and for a moment, I think she's fallen asleep before she yawns. "He's a killer. I can smell it on him. I'd bet at least a dozen souls have been sent to Hell by his hand."

This makes the hairs on the back of my neck stand as I slip from the bed, suddenly needing the weed more than she does. "And you're comfortable having someone like that be an associate hired to *protect* you?"

"All my guards have taken a life. And he's more than a killer, that's why I mentioned it last."

"Yes, sure. I guess give credit where it's due. But what about him makes you so sure?" I open the drawer, pulling out the joint already tightly wrapped.

"He made me think of how fiercely my father protected my mother. How when he was with her—with us—he was someone different, someone softer, but still the don. How effortlessly he commanded his army with a hand that was both feared and respected."

I light the end of the joint, pulling in a deep lungful. The hot herbs fill my lungs and almost immediately span out, coursing through my limbs and warming my body. "Are you saying this new guard gives you the feeling of someone as powerful as your father?"

"Yes," she deadpans. "And when everything is said and done, I'll kill him."

Well, this took a turn.

After another lengthy drag, I return to the bed, handing her the small blunt. "Kill him?"

"He has a power behind him he doesn't understand. One he was born with. Once he realizes it, do you think he will be content with being a guard? An associate?"

"He'll want more?"

"He'll want it *all*."

My lips part to ask her how she knows. How she could possibly have any idea about his intentions when she doesn't even think he knows them himself. But she's the keenest of us all, and she's always been good with picking up on others. Hence why we don't ever question her when she does even the most outlandish things with the sketchiest of people.

And she hasn't been wrong yet.

Onyx's eyes grow glossy, the strong herbs mixing with the liquor already coursing through her. It won't be long now until sleep finds her. "Alright, Boss. We'll take care of the Murphys and then we'll kill him. In other news, Maddy found a new toy."

"Tell me about her. The brunette, right?"

I nod, accepting the joint back and drawing in a deep breath. "Yes. Harlow."

"Harlow. Is she enough to keep up with her?"

"Not quite sure yet, but I did find her naked, covered in Maddy's artwork."

"Hmm."

I glance down just as Onyx loses her battle with sleep. But it isn't until I've tidied up her room, fixed the crooked pictures of her parents, and cleaned up the alcohol that I find my way back to the twins. When I slip back beneath the sheets, her words echo in my mind, a piece slotting into place of a puzzle I didn't realize I was putting together.

"*He'll want it all.*"

EZEKIEL
CHAPTER FOURTEEN

A heavy rain cloud moves over the estate, hiding the sun that was shining through the tall windows mere moments ago.

Part of me considers it an omen—a visual representation of what I feel inside when I first return to the estate from my night off. But the sickly feeling leaves the moment I smell Russ cooking breakfast.

Unlike the other night, a dozen guards sit at the elongated dining table to the right of the kitchen. All of them are paired up, hunched over in quiet conversations as I pass by, finding my spot near the chef. From the bits and pieces I catch, most of them like to gamble. Horses, boxing matches, football, you name it, and more than a couple of times I have to school my features as I eat at the bar, watching as Russ works around the island.

It's always baffled me how some people can risk their money on a whim—on a chance with odds so slim it makes my insides itch. But then again, maybe it's because I've never had the money to waste.

Or maybe it's because I know my luck is shit, and I'll always lose.

Either way, the concept of risks, chances, and hope confuses me.

"Why are your eyebrows so tight, Z? You'll get wrinkles before you're thirty." Maddy's curls flash in my periphery before I hear the thud of her ass flopping onto the seat.

"Isn't that a good thing? It'll make me look more distinguished. More respectable."

She cackles, throwing her small head back. "Hmm, I'd rather have people fear me."

"Judging by the way the room just fell silent, I'd say people already do."

"Indeed. The only downside is they're also scared to fuck me."

My eyebrows lift at this as I take in my last bite of eggs, wishing I'd eaten slower. "Is that so?"

"A fact," she replies, taking my cup of orange juice and downing the rest of it in one gulp. A stray piece of pulp hangs on the edge of her lips. When I point to the dribble, her eyes widen comically as her tongue dramatically circles her entire mouth. "Oh stop. You're looking at me all funny like you haven't done a Ren and Stimpy clean."

"I'm looking at you like this because you remind me of an overgrown child."

"Do I?" She pouts, folding her arms. "Perhaps it's because I don't remember even having a childhood and I wish to live it now."

"Perhaps," I repeat, staring as she blows a stray curl from her face. The small action solidifies my thinking but makes me remember something from the other night.

Cat's words and the small information I've gotten from Maddy flip through my mind. I wonder if all the people here were saved by Onyx and her family. It wouldn't change how I perceive her Boss or anything that is happening here, but it does give me a slight pause. If Onyx is in the business of helping women, maybe... *no*. I'd be dead before I finished my second sentence. I force the idiotic thought away, not giving it a chance to evolve into an idea and glance back at Maddy.

Her eyes drift away momentarily as her mouth parts twice, her fingers rhythmically tapping against her thumb as if she's deep in her own thoughts. But then she sighs, and whatever she wants to say vanishes as she takes on a more serious tone. "Be ready at nine. Onyx has a meeting with a vendor downtown. It's a rooftop restaurant, and the man is new to us."

"How many guards are going?"

"Trick, you, Shi, and four estate guards. Shi will dine with her, while Trick monitors the floor. You'll be at the top entrance, while another guard will be in the stairwell and the two others on the ground."

I stand, nodding to Russ in thanks for the breakfast. "Alright. I'm going to take a shower and get dressed."

"Meet them in the foyer in a bit. Oh, and don't be scared to stop by Onyx's room on the way for a quick cock-a-doodle-doo." She gives me an elaborate wink while her high-strung giggle follows me out.

I take the stairs two at a time, and even though I tell myself not to, I glance over to the right at Onyx's room. It hasn't been much more than a day, but I'd be lying if I said I haven't pictured the smooth trail of her curves, or the peaks of her breasts once or twice.

A deep groan works its way from my throat as the vision invades my thoughts again, driving my dick to a painful length. What she did was a power move, and I can admit it did things to me I won't soon forget.

Things I want to explore. Things I want to feel.

But the most notable is commanding the body of someone who brings everyone else to their knees.

* * *

"You clean up nice." One of the twins, Trick, I think, lays a heavy hand on my shoulder, his other holding out a small translucent piece of material in the shape of a bean.

"Appreciate it," I reply, tilting my head in question as I take the item from him.

"It's an earpiece. It will connect you with me and the other guards. You'll be able to listen, but not respond. It keeps the feed clear for me and Trigger. Also..." He pulls out a small gun, a .380, and taps the left breast of my Armani jacket. "It fits perfectly in the lower pocket."

Holding, concealing, and using a gun are nothing new to me, which I'm sure the twins have seen on my background check, so I don't bother acting as such. In fact, more and more of what I do here feels so natural, I'm starting to wonder if I even need to worry about a front at all.

"Thank you." I accept the gun and tuck it away before taking my place at the door with the other guards.

All four of them are older and remind me of the men you'd see outside Buckingham Palace with their hard, stonelike gazes and upright posture. The closest one to me nods briefly while staring back ahead.

We stand for a few minutes before a crack of thunder breaks the silence, at the same time a pair of heels hit the marble floor. My eyes flash to her, and my body responds instantly, the tap of my pulse becoming more aggressive in my wrists.

Just like the few other times I've seen her, she's in all black.

Today's long-sleeve dress comes to her neck and hugs her curves all the way down to the middle of her thigh, acting as a second skin. Her waist-length black hair is drawn up into a high ponytail, the ends dangling over her shoulder and kissing her covered collarbone.

When she passes by, her focus, as does mine, remains straight ahead. But then the faintest scent of lemon wafts over me, chipping at my resolve. I squeeze my fist, attempting to rein in the suddenly loose leash I have on my thoughts. It's like an itch I wasn't aware I had, and now that I've accidentally rubbed against it, the need to scratch it is becoming overwhelming.

And here I was thinking the other thing I needed to worry about was not getting caught being a rat.

When we all shuffle outdoors, Trick instructs me to ride in the front of the limo with the driver, while the others follow behind in a separate vehicle. Onyx and her right hand, Shi, sit in the back of the cab with the dark privacy glass raised.

For a moment, I consider making small talk with the older gentleman driving, maybe get to know more about the people in the estate, but somehow I get lost in my thoughts the entire thirty-minute ride. With being less caught up in the safety of my sister and mother, my mind has less to keep it busy. Less to deter it from the very real threat sitting only a few feet behind me.

And far less to keep it from succumbing to something I work so fucking hard at keeping in check.

The limo slows to a stop in front of a tall building. It's nothing but high panes of glass, metal beams, and reflective chrome.

"Don't get out, Zek." Trick's voice takes me by surprise as the sound vibrates against my ear, tickling the small hairs. I see the driver smirk before getting out as Trick continues. "Should anyone be watching, we don't want to make it known quite yet that you're the Boss's new guy. The driver is going to let the girls out, then pull into the garage. You'll enter through the side access door and travel to the tenth floor just under the restaurant. Keep guard there and should anyone get through, open the door and let me know. Don't react. We like to keep people alive so we can gather any information they might have."

I nod even though I know he can't see me and stay put, leaning back into the cool leather. The clouds still loom overhead but have yet to spill any rain thus far. Surprising, considering how dark they are.

"Interested in the weather?" the driver asks, reentering the limo.

"Just surprised it hasn't poured yet."

The driver peers through the window, his small smile causing the skin near his eyes to wrinkle. "Miss Embros loves the rain."

"Oh yeah?"

He nods, pulling away from the entrance and around to a garage on the side of the building. "You'd be surprised by how dark a sunny day can be."

My brows furrow, but the man doesn't add anything else as he parks and lets me out.

The mystery surrounding Onyx only grows thicker with the more people I encounter. It makes me curious as to how many layers I'll get to peel and look under before I leave.

If I leave.

The thought embeds in my conscious thoughts, reminding me that while I can hope everything works out, odds are, they won't.

Just as Trick described, an access door rests at the back, next to the kitchen exit where they come to dump the trash. An estate guard is already standing in front and pays me little mind when I walk through the door and begin the long trek up the flights of stairs.

By the time I reach the top, a healthy burn radiates down my quads, my lungs tight as I take in full breaths. There's an itch at the back of my throat I can't seem to clear, and for the dozenth time, my eyes skirt down the stairwell. Similar to the storm outside, waiting for the right moment to crash to the surface below, something feels... heavy.

"The guy seems like a fucking tool." Trick's voice comes through the small earpiece, but this time I'm better prepared and don't jolt at the invading sound. "He's got a woman next to him that looks like she wants to blink twice for help, and his suit isn't even tailored. Worse, he looks grungy."

Grungy?

I huff to myself, thinking of the last time I heard that word. It'd been Fi's latest boyfriend. He was a band guy, playing out of his aunt's garage, and had a thing for astrology. Nice guy, but he was too free-spirited for my sister. He'd let her commit her random acts of kindness and not think twice about cleaning up the mess she made.

There was one time—

The faintest click of a door shutting turns every sense I have off within an instant. My eyes squeeze shut, listening for the telltale signs that whoever just opened a door ten floors down is sneaking.

You see, when someone isn't afraid of being loud, it means they don't mind being caught. This usually translates to them being in the wrong place at the wrong time, but with no ill intentions.

But someone who is quiet, measuring their every step, and prolonging the time between any noises they make, is in the right place for their intended purposes.

One, two, three. A step. Faint, but heavy. A man.

I contemplate telling Trick, but the access hall is quiet. Any move I make will alert them to my presence.

He's good. Two minutes without a sound and he's up two flights. A small squeak echoes up, not much louder than the sound of a pen dropping in the room next door. But it's loud enough to give him pause.

On my way up, I too, check the floors. On the sixth, there are three simultaneously warped boards that will need to be hopped over. The eighth has a loose banister. And right beneath me, the last few steps are new replacements, made of a different nonslip material that adds friction to your steps. If he's heavy enough, I'll hear his shoes scratch the surface and get the upper hand, landing on him as soon as he rounds the top corner.

I keep my eyes closed, measuring how quickly he moves. He's fast, and even a little agile, I'll give him that. But I can tell now that he's a bit closer, he's not bigger than me. As long as I get the drop on him, he'll go down quickly.

Almost as though I've summoned him by thought, his shoes scratch the first step of the level below me.

Where I'm standing, there's no option for being able to press my back against a wall or stay hidden in the nook of a door.

I'm going to have to jump at him.

My nerves begin humming, and the dark fibers that stay idle spread quickly, coiling around my veins and surging through my racing heart. It's as if I'm giving myself over to a force, letting it take the reins as it prepares to pummel the idiot that thought they'd be able to get past me.

Which is an insult, really.

My limbs get ready, loosening and tightening as the victim makes his way up. And the moment I see dark hair, I lunge. His arms fly up quickly, but the flash of shock crossing his face tells me he wasn't anticipating I'd be this big, and the moment of hesitation costs him the chance to defend himself.

His back smacks into the wall, a vicious crack resounding in the air as his head follows suit. He crumples in the next breath, his body falling limp against the cold concrete steps.

It was a bit anticlimactic, and even a little disappointing, but the shadow doesn't ebb and instead whispers something I hadn't thought of until just now.

Onyx is afraid of a rat. Wouldn't it be funny if you're not the only one?

My eyes inspect his clothes.

He's dressed as a waiter.

He came from the kitchen.

There's an estate guard watching the access door next to the kitchen.

My feet move faster than they have in a while, taking the steps three at a time. If the guard's dead or knocked out, he's clear. But if he's missing or still there...

I don't have to wait long for an answer as my body comes to a complete stop when I get to the bottom and reach for the door. Muffled voices seep through the thick metal, and I know Trick didn't hear the small commotion since the guard seems calm when he speaks.

"Trick is going on about the decoy. I knew we should have had him put on nice clothes. Onyx isn't fucking stupid. She'll read through him quickly if she hasn't already."

Another voice comes. It's older and I can hear it shaking as he holds on to his composure. "Willy should be up there by now. Think the guard took him out?"

"The new guy? Fuck no. He's big, but Willy's faster. Maybe he's taking his time. Doesn't wanna get caught halfway up and have the dog run and tell his master."

My fists tighten at my sides, suddenly aching to punch

through the door and smash the guy's head against it. I'm no one's fucking lapdog.

Not only are you a bodyguard, but you're being given orders by a sex trafficking scumbag.

To save my fucking sister. I internally scold myself before forcing my attention back on the conversation outside.

"I'm ready for this shit to finally be over. Get rid of Onyx, get our bag from the Murphys, and leave the city. No way Trigger and that crazy bitch Maddy won't bomb every last building after this, and I have no fucking plans to be here when the shit goes down."

I knew I wasn't the only solution the Murphy's have used to get to Onyx, but hearing them want to kill her is jarring. They only wanted me to get intel about her and the estate. What would be the point if they had other people trying to off her? They could have asked *me* to off her. But they didn't. This doesn't add up.

Copper hits my mouth before I realize I'm biting into my lip. Why am I bothered by it? This isn't my fight.

"Go check on him. I'm headed to pull up the car," the older voice says, seemingly more uneasy now with the reminder of the aftermath to come should they succeed.

Only, they won't and two seconds after the guard opens the door, he realizes it too.

I'm going to take a guess that I've gained at least three pounds of muscle after today. I wonder if Russ will make me a steak. I damn sure deserve one after knocking out two men and carrying one up ten damn flights of stairs.

Finally, back at the top, my lungs scream with the rest of my body, and since the adrenaline from earlier is long gone, I feel every pull and strain in my muscles. After dumping the body on the other, I rap my knuckles against the roof door.

Trick's pale face appears. He eyes the sweat dripping from my forehead, my missing jacket I happily discarded on the second floor, and the loose suspender that came unfastened on the eighth floor. His gaze continues past me toward the two bodies piled on top of one another before he looks back to me.

Instead of asking a single question or the scolding I'd partially prepared for, he nods once, turning back around. The door stays slightly ajar, allowing me to take in the private balcony restaurant. Like you'd expect, it's full of glass tables, fresh flowers, and hanging lights from the side canopies. It's empty besides the one table occupied by the Embros women and the two guests.

I watch as he nears Onyx, whose back is to me, and bends to whisper in her ear.

She nods and says something that makes the man sitting across from her blanch. He shakes his head profusely, but Onyx merely rises and exits through the restaurant entrance.

Shi, however, stands slowly, holding her hand out to the woman, who does in fact look as if she's in need of desperate help. She's nothing more than bones, bleach, and injections. The woman nearly scurries to her feet, leaving the man alone at the same moment he realizes Trick is standing behind him.

The second he does is a second too late and a sharp needle protruding out of his neck does its work quickly.

"I need two ground guards to the roof. To the other one, Onyx is coming down. If she doesn't make it to the limo in the next minute, I'm skinning your dick and putting it in her rose bed." Trick's voice comes through double as he speaks into the heart cuff link on his sleeve.

He hauls the now unconscious man over his shoulder and meets me at the door. "They'll be up in a minute. Head back to the limo."

I almost open my mouth to say I can handle carrying one of them down, but my ligaments snap my mouth back shut and force me to nod.

"Oh. And Onyx wants you in her office as soon as we get back."

EZEKIEL
CHAPTER FIFTEEN

As much as I find myself stuck in this office, I'm beginning to think there's nothing in here worth searching for. At least, I don't think someone as keen as Onyx would leave anything of real importance sitting in a place where she makes people wait alone for extended periods of time.

Unless she figures no one would be bold enough to look around, knowing someone could walk in at any given moment. Either way, besides the large desk with basic office supplies, the seemingly untouched liquor cabinet, and floor-to-ceiling bookshelves, there isn't too much I can search.

Come to think of it, there's only one room in the house I've seen thus far that has extra security—her room.

Ideas swirl in my mind on how the hell I'll be able to get in there—*alone*, no less, with enough time to look for something. Hell, that's another problem. I have no idea what I'm even searching for and staying inside longer than handing her breakfast seems far-fetched at this point.

I may have only been here a couple of days, but it's easy to see how guarded the woman is, and not just physically. There's a thick shield hiding everything about her, and I imagine scratching the surface would be equivalent to cutting down a giant oak with a butter knife.

You could always fuck her and wait till she's asleep.

My dick twitches at the intrusive thought, but thankfully, I'm not given any time to dwell on it. As if my formulation of a plan beckons her, the door behind me opens, Onyx's heels clicking against the hard floor, announcing her entrance. I don't turn to face her, but stand, waiting for her to round the desk and take a seat behind it before sitting.

My pulse hums with her close proximity, the sudden anticipation of what she may have to say playing with the edges of my sanity. I wonder if she'll thank me—though unlikely—or if we'll have some type of standoff like we did when I delivered her food. Not knowing or even being able to guess what she's thinking irks me.

After another beat of her merely staring, she leans forward slightly, resting her chin on a closed fist. "You were told to report anything you might have seen or heard to Trick. Yet, you went against his orders. Orders *given* to protect me, the woman you are being paid to guard, and took matters into your own hands."

Her tone is even and calm, almost as if she's listing off the events that took place rather than reprimanding me for not doing as told. Still, I can't help but reply, since I wish she'd be a tad grateful. "That is accurate."

"At the expense of potentially putting me in harm's way."

"If I would have opened the door, the guy would have heard and ran back downstairs. You wouldn't have him or the snake you let infest your payroll." I don't know why I feel the need to explain to her I was thinking of her well-being, but I want to.

My entire life has been devoted to protecting women, and

her comment feels like a punch in my gut, or perhaps a blow to my ego.

"Yes. Him." The knuckles under her chin bloom white as she clenches her fist. On the other hand, she twirls a playing card I hadn't realized she was holding between her long fingers. "The entire army is going to have to go through regular checks now. We'll begin combing through bank accounts for any sizable deposits or odd spending. He worked for me well over two years. I didn't expect—"

"No one is exempt from betrayal."

"My right hands are," she quickly counters, and for a moment I think I hear annoyance lacing her tone. The small show of emotion has me placing a note on a potential weak spot. I shouldn't try to explore it, but really, I don't have much of a choice.

"How can you be so sure? What do they owe you that would keep them loyal to the end and not to a fault?"

"Their lives."

"Because you saved them?"

She doesn't answer for a moment, taking a long pause as she regains the fraction of her composure she let slip. "Do you know what we do here at Embros? What *I* do?"

I scoff, leaning back into the leather chair. "I know enough."

Onyx doesn't seem offended but instead places the card flat on the desk and interlocks her fingers. "You deem me a villain."

Again, she's not asking, but I decide to answer. "I do."

"Have I done something to you?"

"You may as well have." I cross my arms over my chest. I know I was thinking of diving between her thighs just moments ago, but that doesn't diminish the deep loathing I have for what those in the Mafia do. "You supply drugs and guns to the community. You stake claim on land that people have purchased with their hard-earned money. You ruin lives."

"I have saved hundreds."

"And that absolves you of your sins? You rescue women. Yes, that's honorable, but what about the other shit you do?" I feel my body begin to warm, images of my comatose mother on the kitchen floor fueling my loose tongue. I may be ruining everything—risking it all in a moment of anger—but I can't stop the words from spilling out.

Onyx studies me, no doubt reading the internal battle written over my face. I've always done well to hide obvious emotions, but I've also never confronted the root of my problems. Granted, she may not be the one who started them, but it's those like her that did. "You give mothers and fathers easy access to fill their addictions that make them choose drugs over their children."

"I force no drugs down anyone's throat. They buy them willingly. And if not from me, from someone else. At least with me, they know their drug won't be laced."

"And that makes it better?" My eyes are wide with disbelief, the iconic look of *are you kidding me* scrunching up my features.

Still, she remains calm. "No, but you're a fool if you think I'm not the lesser evil. And an even bigger fool if you think there shouldn't be two to choose from."

I guffaw, scratching my hairline before running a frustrated hand through my hair. "You still allow teens the abil—"

"Any of my dealers who knowingly gives drugs to anyone under the age of legal adulthood is murdered on sight. Everyone knows it's something I don't tolerate." A hardness takes over her delicate but fierce eyes, and I realize there's a story in there she has no intention of letting me read.

"You aid people in killing others." I'm reaching now, I

know, but fuck if I can't stop talking. I need to keep this strained wall I have up, guarding me against seeing her as anything other than a don.

"Think of what you're saying. I can kill you with the books on my shelves over there. With the clip on your suspender. With this pinkie nail." She holds up said nail, displaying the black painted acrylic shining with dark stones. "If someone wants another person dead, they'll figure out a way. A gun would be far less painful. Death by a bullet is honestly a mercy. Something I, myself, don't grant those who cross me."

It isn't until Onyx's shoulders relax that I realize she was even tense. I struck a chord, making her uncomfortable, and I store the knowledge away.

"The people living within this estate would die for me forty times over, and they would do the same if what we do here was threatened in any way. Embros Hearts is our mission. Yes, we are funded by means you may deem immoral, though even that's a debatable perspective at best."

"So you save women."

"I do."

I recall Cat and wonder if Shi and Maddy are the same. "Did you rescue Maddy?"

"Everyone here is a survivor of something."

She could help me.

She'll kill you.

But the moment I used to contemplate trading my life for the possibility of her help was fleeting, crashing into the flames of her next words.

"You've helped me sniff out a rat. And now, I have to make sure there are no others. As I've said, we are running checks, but it's not enough. I'll make a bloody example of the one, and in turn, this will force any others to make their moves. What those moves are, I'm not sure, but I'll need you ready. You haven't been here long, but please see to it that you use your time to explore the grounds, get to know all those that work here. On your days off, visit my clubs, casinos, and bars. Wear the uniformed jacket with the Q and heart on the sleeve. It will grant you access everywhere, including the VIP areas."

Onyx stands, seemingly finished with our meeting that's left my mind conflicted. She's giving me access to everything. Not because she necessarily trusts me, but because she's lost trust in everyone else.

That's what the Murphys wanted.

They had to have known the assassination attempt would fail. They wanted the guard caught. They wanted her to lose trust and question her army's loyalties.

And they did exactly that.

Onyx moves around her desk, coming to stand in front of it, a few inches away from me. She leans her hips into the edge of her desk, accentuating her curves even more. My eyes move of their own accord, raking down her frame and replacing the fabric with the bare skin I saw the other night.

Heat flares in my gut, the air suddenly too thin and leaving my breaths unfulfilling. But I do my best to keep my expression placid as I gaze up.

Her head tilts slightly, her blinks becoming slower as a heat darkens her eyes to a near black. "I need you to find them all. Every last one who lets money dictate who they are loyal to."

"What will you do to them?" I know the answer, but something in me wants more specifics. Perhaps out of curiosity, or maybe to know exactly what she's capable of, I'm not quite sure.

A smirk lifts one side of her pink lips. "There're plenty of things I plan to do. And for every one I find, their punishment will be different. But for their deaths, they will all end the same."

She leans forward, the tip of one of her nails sliding down my jawline until she reaches my neck. I know she can feel my pulse thrumming beneath the pad of her finger as she speaks. "My blade will slice through their jugular, draining them dry with every feeble beat of their heart. Then just as their light flickers, and the reaper comes to steal what's mine..."

She pauses, watching my throat as I swallow, though I partially hope she thinks it's from fear rather than the arousal coursing through me. "Their heads will roll."

I've never believed in taking chances, and now is one of those painful times reminding me why I don't. I can't ask her to help me.

Onyx drops her hand, straightening her spine. "Tell me, Kane. Why work for people you despise? Do you let money guide you as well?"

I ignore the way my name sounds on her tongue. "Are you asking me if I'll let a few extra zeros change who I work for?"

She shrugs, placing her hands on either side of her hips, clenching on the edge of the desk. "I do wonder why you work for someone who you clearly dislike."

"It's not you. It's what you do."

"I've explained my piece. But you're not answering my question."

"Which one?"

She runs her tongue across her pearly teeth and my blood rushes through me, filling my ears with the sudden increase in my pulse. "Either."

I sigh, running a hand through my hair. "The money will get my sister and mom away from here. Start over."

"There is no such thing as starting over."

My eyes bore into her, agitation taking over. "Maybe for you. But for her, for *us*, it's never too late to start fresh."

"So to answer my original question, you'd answer yes?"

"If I was given extra money, would I turn sides and get the hell out of here?"

Before she can answer, I'm up, grabbing the letter opener from her desk and have the flat pressed to the inside of her thigh next to her arterial vein. In the same second, the barrel of the .380 Trick gave me is grasped in her hand, pushed into the underside of my jaw. Our mouths are a breath away from each other, and every inhale we take in unison has her breasts brushing against my chest.

I lower my voice to a gravelly whisper. "As you said before, if someone wants a person dead, they'll find a way. I have nothing to gain by killing the woman who is signing my checks and working with a scum who deals in women."

"And did Madeline tell you what you'd have to do for those checks?" Her hooded gaze drifts down to my mouth, and something deep in my soul says the last thing she wants is a kiss.

The idea flashes through my mind before I have time to think over it. I need to get inside her room, and as fucked up as it sounds, this is my way in.

Fuck it.

I flip the blade over, pressing the handle into her palm before pushing between her legs, forcing her to sit on her desk. She holds the gun steady, observing me with a bored gaze.

The look does something to me. Something deep in my core that incinerates everything, leaving only the thoughts of her mask shattering as she comes unraveled. I want to see her raw, uncovered, completely naked to how I plan to make her feel.

I hate my inherent need to take care of her, but at this moment, I use it to fuel me. Use it to flood my body of each thought, keeping it from acting out something I've wanted since I laid eyes on her.

The need to have this powerful woman at my mercy overcomes me and drives my quick reflexes to take the small knife from her hand and slice down the middle of her tight dress, starting at the hip.

Other than a sharp intake of air, she makes no move to cover her exposed thighs, nor the thin black lace covering her pussy. Instead, she removes the gun, dropping it on the desk, and snatches the knife from me. "I liked this dress."

"I still do."

The corner of her mouth twitches, almost as if she wants to smile but thinks better of it. To put a crack in her resolve urges me on as I kneel, keeping my eyes on hers. My hands find her hips, the soft skin beneath my fingers sending jolts of shivers through my forearms. I slip my thumbs through either side of the lace and tug hard, ripping them away from her body in a loud snap.

This time, she reacts, and leaning backward, her head falls to the side for a moment as she soaks in the bite of pleasure I know she feels. My gaze trails up her body and finds her nipples through her dress. Panties discarded, I grab the torn dress and yank it apart, causing the fabric to tear down the center all the way to her throat.

Besides a delicate gold chain hanging from her neck and looping around her ribs, she wears nothing else to hide her pert nipples. My tongue darts out to combat the dryness on my lips, but the urge to run it along the metal beads hugging her peaks is strong.

Leaning forward, my hands find the curve of her soft waist, but as my mouth nears her chest, she snakes a hand through my hair and pushes down. It isn't forceful, but a silent command, nonetheless. This makes my blood pressure soar, coursing through my ears so loud I can hear nothing but the rapid beat of my own heart.

I want to rip her apart. Piece by fucking piece. I want to devour her cunt in a way she's never had before, driving her mad until she's grabbing on to anything her hands can reach to steady her as her body unravels. No, better yet, I want to take her to the edge of what she thinks she's capable of. To the brink of her sanity until she's sobbing from the stimulation, begging for release.

I need to hear her scream for me.

Letting her believe she's in control, I lower my head until I'm lined up perfectly with her center. The faint scent of lemon reaches my nose first, but eager for her true smell, I press my nose into her, parting her lips slightly. The muscle in her thighs tense as I squeeze her sides, taking a deep inhale of her sex.

Holy *fuck*.

A groan rips from the back of my throat, the very real addiction to her soft musk already embedded in my mind. My hand slips from her hips and to the inside of her legs, just above her knees. I push them farther apart, kneeling between. Even on my knees, she's at the perfect height, my mouth slightly below her warm core.

My eyes flash to hers and to my amusement, nothing besides her heavy-lidded gaze gives away what she's feeling. It's like a challenge. No, my fucking *mission* to break her mask into a thousand pieces. But why, I still haven't figured out.

After another inhale, I lick lightly through her folds. Again, she tenses, but makes no movement, though I'm not sure she can with the tight grasp I have on her keeping her in place. Another pass and she grips my hair harder.

I see it before she makes the move, grabbing the discarded letter opener, and pressing the cold metal to the side of my throat. The act makes my painfully hard dick twitch, but I look up lazily, happy to see more of a fire in her gaze.

She's unbelievably more beautiful from this angle. Her brows knit together, her chest heaving with the breaths she's trying to steady, and her nipples drawn tight, aching to be touched. Still, she finds the words to tell me how much she wants more without saying it outright.

"A man caught up in the throes of passion is an easy man to kill."

She applies pressure with the blade, forcing my face upward and allowing my nose to skim over her clit. I can tell she didn't anticipate the possibility as her eyelashes flutter. Near desperate to see her have the reaction again, I opt for a non vocal response and apply more force with the long, languid lick of her slit with the flat of my tongue.

Her eyes flare, but it's a fleeting tell that she quickly corrects, resuming her inspection of my mouth hovering over her pussy. She's fighting giving in, and fuck if that doesn't make my insides combust into flames.

I break the stare down and focus all my senses on the pretty sight in front of me. She's glistening, her aroma calling to me while the soft flesh of her thighs meld to my touch, making me hungry for so much more. I need more.

My tongue goes to work, interchanging between swift licks and hard flicks. I keep all my efforts on her pussy until she starts to shift, the knife digging in my skin harder the longer I stay away from her clit.

I dive into her sweet core, licking along the edges of her walls. I refuse to move until she asks for it, so I keep up the same torturous pace—dipping in and out, in and out, up and down.

Onyx's body begins to quiver, and at last, the knife falls from her hand, clattering to the marble floor as she threads her fingers into my hair to join the other. She tugs on the ends, bringing my mouth where she needs it. I break away slightly, loving the way she nearly rips the hair from my scalp at the loss of me. But instead of making any demands, she watches me, her cheeks now a delicious shade of pink.

I run my tongue over my top lip before letting the excess spit, mixed with her arousal, pool at the edge of my mouth until it falls, landing on her swollen bundle of nerves. She draws in a sharp breath, and for one moment, I see her.

It's a moment of vulnerability, a moment of pure unbridled need and desperation. And that's all it takes.

My hands leave her thighs. One travels up her back and yanks the tip of her ponytail, forcing her head back while the other swipes through her wet folds and curls inside her tight cunt. My teeth brush against her clit before taking a tentative nip.

The hiss that streams from Onyx's teeth makes my dick throb but also spurs me on. Two digits move at a steady pace, exploring her walls until I find the spot that makes her clench around my hand. Once I find it, I continue to pet the spot while my tongue takes on a brutal pace over her clit. My lonely pinkie moves of its own accord and begins probing at the ring of tight muscle, stroking the edges until she jolts in my hand.

At long last, moans slip from her in a beautiful melody and her breath quickens as her façade falls to the wayside. One of the hands breaks from my hair and catches her breasts. I watch in annoyance as she tugs at her nipple, the very one I almost had in my mouth.

I jerk her ponytail harder, forcing her back to curve into a perfect rainbow as I continue my assault. Again, I bite, only this time it's harder, and the small spike of pain is exactly what she needed.

Her body convulses as she comes, her thighs locking around my head as she attempts to rock her hips and force her pussy harder against my face. Only it's an unnecessary move. I push into her, fucking her with my fingers in long, powerful strokes to prolong her orgasm.

"Kane." It's a whisper, but I hear it. It decorates her shivers and coats my insides with a song I know I'll do fucking anything to hear again.

When her tremors subside, I release her, standing and backing away to take in the glorious glow. I thought she was striking before, but it has nothing on the aftermath of her being sated.

She straightens her spine slowly before lowering herself to the floor. She steadies on her heels and then ties the two ends of the tattered dress, covering my meal. I lick my lips, forcing myself not to groan at the lingering taste.

Onyx takes two steps toward me, and just like the first time I met her in the office, she stops right in front of me, pressing my gun to my chest. "You found one rat. Now find any others so I can take their heads."

And without another word, she's out of the office, leaving me with a hard-on and hunger I've never known.

EZEKIEL

CHAPTER SIXTEEN

Thursday

I wake up at five a.m. Work out in the gym, shower, and eat at the bar while watching as Russ cooks. The guards don't talk about gambling today but instead eat in silence. Every once in a while, someone will mutter their disbelief over their fellow ex-guard out loud, but no one looks my way. I'm sure they want to mourn the loss of a friend they've worked with for two years, but don't know how, considering what he was trying to do.

And that's assuming he's dead...

Cat steals my attention as she fusses over everything Russ does, all the while smoking her joint from the high-end cigarette stick. She's asked me twice now who I am, and each time I answer, she rolls her eyes and takes another hit.

After I finish, Russ pushes Onyx's plate across the bar top, and I wonder if this is a permanent part of my job as her personal guard. Doesn't matter either way, but after yesterday in her office, I'd be lying through my teeth if I said I won't have to fight the temptation of pushing through her door and going back for seconds.

I know I initially planned for it to be a way to sneak around inside her room, but fuck, I also didn't expect for her to taste so good. So... *addicting*. But the feel of her beneath me, her smell, her responses to my touch—just everything—turned me on in a way I'd never even thought possible. Hell, it was damn near painful.

Taking a deep breath, I knock twice, curious to see how her demeanor will be. But when she opens the door, she merely looks at me and then holds out her hand.

Her long black strands are wavy today, falling over her shoulders and closed robe. My hands itch to reach out and grab it. It'd been so silky in my hands, and with the angle, I hadn't been able to wrap her ponytail around my wrist.

"Am I always going to have to wait for you to hand me my things?" One brow is arched in question and much to my disappointment, she sounds bored.

Should that bother me or intrigue me?

Deciding not to push it or piss her off after a day like yesterday, I relent, handing her the breakfast and dropping my hand seconds before she shuts the door.

While I want to knock again and say some shit that will most definitely land me in some type of trouble, I don't, and instead inhale the breeze of lemon that slips through the door.

It's the sweet notes in the fragrance that plague my mind the rest of the day.

Friday

Five a.m. again. Same routine. But this time, a guard approaches me during breakfast.

"Hey, I know they have you checking into us, but look man, none of us would do anything like that. I can speak for everyone here."

A slight prick of annoyance makes my eye twitch. "Would you have said the same about him?"

The guy shifts uncomfortably, scratching the back of his neck as he takes a look over his shoulder. "I mean, no. But—"

I hold up a hand, cutting him off. "Look, I'm not trying to be a dick, but I don't know you. Therefore, your words don't mean shit. If you're not doing anything sneaky, cool. But if you, or anyone else is, I have no problem snapping your fucking necks."

Even with my voice calm and nonchalant, the man grimaces and nods before returning to the table.

Am I being a complete fucking hypocrite? Absolutely.

But do I mean it? Yeah.

I know I don't know much about the woman, but if my sister's life wasn't on the line, I wouldn't do what I'm doing. Not only because she's right about being the lesser of the two evils, but because she's actually no—

"They're on pins and needles because they saw the gardeners planting body parts this morning. But I'll tell you a little secret." Cat takes a long draw of her joint, holding it in for a moment before blowing it out. "It was the other guy. The one you so graciously slammed against the wall. You killed him."

My mouth pulls down in the corners, my brows raising in slight surprise. But then the resounding crack of his skull hitting the cement wall plays back and I nod. "Makes sense."

Cat's eyes narrow, her blue strands falling over her forehead as she tries to read my lack of a response. "Who are you?"

I smirk, standing and taking Onyx's plate from Russ. "Same person I was yesterday and the same person I'll be tomorrow."

She scoffs but doesn't call after me.

When I enter the foyer to climb the stairs, Onyx's voice catches me by surprise. I veer to the right and see her sitting at her desk, the dark French doors wide open. Trigger is pointing to something on the computer as she observes, nodding while he speaks too low for me to hear.

She notices me standing in the open doorway and nods, a silent beckoning. When I approach, I glance at the available chair, tempted as hell to have a seat and play another round of give and take. But it's as though she can read my thoughts and resumes her conversation.

"All clean?"

Trigger nods. "Yes. I've checked the last five years on everyone. Also, I haven't gotten anything out of Manny. How long are we keeping him?"

Onyx glances over as I set her breakfast down. We lock gazes, and my blood immediately warms, moving faster with my increased heart rate. She keeps her dark eyes on me, though her words are meant for Trigger. "For another couple of days. I'll go pay him a visit soon"

From my periphery, I see Trigger nod again. "Alright. I'm going to work on your outing for Sunday." He turns to me, but I can't seem to break away from Onyx to face him. "Take the day to walk around and get to know the guards. Tomorrow, I'll meet you upstairs in the control room."

He doesn't wait for a response, nor for me to ask where the hell the control room is, and instead walks out of the office, leaving me with his Boss who looks too fucking good at six in the morning.

Her hair is tied up, and her usual black outfit hugs her body. Today, it's a bodice, cinching in her waist and pushing her breasts up. I'm tempted to shut the door and rip the damn thing off of her, but her bored drawl cuts through my decision.

"Did you need something?"

"Do I need to in order to be around you? The person I'm being paid to guard." I grab the back of a chair, tilting my head lazily with a smirk.

Her eyes flash to my left dimple before she gestures around her. "I'm in my house. What is there for you to do?"

"Anything can happen in here considering the other day."

The nerve under her eye twitches before she clears her throat, pulling her breakfast closer. She picks up the fork and drags it over the eggs. "Yes. What happened?"

I almost expect for her to finish but instead she stabs into a slice of pineapple and pops it in her mouth. Returning to the computer as if I'm not there, she begins typing. A healthy dose of irritation flushes away the arousal that was once dominating my bloodstream.

This woman both vexes me and lures me. Like the smoke from Cat's weed. I both want it and don't, knowing the pleasure I'll get from it will be both addicting and fleeting.

"Get to know the guards so I won't need you to watch me work in my office." Though I know she's meaning to be dismissive, I hear it. The faintest bit of concern staining her words. So I oblige, standing and leaving her to work as I walk back to the kitchen to meet the guards for their shift.

As odd as it may seem, in some sick type of way, I actually *want* to protect her.

For now, at least.

Saturday

Wake up.
    Work out.
    Eat.
    Same morning routine, only today, Cat takes Onyx's breakfast, while I sit with the group of guards I met yesterday. A few are young, a couple older. Most of them have families that support their job choice and the nice chunk of change they bring home. The ones with no kids to take care of, gamble.
    I have a good read on people. It's something I've always been good at, while my kid sister has always been able to feel them—an empath is what she calls herself. And while I may not pick up on their emotions, I can tell they aren't like me. Their loyalties are with the Embros family.
    With Onyx.
    She's got a good group of men behind her, and if it wasn't for the fact they can't see the snake in front of them, I'd say she's made herself an iron-clad army.
    Too bad they don't see me.
    After they part ways to secure the grounds, I meander upstairs and around the long hall. All the doors are painted black, presumably belonging to the rooms of the twins, Shi, Maddy, and maybe the jittery guy.
    While yesterday was spent exploring acres of rose bushes, the edge of the forest that backs straight into her property line, and the massive pool, today will be on camera duty.
    A loud roll of thunder passes overhead as the hallways open up into a curved bridge surrounded on either side by sheets of glass overseeing the side of the estate and said pool.

The tan body baking on a chaise lounge as if the sun was beaming gives me pause.

It's Onyx, with her amber curves on full display.

She's lying on her stomach, her head tilted to the side and her eyes closed. Her long strands sprawl over her back. Her ass is barely covered by the black bikini bottom and the two guards watching across the pool makes my palm itch.

"Why is she out there?" I turn to see a surprised Trigger standing a few yards away.

His mouth gapes open for a moment before he shifts, so he's not hidden in the shadows of the hallway. "How did you know I was here?"

"Reflective glass," I point out. Though I heard him the second he left whatever room he was in.

He takes the necessary steps before he's next to me, eyes following my gaze to where Onyx lays. Unlike me, he doesn't let himself linger, snapping back to me with a stern look, straightening his lips. I like that he won't look at her. "Are you ready?"

"As I'll ever be."

"Good. This way." He rotates and leads me to the security room.

He stops at a black door with an odd-looking bolt—almost as if it's a keypad missing the buttons, but then he taps the surface, lighting it up a dull blue. Trigger presses two thumbs against it. I comically wonder if a red line will appear to scan him, but instead, little blue waves vibrate outward and the door unlocks with a heavy clunk.

Inside, the space is about the size of my room. One extensive desk has been built into the wall, starting from the door, continuing along every edge, and stopping just before a small refrigerator. Monitors are posted on the expanse of the longest wall, and a year-long calendar on the other. The remaining desk space is occupied with small, locked metal file cabinets, all of which are labeled. SD, MD, BV, and M.

Trick is busy filing something away in the BV drawer before he turns around and smiles. He's definitely the happiest person here. "Hey, man. Good morning."

I lift my chin. "It is. So is this where you hide out all day?"

The twins huff in unison before Trick meanders to the fridge and digs inside for a few drinks. He tosses the cans one by one to me and Trigger. "Nope. The majority of the time we're creating weapons in the workroom, but we let our monitor guys watch Onyx at the pool so we could show you the room, get you an entry code, and all that."

I don't miss the way Trigger tries to gauge my reaction about someone else watching Onyx—in barely any clothes, no less. But I simply nod and open my can of... sparkling water.

"Alright. Let's do it, then."

The rest of the day I spend locked up in the security room. I learn more about the guards, the premises, and everyone in it. I take note of all the places with cameras, which are scattered everywhere, and the angle in which they film. There are pockets of blind space throughout—thin and not enough to miss any action, but enough to bypass two bodies hunched together in secret conversation. None of the guards I watch act suspiciously as they make their rounds, and the only change comes when the rain begins to fall and they open umbrellas.

I learn the files stand for security detail, medical, business vendors, and Murphy. They make hard copies of everything on computers, just in case their computers are compromised in any way, and the twins and Onyx are the only ones with the keys.

A few hours pass before the twins leave me to watch the monitors for the remainder of the night and familiarize myself with the blueprints of the house. The estate already looks monumental, but the paper in front of me shows just how massive it is.

After jotting down my own version of the prints, I slip it in my pocket and return to the monitors. Onyx had disappeared into her room shortly after the rain broke free of the clouds, and I haven't seen her since. Still, every once in a while, my eyes drift to the screen displaying her quiet door.

I'm self-aware enough to know my interest in her is becoming dangerous, but even knowing that, I can't help but wonder.

Who is she?

Sunday

"A farmers' market?" I stare in disbelief as Onyx grabs her satchel and swings it over her body.

Like any other day, she's dressed in all black, but it's a casual look that I'd be lying if I said didn't completely disarm me. Her dark hair lays in soft waves over a cotton tee. The shirt isn't tight, but still conforms to her shape, draping over her breasts before dropping and pooling at her small waist. Her jeans, however, look as if they're painted on, and I don't bother hiding the fact that I'm fucking ogling her.

Even as she clears her throat to garner my attention, my eyes continue their descent until they land on boots. *Boots.* And somehow, she looks as sexy, dangerous, and stunning as with her usual clothes.

"Kane, unless you plan to eat me as the meal you're picturing me as, I'd like to leave now." A sharp manicured hand finds her waist.

"I wouldn't use the word eat. Devour, maybe." My eyes flash to hers in time to see them flare, and I'm almost certain she's picturing me on my knees in her office.

"The best produce will be gone by the second hour," she states simply before walking through the foyer.

I catch up and pass the older man that I've never seen *not* standing by the front door and open it before he gets to it. "Will anyone else be joining us?"

"No. Good morning, Edwards." She nods to him before tossing a set of keys over her shoulder and into my waiting hand and continues down the entry steps.

"And you think that's wise? After what happened? Seems a little fucking crazy to me."

"Whatever gave you the impression I was sane?" She spins on her heels, standing in front of a midnight-painted Jeep parked at the entrance. A Jeep with no fucking roof. In a city with consistently overcast weather. "And I'm beginning to think neither are you with as many times as I catch you grinning at nothing."

I bypass my curiosity about her vehicle choice and move on to the fact we are about to be surrounded by people in an open area. Where someone could shoot or shank her and get away in the crowd. "I thought you didn't leave the house much."

Onyx gestures to her car handle, which my body automatically moves to open. It's a reflex and I curse my mind at the knee-jerk reaction. "I don't. But that also doesn't mean I'm a recluse. Are you saying you can't protect me around stay-at-home moms and rambunctious toddlers?"

"I'm saying there may be more to worry about than MILFs and their kids."

"So you're incapable of doing your job."

I huff, rounding the hood of the car and yanking the driver's side door open. "Give me the directions."

We ride in silence the entire way, and every now and then, when I turn on her cue, I catch a glimpse of her in my periphery. She really is breathtaking. And right now, with the bits of sun poking through the clouds, she's glowing. She's at ease, completely relaxed, and somehow looks more like the Boss of a crime family now than she ever has.

It's borderline frustrating how I can see so many of her layers at once, but not know precisely what I'm looking at.

The farmers' market is exactly what I'd expected. A sea of colorful tents over acres of grass, and hundreds of women with empty bags in one hand and a child in the other. Various banners and signs rest outside each shop, encouraging business with their current sales. Onyx walks at a leisurely pace, stopping at every tent that she finds interesting, meanwhile my eyes are scanning the area constantly.

I take in everyone's body language, noting the squeal of delight when a mother examines her baby's new anklet, or the vendor that laughs too loud at a joke. I see the few husbands that were clearly dragged here against their wills and their wandering lustful gazes when Onyx passes by.

Something oddly close to annoyance forces my brows to narrow at every man, and I don't hide the disapproving scowl when they realize I'm watching them.

"Do you always have stare downs with every man you encounter? I feel as if we're starring in an old western movie." Onyx picks up a large dragon fruit and inspects it. Judging from her lack of a facial expression, I almost think I imagined her speaking. Then the corner of her lip twitches.

"Watching over women has always been second nature. I guess it's become a normal thing for me to ward men off."

She nods, placing the fruit tenderly inside her basket. "And here I thought you were a hair jealous."

"Why would you think that?"

"Because you're a man."

"And?"

"The majority of you find yourselves staking claim to something or some*one* you find interest in. And once you lay the invisible flag on it with your initials, you also have the inherent need to have a pissing match with anyone else who nears."

"Why would you think I'm interested in you?" For the entirety of our conversation, I've been watching around us, but now my attention is solely on her.

She drops her basket in front of the sweet-looking vendor and meets my gaze. Her dark eyes are lighter today, the normally hidden chunks of gold shimmering softly. "What women do you protect outside of me?"

The question surprises me and for the briefest second, I think she's asking something else. I want to string her along, see if I can get some sort of reaction out of her if she's under the impression I'm with someone. But the notion that I'm already lying in the biggest way forces my honesty. "My mom and kid sister."

I'm not sure why the sudden heaviness of trepidation weaves into my heart, but it does. The knowledge of everything I've ever done in my life to protect the both of them emerging from the dark place I keep it hostage. It's pulling at the image I project, slowly unraveling it the longer I give it energy.

"I see." She turns back to the woman and pays her tab before handing me the bag of produce and moving to the next tent. "I used to come to this very same market with my mother. Once a month, the moment they opened. We'd walk to every single tent, and she'd buy way more than she needed."

The shadow creeping around my consciousness ebbs, the urge to ask more, to *see* more under her armor taking hold. "What did she do with all the extra things?"

"We would take it to Embros Hearts. Fill the women's

kitchen with fresh food, give them new outfits to help them feel empowered. To help them love themselves again after feeling unworthy for so long."

"You and my sister are kindred spirits." I think on dozens of occasions my sister has done the same things on a smaller scale.

Onyx's fingers slide over a shawl, her rings somehow not catching in the knitted fabric. "Perhaps I'll make her acquaintance one day."

Knowing my sister's rescue means Onyx's death isn't lost on me, but I can't... I can't fucking acknowledge it, even mentally, without feeling conflicted. Her life means no less than Fi's, yet it's the fact of her being my blood that saves her and condemns Onyx.

Fuck.

It's been a long time since I've felt the weight of guilt, but it's heavy as hell. "I wouldn't have imagined the leader of a crime family to be sympathetic."

This makes her laugh. It's throaty and sexy and does adverse things to combat where my head is. "Don't misread me, Kane. I have no qualms gutting fish and wearing their entrails as a necklace. I just have a soft spot for women who are forced to give men something they aren't entitled to."

I nod, resuming my watch as she moves on and continues her morning shopping. The whole thing becomes uneventful until we load up the Jeep before heading back. She's resting her face on her palm, peering out the window when she asks, "Are you and your mother close?"

"I'd say so. I take care of her on my day off."

"Is she ill?"

I shrug, clearing my throat from the sudden burn. "You could say that. She has some pretty nasty long-term side effects from drug use."

"Hmm."

The noise is so small, so meaningless, but at the same time means so much. It's her understanding my disdain of what she does. Of what she contributes to. That I am the aftermath of what they leave behind.

"And your father?"

I guffaw, ignoring the instant tightness the thought of him causes across my chest. "Nonexistent."

Onyx doesn't respond and instead shrugs. "Mine as well."

We're silent the remainder of the way, and when we return to the estate, she's inside before I have the bags in my hand.

Monday

Like clockwork, I wake at five, work out and eat breakfast with Russ and Cat. She asks again who I am, and I *again* tell her the same.

I take Onyx's plate and find her in the office.

Every time I see her, I'm always captivated. From the intensity in her sharp gaze and elegantly defined features to the attire that transforms her delicate curves into a dangerously powerful profile.

Her hair is straight, back in its ponytail at the top of her head. She's wearing a black silk dress that ties at her hip. The thick gold bracelet on her wrist catches my attention as she twirls a playing card between her fingers. "It seems Maddy has overslept this morning. I'd like for you to join me in her stead."

"Good morning to you too," I say, setting her plate next to where she leans against her desk.

She guffaws, her lips curving in amusement. "I didn't take

you as one for pleasantries, Kane. You gave me the impression you were more of a *to the point* type of man."

I step closer, not hesitating when I press my chest against hers, and capture her chin in a light grasp. Her breath catches, and her pupils dilate, but the smirk painting her face makes me hesitate.

It's a look of question tilting her brows. No, a challenge. I have her physically in the palm of my hand and she wonders what I'll do. Like a dog who finally caught up to the mailman.

Gripping her tighter, I lower my face to have our mouths only a breath apart. My eyes flash to the dip above her succulent lips. "You'd be surprised how many detours I'd make before reaching my *point*, Boss."

When I gaze back up, her irises are alight with something new—something between curiosity and defiance. But before I can read into what I think I'm seeing, she cups my stiffening length through my slacks.

The sudden friction makes me twitch in her hand, causing her to laugh and slip away from my hold and walk toward her shelves. "Let's see if you still have that same determination when you see who I am."

Onyx presses against the farthest bookshelf, which I realize is a door, revealing a stairwell behind it. She glances back at me with an arched brow raised while she waits for me to follow through.

The stairs are fairly narrow, and attach to cement walls, not allowing me to see what I'm walking into. Or allowing whoever may be at the bottom a chance to know what's coming. And there is someone at the bottom.

I smell the metal in the air. The sweat carrying their faint odor and fear. And then there's something else. Almost like grilled chicken with herbs.

We pass a small panel that lights up as I pass, it kick-starts a soft whirl of machinery somewhere and a cool blast of air begins flowing from the vents above. When I reach the bottom, I realize immediately why I'm here.

The guard I knocked out at the restaurant is sitting in the center of the sterile basement. His head is slumped down, touching his visibly moving chest. His breaths are deep and steady and despite the increasingly cold air swirling around the space, he doesn't stir or even shiver.

He's knocked out.

His uniform is still on his body, though I use the term lightly—it's barely hanging on. The dress shirt's been ripped in various places, all of which display areas of flesh covered in what looks like dirt. But I know the gummy texture to be dried blood.

His matted blond hair is dark as well, covering half his face, even as Onyx pushes his head back. A groan rumbles out of him the same time I find myself curious. "Why aren't his pants soiled?"

Her head snaps around, her brows furrowed. "That's the only question you have?"

What else would I wonder?

I nod, and she huffs a laugh before turning back to her prisoner. The sound is fleeting, but it penetrates my chest with its lightness.

"Oddly enough, it's the only smell I don't stomach well. Not that I can't tolerate it. It just doesn't get me off like the sweet tinge of blood." She threads her sharp nail through his scalp, gripping it so hard a very conscious hiss streams from his clenched teeth. "Trigger usually comes down a few times a day to allow him into the back room to relieve himself. Normally, I don't keep people here long enough, but I needed Manny here to fester for a few days."

A quick glance behind me shows a slim metal door attached

to the side of the stairs. Hanging on the wall next to it is a rolled hose. I take my time in observing what little else lies in the room. There's another set of stairs against the wall, this one a normal set of basement stairs, letting me know this place has two ways to get here.

I hadn't seen them on the blueprints, and I begin to wonder what else wasn't on them.

Other than a low metal table holding various tools, there's only the occupied chair in the middle. He's chained with his hands behind his back, his feet bound to either front chair leg. When he finally opens his eyes and sees who has him held, a horrendous scowl crosses his face.

He can act tough, but his straightened spine and a thick swallow down his throat are his tells. He's nervous.

"As my guard likes to say before having a conversation, good morning, Manny. I hope you're well-rested."

His upper lip curls in a snarl. "Fuck your morning, bitch."

A barb of anger pokes into my side and moves my foot a step forward. Onyx sees from her periphery and grins, shaking her head with both a notion to stop me, and to mock him. "Silly man. Though I'd expect nothing else, considering you thought it wise to cross me. *Me.*"

"You were supposed to help keep him alive. He was your personal guard." The man spits and though Onyx tries to move, it's not fast enough, and she catches a bit to the side of her cheek.

The barb is on fire now, and I don't stop, moving the few steps required until my fist is in his soft belly. "Watch your fucking mouth. I have no problem killing you now and dealing with her later."

"Get your dog, On—"

My knuckles ache when they connect with his cheekbone. "Who the fuck said you could say her name?"

Manny spits a mixture of blood and phlegm onto the floor before turning his muddled, shit-colored eyes back to me. "Anything else?"

A small but forceful hand finds my shoulder and even under the tension radiating between us, it unwinds the tight nerves in my shoulders. I relent, stepping back and letting Onyx take my place.

"I'll do you the honor of wasting my time to explain a few things to you, Manny. Know that the only reason I'm choosing to pay you this courtesy is because I feel you should know before you die how pathetic your bloodline is."

She takes a step back, gauging his confused, rapid eye movement and upturned thick brows. "What the fuck are you talking about?"

Onyx turns and grabs a scalpel from the table. "Your brother was a decent personal guard. He could lick my pussy fairly well, but he was an imbecile when it came to keeping his small dick in his slacks. On one of his days off, he stopped a Murphy van. He then used *my* insignia to make the women think they could trust him. They thought he was taking them to Hearts."

A nasty twist of jealousy makes my fingers itch to touch her. To run my hands along every inch of her soft skin until I've brushed away the existence of anyone before me. But I reel in my thoughts as quickly as they came, clenching my fists closed at my sides.

She's a temptation. Nothing more, and I'll do well to fucking remember that.

As if Onyx can hear my internal struggle, she blinks lazily at me with a knowing smirk before continuing her monologue.

"He stole from the Murphys, promised these women he'd take them somewhere safe, and then sold them." Even in six-inch heels, Onyx crouches down to his level, her dark eyes searching his, but for what, I'm not sure. Perhaps guilt to affirm this is something he already knew, or maybe the realization that his brother was the cause of his own death.

"The Murphys got to him before I did, Manny. And for that, you should be grateful."

"You should be grateful I wasn't able to gut you like the pig you are."

"Do you hear yourself? You're so blind by the fact he is your brother that you're unable to see I am not the one in the wrong here. You are painting me as the villain to justify your actions rather than being forthright. I did not force your kin's hand. *He* made his choice and received penance for that choice. Just as you will now."

I can't help but absorb her words into my system. It injects into my veins, spreading like wildfire until my temples sheen with sweat. I'm condemning Onyx for something she didn't do.

But what other choice do I have?

"Is there anyone else here who is working with you or them?"

The man sighs wearily, his resignation evident in the downward curve of his mouth. But as an idea blossoms, a nasty snarl transforms his face. "Why should I tell you? I want you to live in fear each time you step foot outside. No, better yet, I want you to go to sleep every night with one eye open."

"I don't think I will." Onyx twirls the scalpel in her hand before standing, motioning for me to join her with the quick tilt of her head.

As if we are one and I know exactly what she wants me to do to him, I walk closer, grabbing Manny's jaw and prying his mouth open. He struggles against me, but I only latch on tighter, digging my fingers into his skin, ignoring the bite of his scruffy beard.

Onyx moves in, slicing just below his bottom gum line.

He jerks violently, shaking his head and spraying blood along both of our chests. While this pisses me off, Onyx grins, lifting her left heel and jamming it into his thigh. This forces her dress to rise, and the brief view of her lace covered pussy makes my dick stir to life.

She leans in, grabbing hold of his hair again, and forces his face up. Blood pours from his mouth and over his quivering lip. She scoops a bit up with her pinkie finger and traces a heart on his cheek. "Tell me what I want to know, Manny."

The muscle in his jaw works, but I catch him before he's able to spit again, squeezing his lips shut. "You're already dead. Decide how painful you'd like to go."

He narrows his eyes at me but swallows the blood he had ready to spew at Onyx. I release him and let her resume her place, only this time, she has a pair of pliers in her hand.

"I'll start with the molars and work my way to the front." Her words are meant for me, not him, and I nod in understanding, prying his mouth open again. She's done asking him questions and instead will rip the words out as she watches him bleed out.

Wise on her part. It makes her come across as bored, rather than desperate. Like this is no more than a tedious job and she can't wait to just be done with it.

And it works. She's three teeth in before his howls turn into confessions. Some that have nothing to do with Embros, I'm sure shouted from his delirium, and others that are important. We learn that he was approached by the Murphys and given the incentive of sixty thousand to work with some others to stage the business meeting. It was a four-year project setting up the vendor's credentials, which is why he seemed to check out when the twins ran the check. The guard already had a grudge, the Murphys just had to remind him and give him reason enough to act on it.

There are no other moles according to him. Well, just one. Me.

"Is there anything else?"

"Kill me," Manny roars, thrashing back and forth in the chair. "Just fucking do it, you piece of shit whore! You are nothi—"

He doesn't get to finish his statement because his eyes are wide in shock, the pain slowly working through his adrenaline as he realizes it's coming from the blade sticking in his chest.

My own body responds to her swift act, my blood thrumming fast, the sound in my ears much louder than his gasps for air.

"I'm growing tired of insults surrounding what I do with my pussy," she mutters more to herself than him as she releases her fist, and the knife retracts back into the metal bracelet. "Do you still see me as some sympathetic... What are you doing, Kane?"

I'm on her before she realizes, backing her into the table. I've never been more aroused than I am right now, and while I have no idea what I'm about to do, I know I need her to come undone by my hand. I need to see something behind the calm veil she has over her.

I need her.

My hand finds the tie holding her dress together and yanks the knot free, exposing the delicate body underneath. Her nipples react immediately, drawing tight in the cold room while goose bumps spread the expanse of her arms. I snatch the bloody scalpel from the table and slice through her panties.

She watches them fall to the floor before her low, heated gaze roves the length of my body and focuses on my eyes. She's trying to read me. Trying to understand how I can be so fucking turned on by the fact she's just tortured and killed a man while I'm still wearing his blood on my button-down.

But she won't be able to figure it out because even I can't.

I step into her space and capture her jaw in my hand. She seems unfazed by my tight hold and instead leans her head back, a silent command rather than a question burning the edges of her pupils.

My body does as told, eager to take care of her in all aspects in this moment. My lips find her neck, and my tongue darts out, exploring the column of her neck while my free hand greedily slides down her body. Over her pebbled nipple, down her soft curves, and to the heat radiating from the place I want to be the most.

I let my thumb work over her slit, sliding through her dripping pussy until I find the spot that makes her tense. She sucks in a sharp breath, and I smile against her neck, slipping two fingers inside while I massage the nerves that have her moans falling freely.

One of Onyx's hands finds my back, her sharp nails digging through my shirt and into my muscle as she tears at the fabric to find leverage. I hiss, releasing her jaw, and grab one of her legs, hooking it around the crook of my elbow while I fuck her with my digits.

I know she's trying to take back the control she's letting slip, but I refuse to let her, and the harder I press into her clit, the louder her whines of pleasure. She's close, so fucking close, I feel her tight walls flutter around my fingers.

My teeth find her ear lobe, nipping as she begins to rock her hips, chasing the high. "Take what you need, Onyx. Because when it's my turn, I'm going to take *everything*."

Her orgasm is beautiful, rippling through her body until I see the shivers in her leg I'm holding, to the tips of her hair brushing against the tabletop. It's a sight I'm becoming addicted to, just like everything else about her.

She drops her legs back to the ground, tying her dress up

casually. She scans the still warm body slumped behind me in the chair before turning her dark gaze on me, her mask firmly back in place. "If you can manage to take it, it's yours."

Tuesday

"Did you get all that?" I ask my sister again, my eyes scanning the fridge for anything else I may have forgotten.

Again, my mom is out walking with our neighbor, and she ate so much over the course of a week, she only has one apple left in the fruit bowl.

I'm not sure how to feel about the fact her health seems to have improved without me and Fi around. Part of me wonders if she's started using uppers, but after searching the house from top to bottom and flat out asking, I've come up empty.

She's told me I can stop worrying over her and that she feels better enough to cook for herself, but without being able to stop by anytime, I don't trust her enough behind a stove.

"Yeah, I got it. The only good information you've given me is that they have a locked file on the Murphys." My sister's voice has a bite to it that strokes the flames of irritation smoldering in my chest.

"Fi. I've been there a week. They aren't going to hand me the fucking keys to their operation because I've helped them sniff out a couple snakes. Snakes that the Murphys had no intention of actually getting to Onyx other than to make her paranoid."

My sister sighs. "I know, Zek. I'm sorry. It's just Sam said he was giving you three months, and I'm nervous. I'm just glad you're still alive. I've been a wreck."

I run a hand through my hair, shutting the door to the fridge, satisfied with what I've made. "I'll get the information in the allotted time, Fi. Trust me. It's not easy working with people and getting to know them while *also* being well aware I'm sentencing them to death."

Even though I didn't mean to say it out loud, I meant the words. Out of all the gigs I've had, all the fucked-up shit I've done and the people I've met, those in the Embros estate are growing on me.

"Do you like her?"

"No." My words aren't convincing, even to me. "But she's not what I thought. None of them are." I collapse onto the worn couch, kicking my feet up on the coffee table.

She huffs. "I get that. I've started talking to one of the guys that brings me food. He's nicer than the rest."

This piques my interest. "Think you can talk him into sneaking you out?"

"And go where? We'd be on the run, forced to hide."

True. If I tried to bring her and my mother to Onyx, I'd have to explain why. Then we'd all be dead regardless. A sickening knot of dread wedges in my throat. But still, I'm somehow able to keep my voice steady despite the very real notion that there is no winning here. "I love you, Fi."

"You too."

* * *

Another week passes in the Embros estate. Another seven days of strained breakfast passes, heavy eye contact, and watching Onyx in meetings with all sorts of people. If her business wasn't illegal, you'd think she's the CEO of a Fortune 500. She's pure business—cold, calculated, a realist, and uses no emotion to make deals.

She's all facts and data.

Loss and profit.

Unlike most, Onyx has no tell when she's uncomfortable or frustrated. No hitch in her voice when she's annoyed or excited. No show of impatience when something is daunting or dull.

It's incredible to watch—especially knowing how she is when she's covered in someone's blood or lost in an orgasm.

Fuck.

I've tried not to let my mind remind me of how fucking perfect she is coming undone. And I've done well the past seven days. But the more I'm around her, seeing her, being captivated by the sheer power the woman consumes in a room, it's getting impossible not to throw her ass across the desk and just take her.

"Where's your head?" Maddy flops down in the seat next to me, her thin finger wagging toward my crotch. "That dick of yours is sticking up through your slacks. Must say, for a guy your size, I didn't think it'd be as big as you."

I chuckle but make no move to readjust. No point now since she's seen it. "Guess it's been a while."

Maddy looks at me as if I've just told her the stupidest shit she's ever heard. After another moment of her dramatic gawking, she rolls her eyes. "I gave you more credit than I should have."

"And that means what exactly?"

"You're either stubborn or deranged, but whether it's this or that, you fit right in." She glances at the clock on the bookshelf. "Two minutes left. Any plans for your day off?"

It takes more effort than I want to admit to school my features and shake my head. "Check on my mom, cook, and maybe go visit some of Onyx's places."

"Be safe. I worry about you when you leave."

"Oh yeah?"

Maddy nods. "Yep. And Boss may not admit it, but she feels safer after what happened. You may think it did the opposite, but it was already something we were concerned about. You did us a favor."

I stand, knowing if I continue to sit, I'll let what little conscience I'm allowed to have seep through. "Glad I could help. I'll see you tomorrow."

"Tomorrow. Such a lovely place to be. Lovely indeed."

Kilo
CHAPTER SEVENTEEN

Four more drops, just four more.

I'm tired today. We've been so busy. Every day it seems as if I get two or three more places to go, people to meet, deliveries to make. I'm not complaining, not at all, but my legs are tired today. Yes, they are.

Oh. The ice cream shop. The one with the white and black canopy and the shiny red door. They make everything by hand and it's so good. Maddy took me there one time. I must ask her to come again.

When we were here, it was dark. The sun had just set, and I dropped some mint chocolate chips on my shirt. There was a dry cleaner a block up that she said would be a good place.

That's when I saw the prettiest eyes I'd ever seen. The girl, by the corner store, staring up at the stars. It was like looking at green jewels stuck in mud. I wanted to pluck them from her eyes, clean off the muck, then put them back.

But then a few weeks ago, I saw another with eyes like hers. The bodyguard, Ezekiel. He's a good guard. Onyx likes him. It will be sad when she kills him. But I understand. She can't be hurt again.

If she were, I know without another thought, we wouldn't get her back this time.

No.

She'd be lost forever, and without her, there is no wonderland.

Oh! Look at the time. Four more stops and I'll be done, and already I'm late.

Onyx
AGE 14
CHAPTER EIGHTEEN

It's so sunny out. Like something you'd see in the movies, or a cartoon animation of the sky. It's the faintest blue, reminding me of Kilo's eyes, and there isn't a cloud in sight. The temperature is perfect too—a cool sixty-five degrees with the slightest breeze.

Mom woke up this morning like Snow White. Dancing around the estate, assisting Mr. Russ in the kitchen and singing to the tune of a hummingbird. He helped her pack a huge basket for the impromptu picnic Dad suggested, but the contagious smiles lighting up the kitchen quickly turned sour when I realized the boys weren't coming.

They were on training assignments, Dad had said. But I knew that was code for they were being brought to their knees by Uncle Antonio as he *trained* them in torture. They needed to fear nothing—not even the grim reaper himself—if they wanted to work high in the ranks. I should be a part of it too, but Dad says a few more years. And no matter how much I argue, he won't budge.

We're currently in the limo on our way to a park across town that overlooks a lake, and I haven't stopped pouting. I'm not trying to be a brat or have an attitude, but it feels like a double whammy.

They can't enjoy the day while I'm still being treated like a delicate rose.

"You must want to look like your father after all." My mother's tender voice and accompanied pat on my thigh forces me to turn and face her. "It will get stuck in that awful scowl if you keep it like that much longer."

"Momma. They should be here. What's one day?" Even though I'm speaking to her, we both know my words are meant for my father, who is gazing out the dark tinted window.

"It's part of the process, baby. They are going to have to miss some of the good days. But it will make them appreciate and cherish them even more when they have them." My mother tries to reason with me, but it only frustrates me more.

"But how rare is a day like today? It's so pretty, Momma."

I'll forever have a soft spot in my heart for the boys. They have been through things I would only wish on the people that caused them their pain. It was heartbreaking and painful, and everything I never want to see again until I die. And because of that, they deserve days like this more than any of us.

"Life isn't perfect, Onyx." He sighs. "It can be the sunniest days that bring us the most darkness. And the ones with the blackest skies that we find happiness. Please understand, the boys agreed to this. They are growing stronger every day, and soon, they will never have to worry about someone hurting them, or you, for the rest of their days."

I hate it when my father brings logic into my fits. It makes me see not only reason but also makes me feel childish, reminding me why he continually puts off my training. I show him I'm not ready.

I take a deep sigh, resignation unwinding the tight muscles in my neck. "You're right. I'm sorry, Father."

"Don't apologize, baby love. That passion, that fierceness you have to protect them, is what will make you a great *donna* one day." He reaches over my mother and tilts my chin up to look at him. "Don't ever lose your fight. Even during *your* dark days."

"*Especially* during those," Mom adds.

"I promise."

"That's my girl."

We ride through the city, engrossed in conversation about my latest tutor, and how I promise not to let the boys scare him off this time. Even before they came into the picture, I always wondered where my parents got my tutors. They were always so feeble and scared easily.

When we finally take the exit, the driver rolls down the privacy screen. "Sir."

My father's smile disappears as if it was never there, and he looks at the man. "What is it?"

He's not snapping at the driver or angry; he sounds like he knows something is wrong and needs to know what it is.

"Our guys in the back didn't exit, and the ones in the front just switched out with an unidentified."

"Jada." This time my father does snap, and my mother jumps, grabbing me by my arm so fiercely I know I'll have bruises.

"Ow, Momma, wha—"

"In here, now." She lifts up the long seat that runs along the windows. It's like a hideaway box for emergencies.

"No. Let me he—"

"Baby, please. Just listen to me. I need you to get inside." The pleading in her voice breaks something in me. Something deep and defiant, making me trust that she knows what she's doing.

But when I'm lying inside, under the seat and watching my mother lower it back down, I realize too late it was a mistake.

The telltale sign of a lock clinking into place makes a rock drop into my stomach. The hollow plop sends dread into my limbs, causing me to feel heavy and weightless at the same time.

"Call my brother. As soon as you get an opportunity, get my daughter the fuck out of here."

"They're coming, love. Six at the back, one looks like Sam, and eight in the front. Do you want to take as many as we can?"

"No," my father tells Mom. "They could open fire, hit the gas tank, or shoot through the doors and hit O."

"Daddy." I push the seat up, though it only allows me to see about an inch. "What's happening? What are you doing? Please don't leave me here."

Though I haven't gone through the intense training like the boys, I know better than to beg. But how can I not? They are being stupid. Why are they walking out?

"You can have some dignity and get out on your own. Or we can blindly shoot into the limo before tearing your bleeding corpses out anyway. You decide, Embros."

My heart nearly breaks free of its boney confinement. It pounds violently in my ears as I peer through the small slit in the seat as my parents exchange looks. I've never seen it before, and I quickly realize why.

It's defeat.

They are going to step outside because they don't want me to be hurt. They are going to die because of me.

Their weakness.

"Momma, please. Father, don't do this." I feel like I'm screaming but I barely hear the words. I try again.

I'm howling now, the veins in my throat bulge, swelling from the force I'm putting on the cords. But it doesn't help. Nothing is coming out.

"I love you, Jada." He runs his hands down her jaw, then presses a soft kiss to her mouth before tapping her lightly on the nose. "And you, baby love. You are my heart."

"Daddy, please." I try again, pushing my shoulder into the seat, but the lock keeps it from opening more than an inch. "Please."

Hot tears stream down my face, the agony of not being able to touch them, to just speak to them, tearing my insides to shreds.

My mother bends down, her beautiful eyes the only thing I can see as she covers the hole. "Onyx. Listen to me, baby."

"Momma, don't do this. You can kill them. We can drive away. Don't walk out there."

"Shhh. Come now. I need you to be strong. You cannot let this break yo—"

"You have ten seconds, Embros." The voice, a voice I'll never forget for the rest of my life, booms through the limo.

"You have to stay strong, because I need you to finish what we started. And after that..." She pauses, pressing a kiss to her fingers before pushing them through the slit and onto my forehead. "I want you to kill them all. Every last one."

A chill runs through me, coiling with the pain searing my skin. My body is on fire and there's nothing I can do to stop it from burning me alive.

In the next blink, they are both exiting the car and the thick clunk of a lock tells me they've somehow managed to lock me inside.

"On the ground," the man instructs.

"We'd rather stand."

The sound of four shots ring out. Each one a mere millisecond from the last, and with every pop, my chest deflates more. Still, I somehow manage to suck in a breath, holding what little air I can as I wait.

Wait for a cry.

A scream.

Movement.

Something.

Anything.

"Now, isn't that better? The king and queen, on their knees in front of me. I must say, I like this a lot."

A round of laughter seeps through the hole, and it... pisses me *off*.

I throw everything I can into my shoulder, jamming it against the bottom of the seat.

"Miss Onyx. Please don't do that." The driver's voice is barely above a whisper. He's crying. I want to cry. I want to scream. But nothing is coming out.

I try again, but this time when I fall back, my right leg hits something sharp. My hand fumbles in the dark, reaching for whatever is lodged in my calf. When I yank it free, I realize it's a crowbar.

"Nothing to say? Don't wish to beg for your wife? Come now, you make this less fun." The man goads my father as I shove the metal between the lock and seat and use every bit of strength I have to pry it open. "Well, since you have nothing to say, can I tell you how I found you? How I was able to get you?"

The most disturbing chuckle I've ever heard falls from the man, causing bile to surge into my throat. Shaking my head, ridding myself of the nausea, I jerk again and one side of the bolted hinge breaks. My heart flutters, working overtime with the new surge of adrenaline pounding through the vessel. They may be risking themselves for me, but I can save them.

"It was your personal guard. The one that sleeps mere feet in front of your room every night. The one that has guarded and protected you for seven years now. We got to him, offered him a few hundred thousand, and he got everyone on board. Your soldiers drove you to your death. How does it feel, knowing that?"

It takes my entire soul to not react to his words. To not crumble into nothingness at what he's saying. The guard they are talking about is a friend. Someone who helped me with homework when my parents were too busy. The one that snuck me extra servings of dessert when I had a rough day. He was part of our family.

My body shakes as I put all my weight against pulling the lock free.

Thunk.

The sound of the metal hitting the floor spurs me into action. I jump from the space, grab my father's gun from the passenger door and rush to the side they are on.

The sight of my parents on their knees halts me. Both of them have been shot in the thigh, and blood pools down their legs and onto the cement beneath them. My mother's eyes are on my father, and vice versa. They don't care what the man is saying. They only want to look at each other in their last moments. And then...

Blood.

There's blood on the white roses behind her.

Splattered.

Dripping.

I hear my screams now. The pure agony rips my body inside out as I watch my mother's head tumble away from her fallen corpse. Her eyes still open and full of so much life. But there is none. They just took it. *Stole* it.

Someone calls my name. I'm not sure who. All I can think about is her. Her blood.

It's on the roses.

Why am I moving?

Why is the car moving?

Go back.

GO BACK!

My words won't come out. All I can hear is the guttural roar burning my throat.

I have to save my father.

I can still save him!

Please, go back...

But it's too late.

The same machete that was just used to slice my mother's head off is sticking in my father's chest, right at his heart.

I hear the gun I was holding clatter to the carpeted floorboard. I hear the squeal of tires. I hear the beating of my heart.

But I can't see.

There's only white.

White roses and dripping blood.

It's the last thing I remember before blackness finally moves in and takes me.

EZEKIEL
CHAPTER NINETEEN

Another two weeks pass, and I have nothing of real value to tell the Murphys. Each day, my routine is always the same. Wake up, eat breakfast, take Onyx hers, and interchange between walking the grounds, surveying the monitors, and standing by the office while she works.

It's not a necessity, but listening to her, and watching how she reacts to the conversations has taught me her tells I wouldn't have otherwise picked up on.

When something works in her favor without much effort, her lips draw down in the corners, almost as if she's disappointed. It's almost as if she's disappointed in how easy it is, or maybe boring. When she has to throw around her weight and use some lightly threatening words, she sits up straighter, and her eyes get slightly lighter.

But my favorite is when she catches me staring, watching, studying. She always tilts her head back an inch—a power move meant to be a silent challenge. Her blinks become slow, and the smallest grin curves her lips.

What she probably doesn't know is that the very top of her ears turns pink. It's the faintest blush I'm sure no one even notices. But I do.

I notice everything about her.

Like how she chews on the inside of her cheek when she's thinking. How she only tends to the red roses in her garden and never the white. She only goes swimming when the sun is tucked away and the clouds are moments from breaking apart with rain.

She perks up when any member of the family comes into her office, but always schools her features as if she's not happy to see them. As if they're business partners and nothing more.

I want to know why she does that. I want to know why she does all of it. How she can be so fucking commanding and intimidating and hide every soft part of herself, even from the people she trusts the most. There's more to it than needing to project Boss energy. Something happened. Something that keeps her from growing deep attachments.

She's learned a very hard lesson in more than one way, and I need to figure out what it was.

"You're a little lost, Ezekiel Kane." Caterina's low voice steals me from my thoughts.

I look through the open door to my right where Cat sits in a massive beanbag chair, legs folded beneath her, smoking from her hookah. I've been this way multiple times when making my rounds, but never have I seen inside this particular room.

In the bed next to her chair is an older man, asleep in the middle. Thick pillows are placed behind him, propping him up slightly, while the white sheets are drawn up to his stomach and folded at the edge. An oxygen tank as well as an IV hang on the side while the green light on the display shows his heartbeat. His pale face is serene, his breathing calm as he rests.

He must be Antonio.

I drag my eyes back to Cat and grin. "So you remember who I am?"

She sucks in a heavy pull from her mouthpiece, holding it

in until her lungs demand she breathe. "Oh, I've known who you were all along. It's *you* who doesn't know."

"I can't wait for the day you tell me what the hell you mean."

A stream of smoke puffs from her small mouth. "And I await the day you figure it out for yourself."

* * *

Riding through the city at night seems almost foreign now. A mixture of blurred colors and shining lights peek through the dark tint in the limo and dance across Onyx's skin.

It's our first time being out since the farmers' market, but this time, it's for business. She's dressed down in a black tailored suit, her hair slicked back in a high ponytail. A gold stem earring curls around the shell of her ear, the rose at the head wrapping around the top.

As always, her blinks are slow and bored, her eyes scanning the buildings outside as we pass them.

She likes to check up on her casinos from time to time, and tonight, she's decided to accompany Shi to collect some of the money. She and Trigger are in the front, hidden by the rolled-up privacy glass.

"Tell me, Kane, have you come to visit any of my casinos."

Her voice floats across the cabin, and though she's not looking at me, I hear a slight difference in her tone. It's lighter somehow.

"I haven't. My one day off is spent cooking and cleaning before sleeping twelve hours and coming back here."

"I imagine that must be nice."

This forces a laugh from me. "Cooking and cleaning? I mean, I'm not complaining but also, it's nice having those things done for me."

Between Russ and the housekeepers at Embros, I've never had a fuller stomach and a floor so clean I could eat from it. A surprisingly pleasant change, considering...

"Sleeping," Onyx clarifies, and when she lets her dark eyes flash to me, I nod.

The faint shadows under her eyes clued me in early on, she never gets much sleep. Pair that with the other things I've observed, I doubt she sleeps more than a few hours at a time. I think she wants to keep her mind busy. Stay in control of her thoughts.

Because once the veil falls and she slips into the abyss, she has no say of what her mind plays in her head.

Instead of breaching a subject where I have no right, I try to ease the soft tension that's risen. The corner of my lips curl and I lean forward. "I'm up for the challenge if you need to be exercised into exhaustion."

Instead of a smart remark, or ignoring me like I expect, she returns my smirk. "Is that so? You think you could tire me more than Trigger does in the gym? Or when I garden all afternoon, swim laps in the pool, or when I torture a man for hours?"

"I do," I say simply.

Her brow arches, a genuine look of curiosity making her head tilt. "How so?"

"Because you use your darkest moments to fuel those activities. You feed off of it and use it as energy rather than expend your own. You're giving so much power to it, it's all you can think about, hence why you probably dream about it."

I know I've touched a nerve when she adjusts her posture, straightening her spine. I see her and it makes her uncomfortable. But I like looking, because she has no fucking clue how, despite it, she's so goddamn beautiful.

"With me, Boss, you wouldn't be able to do that. Your mind wouldn't be able to run from me, and how I make you feel."

I lean closer, reaching for her chin. When she doesn't back away and instead stares down her nose in a silent challenge, I close the space, gripping her delicate skin. Her citrus scent invades my airways, and it takes too much effort not to kiss her shimmering lips. "As a matter of fact, even now, I think your head is so cloudy all you can focus on is us, here and now. I wonder, though, does that intrigue you, or sca—"

"Careful, Kane." A manicured hand removes mine from her face. "I'd hate for you to say something and force me to take your tongue."

"You'd miss it too much."

Onyx's husky laugh travels through me and I don't fight the chuckle it coerces out of my chest. "It is a rather talented muscle."

I don't get to respond, because somewhere between our bubbled conversation, the limo has pulled into our destination, and Trigger opens the door.

Onyx spares me a quick glance before taking Trigger's outstretched hand. "Shall we?"

When we exit the limo, I take in the back of what appears to be a plain six-story office building. It's smaller than I'd imagined and sandwiched between two much higher ones. We've parked in the alley, which is quiet and clean of any common debris or trash. Hell, besides the lone brown cat lurking near the end, we seem to be the only living beings in the area.

"That cat loves you, ma'am. It's like it can sense when you're coming." A guard closes a window slat before opening the door. He's in a suit similar to the man I saw outside of the Rabbit Hole where I met Maddy. "Haven't seen her in weeks, and then bam, you show up and she's back."

Onyx peers at the animal for a moment before turning to the guard. "How's your wife, Andrew?"

The man smiles, the cat forgotten as he opens the door

wide. "Round and heavy. Due any day now. We really appreciate that truckful of nursery stuff you sent over. She cried for about a week straight."

"It's nothing." Onyx waves him off as we pass by, walking the long corridor until we reach an elevator.

Inside, Trigger taps the button B2 before wrapping a large arm around Shi's shoulders. She moves into him naturally, letting her eyes flutter closed for a moment before the ding of doors opening steals her attention.

Now, this is what I expected.

Bloodred carpets line the floors, while chandeliers and dim lighting illuminate the ceiling. The scene is almost picturesque of Heaven and Hell, while in the middle, purgatory rests. Rows of tables fill the vast space—poker, blackjack, roulette, and craps, to name a few.

Like the guard outside, the dealers and waitresses all wear the same attire, complete with a red heart on their sleeve. And every worker is busy, tending to the full house of patrons.

We walk through the space toward the back, past a window of women dealing out chips and to a black door where Onyx enters a code. Inside the small room, an older gentleman who was sitting behind a desk stands and nods toward us before crouching down. The few telltale signs of a safe lock whirling and thick clunk of a lock gives way to what he's doing.

"Our numbers are higher this week."

"Percentage?" Onyx asks as she studies one of the dozens of security's surveillance cameras mounted on the wall.

"Six."

"How?" Shi's brows furrow as she looks over an open book on the desk. Her eyes scan almost abnormally fast until she smirks. "The savings are in liquor."

The gentleman stands, stacks of money in hand. "We've

had an increase in underage guests after a social media influencer hit one of our small jackpots."

"Spending money and filling seats, but can't purchase booze. Sounds good." Trigger huffs, filling his small duffel bag with the money.

"Until they run out of money they don't have," I say, moving to stand next to Onyx, who is staring intently at one particular screen.

"What do you mean?" Trigger asks.

"This means we are the *it* thing right now. If they are taking their parents' money, it's only a matter of time until one loses an amount too big and the wrong people come sniffing around." Onyx nods to Shi, who writes something down in the book. "Raise the age to thirty for the next three weeks. Run some specials to make our regulars happy. Kane, let me ask you something."

My eyes follow hers to a blackjack table. It's full of men of various ages, all of which have large piles of chips pushed in front of them. Before she utters a word, I point to a younger guy wearing a red hat. "Him."

Onyx smirks and turns just enough that I see both her eyes twinkling in amusement. "Very good eye, Kane."

She snaps her fingers as she twists for the doorknob. "Table one hundred six. A counter in the red hat. Come, Kane. Let's have some fun, shall we?"

EZEKIEL
CHAPTER TWENTY

A ceiling with no texture is easy to stare at. It allows me to listen to the late-night sounds of the house while not getting distracted with making shapes in my mind.

I've memorized the estate's noises. Every alarm, every midnight snack trip and toilet flush. I know the pipes groan when used past two in the morning, and the tapping of Cat's hookah when she cleans it out before walking downstairs to get Antonio's food.

All of it. Every minuscule sound.

It's how I can both ensure no one is headed to Onyx's room at convoluted times, while also getting the drop on anyone who might come to mine. Not that I think anyone is suspicious anymore. Can't ever be too cautious, though.

Satisfied everything is normal, I return to the book I set aside earlier. Though it was so long ago, it seems more of a dream rather than a memory, I'd loved reading. Every Friday after school, I'd bribe Fi to stop at the library on our way home so I could carry as many mystery and *Goosebumps* books as possible.

I loved the thrill. The adventure. The escapism.

It's been a long-forgotten pastime, and one sunny afternoon, when Onyx had retired to her room, I found Trigger reading near the foyer. It was a Stephen King book. I remember counting down the days until I was old enough for the librarian to let me check one of his books out.

Never did get to do that, though...

But Trigger saw me gawking and let me look over some titles he had. Now, I'm my third book in, and fuck, have I been missing out. The thrill, the chills, the excitement. With every page I turn, it seems like I never know what this brilliant man will throw at me.

Fucking Annie Wilkers, man. I know she's really a representation of King's addiction to... The soft shuffling of feet draws my attention to the left of my door.

I consider putting my book down but think better of it and instead continue running my eyes over the pages, waiting for her to make an appearance.

A few moments later, the knob on my door slowly turns, and Onyx slips inside, closing it behind her.

It could be seconds, maybe a few minutes, but it feels like hours that I'm focusing on the words on the page, reading and rereading the lines as I wait for her to speak first.

Finally, she takes a step forward. "You are quite the problem for me, Kane."

I huff, turning the page. Annie is about to fuck this guy up. "I thought I was your solution."

Another step, and my heart beats faster at the sound of her long sigh. "I find myself enthralled with you for reasons I can't explain."

This makes me look up, and my dick immediately stirs. She's in nothing but a black silk robe, the fabric barely long enough to cover her pussy. It's tied haphazardly on the side, causing the top to hang off one of her shoulders. My tongue peeks out, running over my bottom lip as my mouth begins to water, her taste still fresh in my memory.

Two more steps. "Or maybe it's because your hidden darkness attracts mine."

She's next to me now, lingering at my bedside. The heat from her body radiates across my bare chest, and I realize too late I'm cracking the book's spine. "I'm afraid I don't understand what you mean."

Onyx runs a nail up my arm, leaving a satisfying shiver in her wake. Her finger continues to trail upward, sliding over my neck and across my jaw until she reaches my lips. "The only place these belong is on my pussy, but I can admit I've thought about how they may feel on mine."

I catch her by the wrist, letting my heated gaze rove the exposed glowing amber skin. "Why wonder, then?"

"Because I don't know intimacy. I don't want it."

My voice dips, the natural huskiness somehow becoming more gravelly. "And what is it that you want?"

Her dark irises flash to my lips, then down, before coming back to me. I feel my jaw tense as I grind my molars against one another, waiting.

"For you to leave me shaking."

A surge of blood rushes through me, and I yank my bottom lip between my teeth. "If you want it, *take it*."

The air becomes thick, her fingers falling limp in my hand as she leans forward. Her mouth is an inch away from me now, her exhale becomes my next breath. Her citrusy scent consumes me, and soon I'm high off her smell.

Her grin is devastatingly beautiful and equally dangerous as she finds my ear, running her lips along the shell. "Why take it, when you could just give it to me?"

Those words are all I need. An invitation to completely fucking destroy her in the best ways. And even though she has some type of vendetta against men owning women, I fully intend to own her orgasms.

Every.

Last.

One.

"Your throne awaits, Your Highness. Come, sit on my face." I yank her down, forcing her on top of me. She catches herself just in time, hand pressing against the wall as I grab her hips with enough force to leave bruises.

She hisses the moment my mouth meets her wet cunt, while a deep-seated, satisfied groan erupts from my chest. I lift her slightly, running the flat of my tongue along her slit. "So fucking wet for me. Were you already thinking of me? Lying in your room, with your hand between your thighs, wishing it was me?"

She threads a hand through my hair, yanking the strands as she lowers her pussy back on my waiting tongue. Her voice is low and raspy, and I don't think my dick can get any harder. "Fuck me with that mouth of yours or I'll have you watch me please myself with my hand."

I chuckle against her clit, making her jolt upright. "Yes, Your Majesty."

My fingers dig into the soft flesh of her hip, my intentions to both leave my mark while also mixing a bit of pain with her pleasure. I continue exploring the different nerves she has hidden along her slit, dipping inside her sweet cunt every now and again as I do. She can hide behind her soft moans, but she clenches hard when I hit spots she really likes.

I keep my efforts there, sweat beading along my brow as I work her into an orgasm. But just as she begins to flutter around me, she shifts, lifting and turning before I realize what's happening.

Her ass is in my face now, her tight little puckered hole tempting me while she settles back near my mouth. We both move in unison, her grabbing my cock from the confines of my boxers while I sink two fingers inside her. Her muscles squeeze around my invasion, her slickness guiding them in deeper.

One of her hands grip into my thigh, the sharp burn of her nails coercing a deep hiss from behind my clenched teeth, while the other wraps around my length.

Fuck, I would give anything to see her delicate hand, but I must admit, my current view is better. I begin to pump my fingers into her, curling them as the sound of her wetness and moans play like a melody around us.

She releases me and threads her fingers between mine, sweeping through her folds before grabbing hold of me again. She uses herself as a lube, squeezing around my cock from base to head. "That's better."

I groan, jutting my hips up at the feel of her small hand around me. My dick throbs, the thought of how her cunt may feel invading my every sense.

"Oh, Kane. Don't tell me you're about to come. I've only just started."

The snark in her voice doesn't go unnoticed, nor does the ringing pop of my slap on her ass. She jumps, yelping her moan, forcing my fingers to slide out as she leans forward.

I wrap one arm around her waist and yank her back so I can rub my hand over the red print. "Don't insult me. You're the one who had to change positions to buy yourself more time."

"If you ever—"

Another slap, followed by a louder scream. She jerks against my hold but doesn't get very far before I wrench her back, her clit now an inch away from my mouth. "I plan to do far worse things to you than slap your ass. And when I do, you'll beg me for more. Like now. You're fucking dripping down my chin."

I don't wait for a response and instead mimic her, swiping my thumb inside her cunt before pushing it into her tight ring of muscle.

"*Kane.*" My name is nothing more than a breathy moan, but before I can claim victory, her warm mouth seals around my cock.

Fuckkkkk.

My eyes roll so far back it's painful, while the immense pleasure and desire rushing through me threatens to make me come. A guttural groan rumbles my chest as we both continue the assault on each other.

It's a game of who will break first. Who will take the other and control the entire dynamic? It's seeing who will succumb and who will rule.

It's a game I intend to win.

I increase my efforts, fucking her ass harder with my thumb as my tongue lashes at her clit. She mewls, her body starting to move greedily for more, while at the same time taking me deeper down her throat.

Onyx moans around me, the farther she takes me, the more she presses into my face.

It's the sexiest fucking thing I've experienced in my life, and just the notion of someone so fucking powerful sucking the life from my dick has me about to explode into her mouth.

Fuck, I want to so goddamn bad.

But I refuse to let her win. My licks become longer, and her sucks become harder, both of us on the brink until finally I feel her shaking. She's so close she's losing focus, losing a grip on me.

"You're clenching me so fucking tight..." I release her thigh and snake up her back, my fingers finding the tips of her ponytail. I wait until I'm able to get a good grip and then yank so forcefully, my cock pops out of her warm mouth. "Enough with the games. Come for me. *Now*."

And she does. Goddamn, she fucking does.

Her back folds, the cries of her release permeating the air and soaking into the wall until its sounds are all I'll ever hear when I walk in the room.

I release her hair, hooking my arm around her waist and holding her up while slowing to long, languid strokes, drawing out her orgasm. She shudders through it, our breathing matching in unison as we pant for air.

My cock throbs next to her hand, the blood rushing painfully to the spot that's been suddenly deprived of attention. It was worth it, though. I won.

She seems to realize it too as she rotates her frame and rests back on her knees while still straddled on top of me. Her face is slightly flushed, her tan lips swollen and wet. A bead of sweat rolls down her neck and disappears between her breasts, still somehow covered by the small robe.

"That was a dirty thing to do, Kane."

I smirk, sitting up and drawing the silk back over her shoulder. "I like dirty things, *mo bhanrion*." My queen.

Her brows furrow, her beautiful dark orbs scanning mine. I like her like this—fresh from an orgasm I gave her, flustered and now curious.

Her nose is scrunched up, and I can't help but playfully tap it.

And just like that, everything fucking changes.

Her face transforms from something soft and lustful to angry and resentful. She rips herself away from me, fumbling over the bed so quickly, I can't believe she doesn't trip. When she thrusts open the door, the hinges creak, threatening to snap off.

By the time I'm up and grabbing my boxers, she's already gone.

EZEKIEL
CHAPTER TWENTY ONE

I won.

She gave in.

Yet, instead of getting to gloat, I'm having to chase her out of my room to figure out what the hell just happened.

"Onyx." I keep my voice low, but don't hide the aggression in my words.

I don't like the disgusting feeling she's left me with, like I've done something so offensive she can't even fucking look at me. And I hate that I care. But I do.

She doesn't turn back, of course, and instead ignores me, striding the short space between our rooms as if she's fully clothed and headed to her next business meeting. As if she didn't just flip a fucking switch and leave me reeling.

I catch up as she reaches her keypad and tug on her shoulder. She shucks me off as if I'm nothing more than an annoying bug, and types in her code.

Nine. Seven. Four. Six. Three. One.

Something I don't want to think about forces me to look down before she taps the last number. She pushes the door open, and I let out an amused scoff when she attempts to shut it behind herself. I slip in, careful not to slam it shut and attract any unwanted attention as I follow her to the bathroom.

"Why do you do that?" I snap. "Stop for one fucking second."

I should know better than to push her, but over the past month, we've crossed lines. We've crossed boundaries. And despite how any of this is meant to end, right now, we are in new territory.

Again, I have to fling open the bathroom door she tries to close in my face, irritation flaring in my gut.

Holy shit.

Her bathroom is nearly as big as my room. The shower she walks to is in the center, enclosed inside four, seven-foot walls of glass. The black tile floor is a stark contrast to the rest of the white and chrome room, and when she turns it on, water falls down like rain from long strips of metal.

Onyx didn't turn on the light, but above the bathroom is a moonroof, letting the glow from the stars illuminate the entire space, including her. When she takes her robe off, she turns to face me, her natural look of power pulling her features tight.

The moon spills over her delicate curves, turning them into a golden river of pure bliss. They lead the way from her throat, down her perfectly tear-shaped breasts, over the toned flat abdomen, and around her wide-set hips.

I feel like I say it every time I see her in a new way, but I have never seen something as stunning and utterly fucking perilous in my life. She's the waterfall over a one-hundred-foot cliff, and even knowing so, I still want to fall into her abyss.

"Go back to your room, Kane. I don't need you to guard my shower."

She's not upset anymore. At least not on the outside. But I've been doing nothing but watching and studying her for a month. I know better.

I take a step forward. "No. I want an answer as to why you did that."

"Because I'd gotten what I wanted. I didn't feel the need to be in there anymore."

I guffaw, annoyance mixing with the arousal that never left. "Bullshit."

Onyx's lips twitch momentarily before she smiles. "You'd do well to remember who you work for. Who signs your checks."

Another step. "And you'd do well to remember whose tongue makes you collapse from the orgasm it gives you."

Her eyes narrow but she doesn't offer a rebuttal and turns for the already steaming shower.

I move fast, stripping off my boxers and stepping inside the gap of glass serving as an entrance. She whips around, her hand up, but I catch it before it connects with my face. "I'm tired of you walking away from me."

"And I'm exhausted with you thinking I care."

My jaw clamps shut, the nerve in it pulsing as I shove her into one of the walls, keeping the offending hand over her head. There's no space between us now and it takes all of my restraint to focus on her cute, angry expression rather than the feel of her soft skin against mine.

I let a grin stretch across my face, the smug look of victory painting my features. But the moment I stoop down to take her swollen lips between my teeth, a hard fist meets my ribs.

An *oof* whooshes out of me, but I manage to act rather fast, snatching her other hand and using it to whirl her around and ram her into the glass. With the new position, she's facing the long mirror, granting me a view that has the blood running marathons through my body and my dick unbelievably hard. Her breasts and the side of her face are smooshed against the partition, while the rest of her struggles to free herself from my firm hold.

"Let me go, or so fucki—" She bucks her hips back into my

length, but with both her hands bound in one of mine, I use the other to slide my tip through her wet folds, replacing her curse with a sharp hiss.

My knees threaten to buckle at her warmth, but I keep them locked, lowering my voice to a raspy growl against her neck. "I don't think you want me to let you go."

I caress her folds with the head, watching in the mirror as she squeezes her eyes closed and lets out a breathy moan. "No, I think you want me to fuck you until you can no longer stand." Another pass. "Until you're so sore you think of me every time you move."

I line up my tip with her entrance and run my tongue up the nape of her neck to the shell of her ear. Her shivers spur me on despite the constant tug of her hands in mine, and when she tilts her hips up and presses the tip through her entrance, I know for certain. "Until you know, despite what you want to believe, this tight little cunt belongs to *me*."

Then I slam into her.

A strained cry rings out, forcing me to pause, letting her adjust to my size while also taking the opportunity to rein in my adrenaline. I already knew she felt good, but I underestimated just how much.

Her warm muscle wraps around my cock, the slickness of her cunt letting me draw out and thrust back in a little harder.

Onyx sucks in a sharp intake of air, her lashes fluttering closed from the sensation for a moment as she works on regaining her control. I'm sure what I said ruffled her feathers, but now that I've let myself slip this far, there's no going back, and I meant every fucking word I said.

No part of this is going to be soft and sweet.

It's about taking what I've wanted this entire time.

Again, I pull out and drive into her with such force, she's lifted off the tile floor. Her moans grow louder, but once she gets the rhythm, I see her dark gaze find mine in the reflection of the mirror. And it's the moment I see it. The fire, the determination, the hunger, and pure lust raging through her.

The next time I withdraw, her feet find purchase and her hips lift, meeting my next thrust in the middle, the resounding slap echoing in the space around us.

We do this again and again. My long, hard strokes fill her to the hilt, but still, she fixes her hips to stroke my fire.

"Harder." It's a breathless command, but a command, nonetheless.

I smirk. "You're going to have to beg me for it."

She bucks her hips, hitting me with more force. "Or I can take it."

This coerces a stilted laugh from me. "Have it your way, darling."

I release both her hands and grip on to her sides, yanking her with me as I take a step back. The hot water rains over me, falling down my chest and onto her. And when I pull out this time, I drive in so hard her hands fly out and connect with the glass. She attempts to use it to push back, but it's too slippery and I'm already out and sliding back in. My thrusts are punishing now, the constant slap of our skin matching her loud moans.

"Your pussy feels so fucking good." The praise is a whispered hiss I think is lost in our sounds. "It's so goddamn wet."

But a small chuckle falls from her mouth, indicating she heard me, as she does the only thing she can, and arches her back. "I know."

My own lips curl into a smile, but not at her words. Her cunt is fluttering, her legs quivering as her release nears. I thread a finger in her hairband and yank it through her strands until her hair falls onto her back.

I only allow myself to admire the view for a moment before

I collect the now wet hair and force her head back. "Eyes up, *Boss*. I want you to see what I do to you. How pretty you look when I make you come."

To my surprise, she listens, watching herself in the mirror as my hand reaches around her legs and circles her clit. With her already being so close, it only takes a few passes before her face transforms. Her eyelashes flicker closed, her shoulder tensing, and the small crease between her brows appearing as she draws them together.

"Ah, that's a good girl." Her muscles clench around me, forcing my own release to come from seemingly nowhere—the heat spreading through my veins as I fuck her through both of our orgasms.

We pant in unison, our chests rapidly rising and falling as we come down, but the lingering twitch of my cock and her pulsing cunt keep me inside her until we've nearly completely caught our breaths.

Onyx rises, and though she has her mask firmly back in place, I see the slight wince as my dick slips out. She turns for the glass containers affixed to the opposite side and pours soap on a loofah.

Before I can begin to formulate a thought or register the irritation swelling in my chest, she tosses the fluffy material at me. "Wash your mess."

I bite into my lip to keep from smirking and do as told.

The smell of the lemon soap overtakes everything as I take my time, washing over her shoulders, down her arms, and across her breasts. The entire time, she keeps her eyes on me. It's nothing more than a bored look of observation, but she can't hide her tells. The tips of her ears turn red when I run a thumb over her pebbled nipples, cleansing the barbells, and sliding them back and forth.

She can't stop the swallow she washes down when I move

down her stomach, between her legs, and in the small spaces between her black painted toes. And when I come back up and run a hand over her slit, the muscles in her abdomen tighten while her lashes flutter.

When I'm done, she doesn't wait and lets the water sweep over her before stepping out of the shower. I make quick work of washing myself before following her back into her room.

Onyx is already dressed in a silky black nightie, her wet hair braided to the side. She's sitting at the edge of the bed, rubbing a thick cream over her legs. "Why are you still here?"

Though I hadn't planned on staying before, her inquisition makes me decide otherwise. I drop onto the leather couch facing the open window next to her bed, readjusting the towel hanging loosely from my hips. "Because I want to be."

She huffs but doesn't say anything else, shifting to the other leg.

"I can put that on you too, if you'd like."

Her gaze flashes to me, and I lift a brow. She's trying to gauge just how much I meant a few minutes ago. I can tell in the way her eyes narrow. "Kane."

I ignore the way my name rolls off her tongue, and instead focus on her loss for words. "You're mine," I clarify.

"I am no one's."

"That was before."

"Sex changes nothing," she retorts. "Remember your place."

I guffaw, leaning back into the firm cushions. "Yes. How can I forget? But I doubt *you'll* ever forget what I feel like between your legs."

"Your point, Kane?"

"Is obvious."

Onyx draws in a deep sigh. "I don't anticipate this ending well."

I shrug, letting my eyes close. "No. It probably won't. But I'll revel in the warmth until the flames consume me."

Rubbing at the sudden tightness in my chest, I chance a peek at her. She's in the bed now, on top of the covers, her back against the tall plush headboard. Her eyes are closed. "Burning is such a painful way to go. A bullet is more merciful."

I nod even though she can't see me, an understanding washing over. "Until a bullet stops me."

Trick

CHAPTER TWENTY TWO

"**F***uck*. Right there, kitten," I grit out, the tingle starting to bloom in my spine.

Shire's fingers dig into my thighs as she uses them as leverage to pull up slightly, then slam down again. Her legs are quivering now, she's barely able to bounce as her orgasm nears.

I grip either side of her hips and take over, careful not to move too fast as my brother's tongue laps at her clit, forcing her over the edge. The fluttering in her pussy changes to tight clenches as we both come apart together.

She collapses back into my chest, her aftershock trembling and purrs vibrating across my sternum. I bury my face in her soft hair, inhaling her musky scent. We've been at it for hours and her power—her hunger—will never cease to amaze me. But now, as the high wears off, I know the soreness and pain are coming.

As will the fog.

I stroke her hair with one hand while the other caresses the marks I can see. I soothe the little bites and nibbles I left on her inner thighs. Then move to the red welts on the outside left by Trigger's flogger.

He helps lift her off my semihard shaft, then leaves us

while he tends to getting the things she needs.

I hover over her worn body, continuing to run my knuckles lightly over her jaw. "You did so good, kitten."

Though her eyes are closed, her wide smile appears as she presses her face into my hand.

The harsh sounds of my phone vibrating on the wood stand next to us jars me, but Shi's soft nod lets me know she's fine. I lean back on my haunches and reach over and grab it, answering on the third ring.

"Hey, Boss."

"You're out of breath. Are you busy?"

I run a hand over my hair, my eyes flashing to the bathroom at Trigger to make sure he's running Shi's bath. "No, I'm good. You need me?"

"I do. Basement."

"Yes, ma'am." I tap the red button, tossing the phone back on the nightstand.

I scoop Shi's body up in my arms, caressing her hair as I take her to the bathroom. Trigger's already in the filling tub, dropping a few oils inside and knocking in some dried rose petals. I set her down slowly, giving my brother time to open his legs and let her settle between.

"Going down for the driver?"

Nodding, I dip a washcloth inside the warm water and make quick work wiping myself up. "Yeah. One of the women ended up dying in the hospital."

My heart squeezes as I mention Natalie. She was one of the women we just picked up a few weeks ago. Me and another guard intercepted the van she was in, and I remember her being the one we were worried about. She was so far gone, so addicted, we had to give her reduced doses of methamphetamine or else we knew she was going to run.

Turns out our efforts weren't enough. She left, returned to

her dealer, and ended up being forced to lead a couple of new Murphy soldiers to Embros Hearts. Dumbasses must have thought if they were able to steal some girls back, they would get some kind of fucked-up accolade from their Boss, but even the don, Phineas Murphy, knows Hearts is off fucking limits.

The two guys were nothing to handle, but Natalie was in the car with the driver, and he slit her throat before we caught up to him. Guess she had something to say he didn't want repeated. But when I went to kill him, Onyx asked for me to bring him in. I'm not sure why she wanted to keep him, but I didn't question her.

That woman has a reason for everything, even if it's not part of our bigger plans.

"Don't stay up." I kiss Shi on the head and nod to my brother before throwing on some clothes and heading downstairs.

When I reach the basement, I find Onyx already there, leaning against the back wall. She's eerily calm, slowly French braiding her hair to the side. Her slim-fitting jumpsuit is snug against her frame, the front cutting to her navel and exposing the insides of her breasts.

Even though we aren't related, my love for her as my blood is so deeply embedded, I almost feel uncomfortable when she displays her curves to scum. Even tied up and on the verge of dying, I know how they look at her. And it never fails to make me want to stab their fucking eyes out.

I glance over to the driver. He's upright, held in place by chains attached to the ceiling and clamped around his wrists. He's young, no more than twenty-five, fit, and about Onyx's height. His brown, shoulder-length hair is tied back at the nape of his neck, but a few strands stick to his sweaty face.

The metal table is pushed against the far wall, and I realize immediately something's happened. Instead of a scalpel, there're scissors, and rather than pliers, there's a bone saw, and most concerning of all, there's also a pickaxe, bat, and machete.

She didn't come down here for information. She came to blow off steam.

"Should I get Shi? Or Maddy?"

Onyx pushes off the wall, a smirk gracing her face. "I thought we'd have some fun, you and me. It's been so long."

My ears perk up. It has been a long time.

Out of all of us here, I'm the obvious choice if you want to get into some trouble. I'm much further gone in the head if I'm being honest, and I enjoy scalping people more than what's deemed normal.

I think it happened the day we saved Shi. She was the first woman we saved while just out, walking around in neutral area. She'd just turned eighteen when we found her. She was bloody, beaten, and banging on death's door, begging for her end. Her story is one you hear about on the news and are grateful to learn the girl died so she didn't have to endure the pain just from breathing anymore.

Still to this day, I don't understand why she didn't give up and end it all herself. And that's what makes me love her more —she's the definition of a survivor.

But even though she survived, she still deserved justice. And since she would never get it in the way she so rightfully deserved, I was down to give it to her the way she needed it. For her, that meant the piece of shit soldier that snatched her off the street. We tied him to a tree deep in the woods off the property and filleted him from toe to nose.

The whole ordeal took three days, and he was alive and aware for most of it.

It was exhausting, and my ears hurt like a bitch, but Shi was cleansed. She'd taken a piece of what he'd stolen from her. And for me, that was enough because she deserved so much more.

I glance at Onyx. There's a weariness in her eyes, faint shadows under each. "Tell me what happened first."

A full-blown smile breaks across her face, the whites of her teeth stark against her tan skin. She struts to the table, taking the bat off the surface while twirling a playing card in her other hand. "How about during."

She's not asking, so I accept, nodding and standing in front of the man who's been quietly observing until now. His eyes are wide, but somehow still angry, his brows furrowed and a grimace drawing down his mouth. "What the fuck are y'all talking about? I'm not telling you shit about—"

"If I wanted you to talk..." Onyx swings, connecting with his back so hard it sends a brutal crack echoing in the space. "I would have asked you a question."

The man's yelp falls on deaf ears as I walk to the back by the bathroom and grab two folding chairs. I put them both out and take a seat in one, lazily stretching my arm across the back of the other and crossing one leg over my knee. "So who's it about?"

"Him," she says over the man's grunts.

His breathing is rattled, but he remains angry. I've always found these Murphy clowns fairly entertaining. Whether they are tied to chairs, walls, or staring down the barrel of my gun, they all keep their defiant faces to the end. Like they actually do any of their dirty work themselves. Their false bravado is outstanding, really.

"This him or that him?"

"That one."

I bite into my lip to keep from smirking. It was more than obvious something was going to happen between her and Ezekiel sooner or later. When he first laid eyes on her, he was smitten. Not in the creepy way that makes me want to scoop his fucking eyes out, but in adoration.

And Onyx... well, she's not one to give a fuck. So my curiosity is piqued. "Did he do something?"

Onyx takes another swing with the bat, knocking into the side of the guy's knee. It folds inward, and if it wasn't for his scream, I'd still be able to tell from the displaced bone it's broken. "Yes."

I know it isn't bad, or else he would be here rather than the driver we didn't need. The driver who can't stomach a broken knee and is yelling slurs left and right.

"Fucking stupid bitch! What—"

I'm up before he can think about finishing the statement, my elbow at his neck. He's pulled back as far as he can go, and with a bum knee, only one is able to kick out. Onyx takes care of it by jutting the fat part of the bat into him, breaking the other one.

"He made me feel vulnerable," she sighs, throwing the bat toward the table. It clanks against it before clattering to the floor.

I'd dare to say the confession was hard, but the way her shoulders relax, it seems like a relief.

I let the man go, falling back into my chair with a dramatic shriek. "What*ever* will we do? He made you feel!"

She narrows her eyes at me, grabbing the scissors. "Your theatrics aren't required nor desired, Trick. You know the issues at hand."

Leaning over, I rest my elbows on my thighs, watching as she cuts his shirt from his body. "I know. But Onyx, I was taught the same things. If I'd lived by Antonio's words, I'd never have Shi. Trigger and I would be lost. Souls bound for Hell without ever having a taste of Heaven."

And Shi *is* Heaven. Her spirit is our clouds, her heart our sun and her cunt our euphoria. Life without her is worse than any hell.

"You and I are not the same."

"So? That means you can't enjoy him? Even if he makes you uncomfortable?"

"Especially because he makes me uncomfortable. Besides, his fate is decided. After we deal with the Murphys, I'm killing him." Her last words don't come out as strong as the first.

She snatches the man's ponytail, wrenching his head back while sliding the opened scissors next to his throat. "Tell me, how many women have you stolen? I'm curious."

"Fuc—arghhhhhh!" Blood immediately pools near the small cut she makes. It's low, near his collarbone, but now she brings the sharp end up.

"A cut so similar to the one you gave Natalie. Now. How. Many?"

"How the fuck should I know? I just do what I'm told."

She takes the scissors and moves to his cheek. I near them, grabbing hold of his jaw so he can't move as she makes small nicks on his face into the clear shape of a heart. "How many did you rape? Give a test drive before selling them off? Tell me the truth or I'll make this so much more painful than it needs to be."

"Only two," he yells out, thrashing against his chains.

"Liar," I whisper.

Onyx slices across his abdomen twice.

"I swear it!"

Two more gashes.

More screams.

She won't ask again, and when he realizes it, he relents. "All of them. It's our job as scouters to make sure their shit is good."

Onyx sneers, looking over to me briefly, and I know I'm about to have a lot to clean up. "To make sure their shit is good," she repeats. "So, how many have you raped? Give me an estimate."

"I don't know! A few fucking dozen. Maybe more. Maybe less. How am I supposed to know?"

Her voice becomes low, filled with venom even I can feel. "The same way I know I've killed forty-two of the vile pieces of shit on your side. The same way I know I've rescued over five thousand one hundred of the women you tried to pass through my city. And the same way I know you won't be able to use that limp worm between your legs ever again."

"What do you want?" he bellows, tears and snot running down his face and into his mouth.

Onyx lets him go, walking around and standing in front of him. She tilts her head and runs a nail down his jaw. "I don't need anything from you. Your screams are enough to give me orgasms for weeks."

I grin, redirecting our conversation. "I think you should enjoy Ezekiel while you have him, fuck him, then kill him." Shrugging, I scratch behind my ear. "I don't see what you're stressed about."

She ignores the man's sudden pleas as she trades the scissors for pliers. "You think me a masochist?"

"So you like him?" This forces my spine straight. Onyx doesn't like anyone. Hell, I don't even think she likes us, so I'm glad we're family.

Wails of agony bounce off the walls as she shoves the tool down his pants. Not once does she look before twisting and ripping his member off in one fell swoop. She tosses it to the ground and backs away in time for his vomit to splash to the floor. It's rancid and brown, and I'm pretty sure he'd need to go to a hospital if we weren't about to kill him.

Once his bowels are thoroughly empty, he passes out. I stand slowly, carefully stepping through the growing puddle of bodily fluid for my cauterization kit on the side. It's nothing more than a wide flat branding tool and a small butane kit.

"Answer me, Onyx."

A muscle in her jaw twitches, but she knows she's already said too much. Might as well finish. "He makes me feel less in control. But still safe."

A hearty laugh vibrates my stomach muscles. "And how is that a bad thing? That means he's a damn good bodyguard. And maybe good for *you*. Why do you want to kill him?"

She yanks the driver's pants down and holds his hips steady, watching me warily as I hit the tool until it begins to bloom red. "Because once I take care of the Murphys, who's to say he won't try and take over what we have here. Perhaps he becomes comfortable with this life and wants more."

"And if he doesn't?" I touch the metal to the driver's new hole. It takes a moment but when he comes to, the screams are piercing.

Onyx moves next to me, and together we watch as his body forces him unconscious again. "He will."

"Then we kill him. But for now, live a little. We all *want* you to live, Boss. Otherwise, your entire existence, your *survival*, is only to avenge them. Then what after? I'm afraid we'd lose you."

She sighs, brushing me off. "You don't think someone else will rise and take over the Murphys? There's always going to be someone."

Though she makes my worries seem superficial, I see the thoughts working through her mind. The pain, her loss, her desires, and fears. All of it works across her face in tandem, darkening her eyes, forming creases at her forehead, and pursing her lips. She's so conflicted and I'm not even sure she is ready for what comes after.

I mean, how could you be when it makes up your whole persona?

"Is that why we're here? So you can feel in control again?"

Her head lifts, the words evident on her face without the need for her to confirm. I nod and walk back around to the table to grab the bat and a bit of smelling salts from my bag. "Then let's have some fun."

Onyx
AGE 15
CHAPTER TWENTY THREE

My butt slams against the mat for the tenth time. The bruise I already feel forming around my tailbone is doubling in size, and I wonder if the possibility of a blood clot should have me worried. Even if it does, I can't complain. I wanted this.

I asked for it.

"Up, Onyx." Uncle Antonio takes another swig of water. Even while fighting cancer, the man is an unstoppable force.

He wakes up, goes to chemo, comes home and eats, before beating my ass for four hours straight. Well, not always beats. Sometimes he drowns it, smokes it out, then drowns it again before beating it. I've learned every possible way I can die, be tortured, or used in any way. And while death is no longer something I fear, the pain is. It's everlasting, and just when I think it can't possibly hurt any worse, it does.

He wants me to beg for death, and when I do, he always finds a way to make it hurt more.

I see now why my father wanted me to wait for so long. This is... it... it fucking sucks.

And without the boys, I don't think I'd make it. Every night, they come to take care of me. Kilo runs around the house, grabbing everything Cat needs to heal my day's wounds. Trick plays *Donkey Kong* so I don't dwell on the pain, and Trigger massages my muscles, telling me what I can expect next, and helps get me prepared.

They've been through this whole ordeal with my uncle already and knowing that they went through those terrible withdrawals as mere children, then had to survive *this,* makes me see them in a much different light.

No matter what, you have to get it. No one is going to be able to finish this but you.

Trick's words act as my mantra, looping in my mind until I force myself to my feet.

My uncle's dark gaze pierces me, but he nods. "I know you have the boys, and guards, and all the protection in place that money can buy. But you're not invincible." He looks down at his hands and sighs. "My brother wasn't."

My heart burns at the memory of my parents. It's been four hundred and twelve days since their deaths. Since their murders. Yet it feels as if it just happened this morning. The pain is searing, burning through my veins when I let my thoughts linger. The air becomes stifling and suffocating at the same time until no amount of air is enough and I'm gasping for it.

They were everything. *My* everything.

And they were stolen from me.

"Stay on me." It's the only warning I'm given before he swings his right arm.

I block, shuffle back, and only end up absorbing a fraction of his hit. But he keeps coming, moving faster than I can keep up. One after the other, he throws his fists. I duck, dodge, and do my best to not get my teeth knocked out.

"How will you kill anyone when you can't advance? When all you do is block and run? Find an opening, Onyx!"

Frustration bubbles in my gut, his constant probing and

prodding like a fireplace poker to ignite the dormant fire. But it does nothing more than overwhelm me. If I had my father here, he would empower me. My mother would encourage me.

If they were here, I'd have another year before needing to learn how to be beaten down by a man four times my size.

I'd get to scream at them and tell them how the black belt I have didn't prepare me to be whipped with the blunt end of a gun while still keeping my head straight. How it didn't explain what to do when hanging from chains or ropes or being bolted to the wall as someone poked a needle under my nails.

If they were here, I wouldn't be drowning.

I'd be able to breathe.

I'd find a hole to advance and show my uncle that I can protect myself.

But they aren't here, and I'll be damned if I join them without killing everyone involved in ruining my life.

Finally, I see it. The small shift he takes on his feet when he's about to swing with his right. I duck under and connect a quick jab to his kidney, and swing around, hooking an elbow around his neck and putting all my weight into yanking him down.

He falls back, collapsing on the mat with a chuckle. "There we go, princess."

My head whips around. "I'm not a princess."

"You're damn sure not a queen yet. Again." He stands, brushing his hands over his joggers.

So we fight. Again. And again. For what feels like days until my legs beg to give out, my lungs can no longer hold more air than half a breath, and my muscles seize with every move I make. That's when he shackles me to the pipes and leaves.

Five hours later, with the stench of my own urine clinging to me, I climb the steps as though I've rested a full eight hours. I keep my head high as I pass the guards, though even in this state, they know better than to chance a look. My feet are quiet as I ascend the stairs.

My shower heats quickly, and when I step inside, I contemplate breaking apart. I think perhaps a good cry could help release some of the pain that grows inside me every day. Perhaps it will irritate a bit of the darkness that threatens to swallow me whole.

But then what?

What if it does do all those things?

Will I still feel the need to carry on with my plan?

The need to rip them all apart?

It's too big of a risk. So I push the burn back down my throat, wipe away the sting radiating across my eyelids and wash the filth from my body.

Though I'm leaving myself to wander through the dark, I know two things.

One, I'm not alone.

Two, I'm not lost.

* * *

I sit to the left of my uncle in the long meeting room, surveying the many faces I've gotten to know much more than I'd ever wanted to in the past.

We have these gatherings every quarter and all the heads of each area come and have something like a brainstorming meeting. One of the twins is shadowing the man in charge of weapons and another over security. Both of them are older and while death is usually the retirement plan, they have been made privy that they get to spend some years on the beach when the boys hit twenty-one.

Kilo fidgets next to an even more erratically moving woman. She hasn't worked for us long, and judging from the dark circles encasing her eyes, the constant scratching, and the tweaks of her head, I don't think she'll head the drug distribution much longer.

It seems as if for every part we gain, we lose, and I know my uncle feels the same frustrations as he goes over our numbers. We've profited a ghastly amount of money in weapons and cocaine. Our clubs are doing okay but need a bit of work to modernize them, just like our rentals.

"There's a social media influencer that does interior design. Let's pay her and dust our hands of it, uncle. One less thing to worry about. We need to focus our efforts on the consistent loss of heroin product." My dark eyes flash over to the woman who has the nerve to look irked.

"What are you trying to say, girl?" the woman snaps, her head tilting to the side.

"This *girl*, the one restraining herself from slicing your throat across our beautiful table, is your Boss." I keep my voice calm, but pointed, an itch starting to irritate my calm. "Have you checked with your runners? Made sure they are not skimming something for themselves?"

"So what if they are? What is a little bit of compensation in the grand scheme of things? It's not as if the money would be missed."

My uncle adjusts at my side, but I don't take my eyes away from the woman. I examine her unmanicured nails, filled to the brim with dirt and probably dead skin. Her suit is far too big, letting me know she must have ruined or sold the ones we give all those who work for us and replaced it with a cheap replica. Her hair is pulled in a bun, but the strands are haphazard, and look as if they haven't been brushed in days.

After my parents' death, the Murphys took advantage, killing some of the people we've had for years. They can't come anywhere near the Embros estate, but they have done well, ridding us of good soldiers—of good people. We were left to choose the best among what was available. People we knew we needed to watch until we could trust them.

Now, it seems as if the unfortunate soul in front of me will have to join all the others that couldn't make the cut. "I want to make one thing clear. You're saying it is okay to steal. From me?"

Her dirty green eyes widen, the realization settling over her.

I am not my mother, nor my father, but something in between. Something that was once light and full, now tragic and barren. My reign as their predecessor will be made from the blood of anyone who opposes me, and my throne will be fastened with their bones.

Everything that kept the hidden monster at bay is long gone. All that is left is something hungry for screams, and I must feed it.

By the time I'm up and behind the woman, she barely has time to turn. The knife I keep between my breasts is sliding across her narrow throat. Tingles erupt through my body, the sensation euphoric as it sends shivers down my spine.

Blood spurts in a perfect one-hundred-and-eighty-degree line, decorating the table, and the sleeves of those she sat next to.

After wiping both sides of my blade on her horrific suit jacket, I return to my seat, my words meant for Kilo. "Find out if it was her, or her runners."

He nods and stands, moving with the twins, who are already up and disposing of the body, filling the room with the faint copper smell.

"Yes?" My uncle's deep voice garners my attention. I hadn't realized someone had called him, but a phone is to his ear, the folds of his skin prominent as he furrows his eyebrows. "We'll be right there."

"Who was that?" I question, my high slowly subsiding as I rise with him, hurrying to the door.

"The Murphys tried to pass some women through the port. Nothing new, but it was a setup. Soldiers were in the van with some women they must have planned to dump and attacked our people."

Fire blazes through me, the mere mention of their names closing my throat while burning me from the inside out.

I haven't done well when they're mentioned, which is one of the reasons my uncle has yet to let me leave the house besides laying my parents to rest. But now, as I climb into the Jeep, he doesn't stop me.

We speed through the city, four cars following behind us as my uncle gets updates on his phone. The men on the other side have all been killed but one, and four of our employees are dead. The few women alive are all in need of immediate medical attention but they suspect none of them will make it with the blood loss.

My adrenaline skyrockets as we near the port, my hands growing clammy despite the stone exterior I put on for my uncle. He whips the Jeep around the corner and into an alley before parking.

"Stay here. I'll have guards watch you while I clean up the mess."

I nod, not wanting to argue. For one, I can admit I need more time before I risk getting injured by some lowlife when I have much bigger men to behead. Second, I don't want him to regret and add another reason as to why he keeps me locked away in the estate. And also, I think this may be a test like I'm sure the woman that's probably being ground into rose fertilizer was too.

I'm only alone for about a minute before one of my men yells for me to get in the front. Before I jump between the seats, I turn and see him running closer, a frail, limp body in his arms. Red frizzy strands fly out in every direction.

"She's alive," he tells me. I don't go to the front, but do stand, allowing him space to lay her across the back seat. "I'll be right back with your uncle. Please don't move, Miss Embros."

I nod my head up and down, but don't look at him. Instead, my eyes trail down the battered woman in front of me. Her small face is covered in bruises and small cuts, and her body appears like the aftermath of pictures you've seen of victims found in the woods.

"What's your name?" I kneel down, brushing her wild hair away from her face. There's blood pouring from the cuts to her arms and thighs, and I wonder how she's even conscious.

She's a fighter.

"Why is a raven"—her head falls to the side, and she coughs, excreting a mix of phlegm and blood—"like a writing desk?"

Her last words are only a whisper as her eyes flutter closed. My heart sinks. The notion that the poor girl can't be much older than me and has been subjected to the worst of fates weighs heavily on my soul.

Girls like her are the reason Embros Hearts was founded, and I hate that I can't save her.

Still, I lean down, pressing a soft kiss to her forehead, keeping my voice low. "Because it can produce a few notes."

When I back away, the first tear I've cried in years spills over the edge. It's a lone drop of wetness, but when it falls onto the girl's wide smile, I can't say I regret it.

In the Garden

CHAPTER TWENTY FOUR

Maddy

Twirling a stray curl around a finger, I skip outside. It's mostly sunny, so I don't anticipate seeing Onyx. But since I keep her company on Z's days off, I decide to surprise her with a bouquet of roses.

I wave hello to a few of the guards walking around and pass by the bushes flourishing with white roses.

They're so pretty, even more so than the red, but since her mother's death, she refuses to look at them. The only reason she doesn't rip the bushes down is because they were her mother's in the first place. Still, I stop and admire them, running a finger over the soft dewy petals.

"Such a pretty little thing. Unstained and vibrant."

"Funny to hear someone admire them."

I spin around, my heels tearing up the dirt as I turn and meet the light eyes of Z. The dimple in his cheek deepens as he finds amusement in my moment of surprise. I press a hand to my chest. "Why are you here? Shouldn't you be enjoying your day off?"

He shrugs, brushing past my shoulder and snapping a petal from the rose I was touching. "Is it bad that I like being here more than being at home?"

"No. Embros estate is comparable to a place like a wonderland, I'd imagine." I gesture to the grounds, full of greenery. The huge house, surrounded by gardeners and guards walking around the forest's border. "It's full of wild people, and only the brave dare to wander here."

His eyes linger on the sight before him, but after a moment his smile fades, and the corners turn down. His shoulders drop as he swallows, forcing his gaze away. "It's nothing I expected, that's for sure."

"And what did you expect?" I take a step forward, waiting until he follows before walking deeper into the maze of rose bushes. I find a lone bench and take a seat, patting the empty wood next to me.

He sits, still in some type of mood I can't quite decipher. "I thought things would be cut and dry."

Things. A check? Guarding her? I want to ask him but decide to let him take his time. I can tell by the way his lips divot from him chewing the inside that he's weighing his words carefully.

"I guess I figured it would just be another job. A higher paying one, but a job no less. I didn't expect to like the people here. Find good breakfast conversation. Or find a woman who consumes an uncomfortable amount of my headspace."

I wag my finger at him and find myself oddly relieved when his smile returns. "Ah, so there it is. It's the Boss."

He shakes his head, dismissing my comment. "She's this never-ending conundrum I want to figure out. Nothing more."

I sigh, folding my legs under me as I turn to face him. "That she is. And for you to have seen any layer below what she shows the world means something."

"Whatever it means won't be enough to change how it all ends."

Z says it with such certainty, it's as if he knows her plans. Yet he's still here. *Why?*

He stands, patting my shoulder. "I didn't mean to scare you earlier. I was just walking around, taking my time before heading home."

"Still riding around in that cute little deathtrap of yours?"

This causes him to bark out some laughter, and in turn, sends me into a fit of wild laughter. My sides hurt almost immediately as the sound rolls from me freely without end.

I understand my quirk wasn't nearly as funny as I'm making it out to be, but once the giggle fits start, you have to see them through.

"I'm not sure what's more entertaining. The fact he's worked for me well over eight weeks and has earned enough money to replace the car two times over. Or that you are turning into the shade of a plum."

We both jolt upright, our faces snapping to Onyx. *Onyx.* Who is standing outside, near the white roses, in the sun.

Even if I hadn't been observing Onyx for nearly two months, the look on Maddy's face is enough for me to know this is a rare occurrence. She's openly gawking, her wild red curls now a mess from laughing so hard.

I almost expect Onyx to comment on it, but instead, her eyes are locked on mine. It's been a couple of weeks since what happened in the shower, and ever since then, things have been strained. We're both playing the game of who will cave first, and I'd be lying through my fucking teeth if I said I haven't almost given in a dozen times over.

My body is craving hers, and every time we come in contact, it's almost excruciating. Breakfast hand-offs come with low eyes, hooded gazes, and the soft brush of her fingers as she takes the plate. When I stand by at the pool, she's usually topless, and I have to keep watch over the guards to ensure they don't fucking look at what's mine.

I'm well aware I'm becoming obsessive over something that can't be claimed. Like trying to put a collar around a wolf—she'd tear me apart before her pack even had to rise. But even knowing that, I can't help it.

I want her.

Despite what I know.

Despite who I am.

I want *more* of her. Both to know and to claim. I want it all.

"What are you doing out here, Boss? It's awfully sunny." Maddy shifts at my side, reminding me she's still next to us.

"I thought a walk would clear my mind a bit."

Maddy rocks on her heels, and even though Onyx and I haven't taken our eyes away from each other, she continues her interrogation. "I would have thought that the driver you and Trick disemboweled last week would have cleared your mind plenty."

This makes Onyx grin, lighting a fire in my chest. "It served its purpose, but new challenges have arisen since then."

"Like wanting to jump Z's bones?"

"Like wanting him on his knees before me."

Now it's my turn to laugh. "All you need to do is ask, darling. I'll be happy to do as I'm told."

Like clockwork, she doesn't miss a beat. "Why ask for it, when you could just give it to me?"

It's like a damn mantra with this woman. "Then I guess you don't want it that bad and can continue to wait."

"I'm a patient woman, Kane. I've been waiting over a decade to kill an entire family of men, I'm sure I can wait a while for your tongue to meet my cunt."

My dick surges to life, our continuous banter wearing at the thin thread of my composure. It doesn't make it any easier now, staring at her dark waves falling over her shoulder. My hands twitch at my sides with the overwhelming urge to thread my fingers through it and pull her close to me.

But somehow, I do what I always do and refrain, trying to remember despite all the things I desperately want, they are things I can never really have.

Not for long anyway.

Maddy

They didn't even notice I walked away. Or maybe they did and didn't care. And now? Now I am being a total fucking creeper and watching them from behind a row of bushes. Harlow would make fun of me for the rest of time if she saw me crouched down with my face pressed into the sharp shrubs.

Who am I kidding? That sweet beam of light doesn't have a

wicked bone in her body. In fact, it's been quite fun stealing some of it for myself. Because until this very moment, light, in general, has successfully avoided Embros estate altogether.

When Onyx's parents died, it brought one catastrophe after another, but somehow, they held through the storm—the need to avenge, stronger than the desire for death. But that's all it's ever been. Survival.

Living long enough to kill those that wronged her. But then what comes after? We've discussed it before, but she only ever dismisses our concerns. She can't hide from us, though. We all see it.

Life is a struggle for her now. She finds pockets of relief when causing pain to the filth we collect for intel. We both know she doesn't torture them for what they've done. To try and make them feel the agony they caused others. Nope. I think Boss hurts them the way she does, so for a moment, she isn't the only one in the room suffering and wishing for death.

I believe it gives her a moment of peace—watching them suffer physically the way she does internally. And the moment she grants them mercy and kills them, I see the way her eyes flutter closed, pretending that it's her.

A warm droplet splashes on my arm. I look down and realize I've been crying.

Part of the reason is simple, knowing she lives in torment and there's nothing we can do to help her. But the other reason, one I hate to admit out loud, is that none of us are enough to make her want to stay after all this is over.

I love her. We all do. And not because she saved us. But because she gave us a reason to *continue*. To live. To laugh. To *love*.

The necessary things to have a decent life. It's the reason I always tell her personal guards that twisting up her cervix is part of their job description. It's never worked, though. She's never slept with any of them.

Until now.

Unlike her normally passive and bored expression, she seems... serene. There's a small tilt to her lips, and her eyes are soft around the edges, even her eyebrows are relaxed.

They've definitely played hide the sausage.

But something else has happened too. Something changed. Nothing big or monumental. More like small and delicate.

Yet, even with the smallest chip in glass, it's only a matter of time before the next hit makes it shatter.

EZEKIEL

"Why do you hate sunny days?" I ask, leaning back against the warm wood bench.

Onyx sucks in a bit of air, finally breaking her gaze with me to look around the garden.

She's beautiful. Her amber skin glows under the natural light, while contrasting against the bright green. When she returns her eyes to me, she sits down.

It's odd, we're only about a foot apart and yet I want to draw her closer. Inhale her fresh citrus scent.

"One of my worst days happened while the sun was shining. It was like a spotlight, big and bright, directed at something that will live in my mind forever."

"Your parents."

She nods, her hands folding together as she rests them on her lap.

"I'm sorry you had to experience that." I fight the urge to touch her, and instead lean forward, resting my elbows on my knees. She tracks my movement, her eyes flickering over my frame.

"It was to be expected. They were the most prominent Mafia family in Washington."

"And now you are," I reply. "And that doesn't change the fact that it was unfortunate. Even more so because you had to witness it."

Her stonelike face falters, her lashes fluttering quickly as she swallows thickly. "It was unfortunate."

"I can never begin to understand how you feel. No one can. But I hope you've given yourself time to work through your grief."

Her expression changes, shifting from something of surprise with wide eyes and raised brows to confusion, the line in the middle of her forehead creasing. "I don't have time to work through any type of grief. I didn't then and don't now. Nothing will help me heal until those who are responsible are buried beneath my rose bushes."

I pull my bottom lip through my teeth, nodding. I know better than anyone that depending on your enemy's death, to deal with your own shit is the worst thing you can do. "You need to heal outside of that. Their deaths should be a penance, but not your salvation."

"How do you suppose I do that, Kane?"

Though her words have a bite and come out more rhetorical than serious, I hear the slight edge—the real curiosity. "Confront your pain."

"It will kill me."

"Then let it." I watch her work through what I'm saying. "Feel it—*all* of it, without letting anything filter the blow. Let it consume and tear you to shreds, burn you to ashes. And then be reborn."

"Like a phoenix?" she scoffs.

"Like a queen."

"I already—"

"No." I shake my head. While I don't want to piss her off, I also want her to know that she is capable of so much more if she'd let go of the things anchoring her down. The things stopping her from truly living. "A queen doesn't sit idle in her ivory tower."

I stand, shoving my hands in my pockets. "But fuck, I do hope I'm around to see when you fit the crown on your head."

Then, I leave her to walk her garden in peace.

CHAPTER TWENTY FIVE

I don't care for the tedious workings of meetings. Data can be organized and shared without the need to sit in front of one another and discuss something that is already complete. That's why I reduced my uncle's quarterly meetings down to annual. The heads I have manning my departments don't need to check in with me. They've been doing it long enough, and should the need arise, they come find me.

But even that is becoming less and less, which tells me things are lining up nicely. I want them to be able to run the entire operation without me. It's a necessary part of my endgame, just in case things don't go smoothly with ending Phineas.

Or even if they do....

I glance at the man in front of me. He's requested an in-person meeting for a renewal of a contract I have with him. His is just one of the many businesses that donate to Hearts. They get the extra tax break, and I'm able to spend less on Hearts, and more on soldiers' salaries and incentives. Helps keep them happy and loyal.

"Ms. Embros, I—" Mr. Bardot starts, but I hold up a hand to

interject. There are many things I can tolerate but being called something that dredges up past memories is not one.

"I am not my mother, Mr. Bardot. Onyx will suffice."

He clears his throat, clearly uncomfortable calling me by my first name, but he nods regardless.

"Onyx. I appreciate what your organization does, but with your direct affiliation with the Mafia, it poses not only a legal threat, but a safety one as well. I'm sure you can understand that I'd hate to put any of my clients in a situation where they could be hurt."

I run a nail down the column of my neck, the small bite of pain waking me from yet another boring meeting in which I have to read my business partner. It's a necessary nuisance to help them see reason and know that what I do, aside from Embros Hearts, is not something they need to concern themselves with. That it doesn't lessen what the organization does, but propels it. Still, a good dash of fear doesn't hurt anything.

My eyes scan down at Mr. Bardot's appearance. He's handsome and well-groomed. A strong face with heterochromia. I'd bet money it's not from birth, though. No, his discomfort with not using my surname and straight spine as he sits erect tell me he's been trained for this position since he was old enough to walk. I recall my meetings with his father. A man who may be feared by the wall street rats he socializes with but is nothing more than a mere dog to me.

He'd been happy to work with me, made him feel like he had the power of the Mafia behind him or some nonsense, but it seems as if his son here is not the same.

Blaze's designer suit is tailored, fitting his toned muscles, but the shadow under his eyes tells me he's living on minimum sleep. But with the well-established business he runs, I know it's something different keeping him awake.

That's when my eyes find his ring. "You're married."

"I am." He didn't hesitate, which tells me he is proud. Perhaps happy even.

I ignore the faint burn in my sternum and force my gaze on him.

"And she's either sick or pregnant, keeping you awake at night. I can see from the slight discoloration under your eyes, and your anxiety is higher than usual. You've shifted your watch band four times in the last two minutes. Let me guess, it's the latter and you have a baby on the way. Entertain me, Mr. Bardot, and pretend the child is a female. As I'm sure you're well aware, women are born with targets on their backs and eyes on their fronts. Knowing there is an organization, legal or not, that defends women, their rights, and most of all, their safety, should give you ease. Does it not?"

I can tell from the way his jaw clenches together that our meeting here is done. A man who is enthralled with his wife, in love to the point of sickness, would do anything for her. And that love increases tenfold when they have a daughter. I should know. I am the reason my parents became elevated targets after working peacefully away from the Murphys for so long.

I'm not sure if I should be happy for the baby he is soon to cradle or sad for him, knowing he now has a weakness that is free from his body. Easiest way to control someone.

He opens his mouth to respond, but Madeline bursts through my office doors, trotting behind my desk like a lapdog. She leans toward me, her frizzy strands tickling the shell of my ear. "I think your new bodyguard is jealous. He's outside the room pouting."

I feel my lips pull tight, the corners lifting—something once foreign, now becoming a habit. My eyes flash to the door behind my guest, and I idly pick up a card that was lying on my desk. "Hmm."

I'm not sure how to feel about knowing Kane is jealous. I do think it's cute that he assumes he has the authority over my body, but I can be truthful and say giving it to him has been an absolute pleasure. Even if I don't like the soft pieces he seems to find in me, the unbearably good orgasms he gives make it worth the temporary weakness.

"Oh, are we?" Maddy's serious tone draws me from my ruse, and I set the card back down.

"Oh no, Maddy. Just thinking."

Steepling my fingers, I angle forward, my lashes batting slowly. "I would love it if you would give this more thought. Perhaps get back to me at another time? I can have a new contract sent over as well so you don't feel as though your clients' donations are dishonest."

He adjusts his watch yet again and gives a curt nod. "Thank you, Onyx. I'll read over it when you send it."

I stand with him, shake his hand, and look over to see Maddy pointing a gun at the back of his head. I wait until he's through the double doors before holding up a brow in question.

She shrugs, putting it in her back pocket. "You were playing with the card. I wasn't sure if you were truly lost in thought or not."

Sighing, I drop into my seat. "I seem to be doing that more and more these days."

Maddy hops onto my desk, swinging her feet playfully while twirling a lock between her fingers. Though the small woman is mad beyond anything deemed sane, her ability to hold on to some of her perky quirks will forever impress me.

Her life was nothing but dim alleys and picking for scraps in the dumpster. When we saved her from being thrown to drown in the port, she'd attacked every nurse and doctor who entered her room. She was so angry we'd stopped her misery from finally ending.

But I was young then, and selfish. I wanted someone to

suffer with me. To work through the despair and become the monster they saw me as.

Only that didn't happen. When she was finally in the acceptance of what had happened, I'd convinced Antonio to bring her home—she was too far gone to rejoin civilization anyway. And then she met the boys. They made her smile.

And laugh.

And feel.

She ate breakfast with us at the table, trained with me during the days, and nursed her wounds alongside me at night.

Madeline was able to overcome what had happened because she found something better out there. She didn't know what we had here had been a possibility. It made her work harder to keep her place. To earn a better one.

I admire that about her.

I only wish I could be jealous of it. Maybe then I'd strive to stay...

"I sent you an email. We have a small problem." Maddy points a small finger to my black computer screen, prompting me to bring the beast to life. The small whirl begins as I tap the spacebar and nod to Shi, who appears in the doorway.

"I wouldn't label it a small problem, Madeline." Shi walks inside, her newly dyed pink-and-purple strands prominent against the sheet of black. She tucks a piece behind her pointy ear as she sits gently in a chair. "They're buying property in the neutral zone."

A spasm of anger flares in my gut. My girls wouldn't tell me if they hadn't checked multiple times for accuracy. But still. Never have they gone against what little understanding we've always had. They are complete...

"They're trying to draw me out."

The women nod in unison. Maddy hops down, opening the file she sent me and pointing to the location. It's small, maybe an acre or two, and nothing but land. But a statement, nonetheless. They no longer respect what was once agreed upon.

"They can't get to you. Not in the ways that matter, at least. So they are making a move." Shi crosses her arm, her face cautiously observant. She doesn't know how I'll react and doesn't want to guess incorrectly.

Even after all her time in safety, she's still careful. Still constantly at the edge of her seat.

"Buy the rest."

"What? I knew I was out of my head, but, Boss. That would start a war." Maddy's eyes are as big as marbles, her pupils hiding the pretty color underneath.

"Let them start it. It will be all the easier to kill each and every last one. Angry men are reckless."

"But are we ready for that?" Shi asks. I can see her reservations. I understand them. But if the Murphys would like to play, they need to understand I'm the queen of the board. I am not held by the same rules and restrictions they are.

I will slice the throats of anyone, while they dole out the duty to those who can stomach it. I once thought it was to absolve them of any wrongdoings, but later realized those in power cower behind their men—using them as shields while they sit on their horses.

"It's a strategic move. If they wish to draw me out, they need to try a little harder." I stand, brushing my hands down my dark slacks. "Because when *I* move, it will be to claim checkmate, not check."

"And what happens then?"

My eyes flutter closed, weariness working my muscles tight at the same questions being asked when not even I know the answer. But then, something happens that doesn't happen too often. I'm surprised.

"I don't think you should kill him. Your guard."

My eyes snap open, finding Shi's solemn face. "And why is that? He's dangerous to what we do here."

"Dangerous to you, you mean," Maddy pipes up, hopping from the desk and circling around to join Shi.

"Elaborate without wasting my time, ladies." I continue to stand, an indication I'd like to leave the suddenly suffocating confines of the office.

"He makes you smile. And you don't know how to process it. It's been too long since someone made you feel, Boss." Maddy leans into Shi's chair.

"He'll want more than what he can have," I counter. All of them have felt the darkness exuding from Kane. He does well keeping it locked away, but I've seen glimpses. One of which was in the shower.

His face was comparable to an angry god. He commanded everything, taking what he wanted without any regard to how I reacted. He only listened to my body and gave me what I'd deprived myself since laying eyes on him.

My heart picks up pace, the memory of giving him control, even for a moment, was too easy. I can only imagine what he'd do if I gave him a little more.

Yes, he makes me feel something besides the constant pain. And that's even more reason to kill him.

"He doesn't want to take this away from you." Shi's gaze is pointed down, but after a moment she must find what she's looking to say and stands, grabbing the tips of my fingers. "Get what is owed. Then, let go. I think that was always the plan, but without something to continue for, we'd lose you. We all know it."

"So you'd have me depend on a man t—"

"Of course not, Boss. But if the dick makes you want to stick around with us, I'll take it." A lone tear streams down Maddy's face, but she's quick to wipe it away.

My racing heart swells, and pinches, and feels as if it's going to stop at any moment. I wish I could show them what I desire to free myself from. The pain of two loving parents is great. To watch them be brutally murdered because of something you started? Devastating. Being tortured, beaten, mentally stretched and forced to sit on a throne ten times too big without them to guide and encourage me? Unbearable.

My silent screams in the limo still ring in my head. Sometimes so loud I feel as though my brain will burst into mere jelly fragments. I want to be free.

And the only times I am, are when I'm tearing into the flesh of one of the Murphys, or when I'm with him.

I've let it go too far. But also, I don't wish to stop it.

I swallow the bit of reservation I have. "I must be mad, a dunce, or perhaps both, but I'll hold off on killing him for now."

Maddy giggles manically while Shi's wide grin takes over her face. "Oh, Boss. We're all a little mad here."

EZEKIEL
CHAPTER TWENTY SIX

Why the fuck am I jealous?
And I am jealous. Murderously so. I've been around for all of the meetings Onyx has had to attend in person. *Every last one.*

Yet when the pretty boy showed up, she told me to go walk the estate. I could have argued the fact I'm her personal guard and need to be near her when she deals with people. But in the end, I decided against it, realizing it may just be another thing she uses to win the game we're still playing.

A game I'm ready to lose now.

Our time is... limited. So what's the point of denying us something we both want? Of the last bits of luxury I'll ever experience.

Pacing by the side of her office for the hundredth time, I pause, the sound of Maddy's boots clambering down the stairs. She hops the last few steps, landing on the floor with a heavy thud. "Whatcha doing out here?"

"Guarding." I jut a thumb toward the door, a fresh wave of envy washing over me. My muscles draw tight, and it makes Maddy giggle.

"Hmm. Looks more like brooding to me." She steps in the

line of sight to the office and her smile grows unbelievably wider. "Ah, yes. I'd say broody for sure."

"It's just a meeting, Maddy."

"Z, if you can't see that man is something any woman would lick from head to toe, you are blind."

Her words fan the flames, and my chest grows hot. It isn't until Maddy glances at my hands that I realize I've nearly cut through the flesh, red angry crescents in my palm acting as evidence of my tight fist.

"Don't worry. I'd dare to say you look better with that adorable little dimple and your scruffy hair." She moves to ruffle my already disheveled ends, but I take a step back.

"I think I heard Onyx call you. Maybe you should see if she needs m—you."

She barks out in belly-rolling laughter. "You're even hotter when you're jealous, Z."

But before I have time to respond, she opens the door and disappears inside, leaving me to chew on the inside of my lip.

After another minute, I turn and walk the long hall, hoping by the time I return, the guy is gone. But as I reach the end, Shi exits a lone door on the side of the hall and grins at me. As grim as she is, it's always a bit jarring to see how wide her smile can get. Then again, she's the one I know least from the bunch.

The twins I communicate with daily on check-ins, and when helping them test new weapons. Maddy is literally everywhere, and I eat breakfast with Cat and Russ every morning. Kilo. Well, he's kind of a hit or miss, but when I do see him flash by, he's a pretty interesting fellow. Erratic and high as fuck, but fascinating all the same. Shi, however, is a rare sight to see. And even then, it's all smiles and vague riddles.

"Ezekiel. To what do I owe the pleasure?"

"Making myself busy, waiting on Miss Embros to finish a meeting."

"In person?"

"Yep." I pop the P, and rock back on my heels, trying my best to seem unbothered.

Shi thinks over that for a minute, watching as I awkwardly wait for a reply. "I see."

"See what?"

She shakes her head, that damn grin frustratingly large. "Nothing. Might I pick your mind and ask you a question?"

My brows rise in genuine surprise. "Of course."

"What are your long-term plans? Do you plan to be here, as a personal guard, for the foreseeable future?"

I shrug, pressing my shoulder into the wall. Every night, I think about how this will all end. What will happen to me, to her, Fi, and the people I've come to know. And each time, it's always different, only one thing is constant—one of us ends up dead.

Somehow, the heavy weight in my stomach grows bigger, making me nauseous.

I swallow it down. "I mean, no. But I also don't think I have much of a choice. From the sounds of it, it seems as though she's going to get rid of her problem soon."

"She is."

"So then she'll have no use for me."

"What if she still wants you around? Would you leave her if there was no greater purpose than to be by her side?" Shi's words are slow and drawn out, her head tilted in question.

Unlike the first, this one is easy to answer more honestly. "Hypothetically, I wouldn't have a problem staying. My life out there has always been about taking care of one problem while waiting for the next to happen. I spent a lot of time being angry and resentful, and here... well, to be frank, I don't. I have time for things I'd forgotten I enjoy. I've opened my eyes to things I thought I'd understood but misjudged. I've found contentment I never thought possible."

But I also feel guilt so deeply embedded in my soul that I'm not sure anything I do will absolve me of what I intend to do.

"I see," is all she says before her shoulder brushes mine as she walks past. "I'll be quick. Then you can have her to yourself."

* * *

It feels like an hour has passed before Maddy and Shi finally leave Onyx's office, and I've gone through an array of emotions I never wish to again. The first of which was annoyance, fueled by the notion that somehow Onyx has soundproof glass doors.

The second and third were envy and intrigue.

And the last was realization over how obsessive I'm becoming.

I should think twice about what I'm about to do. Or maybe even think it over *once*. But it's impossible, my feet and brain now overruled by my need to dominate and lay claim.

Barbaric, perhaps, but the urge is too overwhelming to ignore.

I push open Onyx's French doors more forcefully than necessary before slamming them shut. She doesn't move a muscle, her eyes focused on whatever task I plan to interrupt.

"Here's what I don't like." I take wide steps toward her, my adrenaline pumping through my ears so wildly I almost don't hear her.

"What makes you think I care about your dislikes?" She raises an arched brow, shifting her gaze away from her computer only briefly.

"You do, so cut the bullshit. And while you're at it, admit why you sent me away to have a meeting with a model."

"A bit melodramatic, Kane."

"I don't give a fuck what you call it. I didn't like it."

She turns to face me now, her eyes following my path as I round her desk and force her chair to me. "Oh, my. Do I need to remind you of your place? How you are here to do as I bid, and I couldn't care less about what you like or not?"

I pin both her hands to the armrest of her chair and lean in, so my breath coasts over her nose as my voice lowers to a near growl. My vexation only strengthens when my eyes rove over her open suit jacket with the gold necklace falling between pressed-together breasts. Fucking corsets are the devil.

"Do I need to remind you who you belong to, Boss?"

A grin splits her face, and my veins physically hurt from the anger swelling them. This only encourages her, her eyes lighting with challenge, and her lips wet with temptation.

Fuck it.

I smash my mouth against hers, fighting her struggle as she tries to slip from under me. Her lips are soft, yet firm—molding to mine while resisting at the same time. She's everything I'd thought she'd feel like, but more, and already the addiction I have to her spreads. And I decide in this moment, I will kiss her every fucking day for as long as I'm breathing.

Before I can deepen the kiss, a sting of pain radiates across my lip, followed by the distinct taste of copper.

She bit me.

I smirk, pulling away from her and expecting to see her furious. But instead, I see something else entirely. From her neck to her nose, she's flushed a soft pink, her mouth swollen and painted in my blood. Her eyes are low, a lust burning through them like I've never seen before, while her chest moves rapidly as she takes quick breaths.

My cock becomes rock hard, the sudden need to forgo everything and fall inside her too overwhelming.

I grant myself a moment to reclaim her lips, my tongue darting inside as she opens for another breath, and it's then she finally succumbs.

She threads her hands through my hair, tugging me closer while pushing me away. She's conflicted, and it only piques my interest. My curiosity.

I grab either side of her hips, lifting her from her chair and dropping her roughly on the desk. My mouth finally breaks from hers, nipping harshly at her jaw and down her neck as I rip the slacks from her legs.

Her gasps fuel me as I seize the delicate lace hiding the pussy I need to sink into and jerk, snapping the fabric and tearing it away. I don't take time to admire her soft curves or the look of her spread and waiting, but instead I slip my own slacks and boxers down enough to free my throbbing dick.

I barely allow myself enough time to line it up before impaling her to the hilt.

She screams out, and I immediately slap a hand over her mouth. "Aht, aht. Not until you tell me what I want to hear."

Her eyes widen, rage and need fighting for who wants to be appeased more. But when I pull out and drive back in harder, lust wins. Her eyes flutter closed, her head falling back with a heady moan.

"Attagirl," I purr, dragging my cock out and powering back in. "Open up for me."

And she does, her legs wrap around my waist, and my hands return to her hips, keeping her steady at the edge of the desk as I fuck her.

Nothing about it is sensual or soft. It's about a mutual understanding. But of course, she has to fight me on it.

She plants her heels at the edge of the desk and pushes at the perfect time. We both fall back and my ass lands into her chair with her still on top of me. A vicious smirk curls the sides of her lips as she lifts her cunt almost completely off my dick, then slams back down.

"*Fuck*," I groan, loving the way her warm muscle wraps around me. But once she does it three times over, I realize what she's doing.

I shove to my feet and place her back on the desk, and this time, position her feet around my waist. She leans back, her hands finding the edge to keep her steady as I deliver long, hard strokes.

It gives me a moment to admire her beauty and power. Her suit jacket thrashing at her side, her corset barely holding in her bouncing breasts, and the red mark still vibrant against her skin.

My hand finds her jaw, my thumb stroking over the residual blood still on her mouth. I spread it over her lips, and down to the column of her throat where I grip, squeezing tight enough she strains for her next breath. Her moans only grow louder.

"Say it," I growl.

She manages to shake her head despite my tight hold.

I let go, dropping my hand to the place I know she wants it. But instead of what she expects, I pinch her clit. "Say it."

"Fuck you!" she snaps, her body pulsing around me. She's so fucking close, and I'm running out of time myself. She feels too fucking good, and she knows it.

I pull out with a wet pop and slap her swollen lips.

The sound that comes out is somewhere between a scream and groan, sending my blood soaring.

I plunge back in, slamming into her before drawing back out. Another slap. Her eyes are wild, her mouth parting open as she struggles with what to say. How to feel. But she needs to understand.

"This is your kingdom, there's no disputing that." Again.

In. Out. Slap. "But when we're here, like this." Again. "This tight little pussy is mine, and I'll fuck it however I please."

Her dark fan of lashes flutter slowly, the look of a challenge blooming on her face. But she can't hide the fact her legs are quivering beside me.

I can't help but grin. She wants control, but I want it more.

This time I keep myself inside her and use my thumb to circle her tender nerves. She moans loudly, filling the space with her impending ecstasy, her eyes closing as her head falls back.

"Eyes on me, *Boss*." I grab her jaw, forcing her gaze back down.

Onyx's jaw clenches but she can't hold back anymore.

After another long, painfully hard stroke, I give her a command. "I want to feel you clench around me. Come."

Another pass over her nerves and she combusts, shuddering and shaking as the orgasm rips through her. I keep my hands in place, continuing to stroke inside her to prolong the end, my own release sending jolts of pleasure up my spine.

I yank her flush against me, claiming her mouth as I spill everything into her. When I come down, I don't let go, but instead keep my lips pressed against hers, rubbing her hips where I know bruises will later form.

It's intimate as hell, but after something so rough, I feel this visceral need to show her I care.

And I do care.

Fuck.

CHAPTER TWENTY SEVEN

I can't get out.

I don't understand. I've run the mazes in our garden every day in my youth. Why can't I find my way out?

My heart beats erratically in my chest, while my lungs burn for air.

Faster.

Around this bush. A left at the next. It's so sunny outside yet I can't see anything. There're only the white roses. Where are the red? Where is everyone?

"It was your personal guard. The one that sleeps mere feet in front of your room every night. The one that was supposed to guard and protect you."

The voice I've committed to memory calls out, stopping my blood and feet at the same time. Instead of the panic that once overwhelmed me, fury and death take over. I'm ready to kill him. To skin him inch by inch until not even the reaper wants what I leave behind.

Another corner.

"Come out, come out, wherever you are."

My adrenaline spikes. The knowledge I'm so close to ending just one of the many fools makes my nerves tingle.

Another turn.

I see my red roses. This way, his face is visible from behind the red roses... something's wrong with the roses.

They're shining.

Why are they shin—no. They're dripping.

White petals I didn't notice before stick out from the red. It's blood. There's blood on the roses. Splattered. Painted.

Where is Maddy? Shi? My boys?

WHERE IS MY FAMILY?

"You're too late. Just like you were for your parents."

I turn. And then there's only black.

"Onyx." Strong hands catch me, jolting me awake. "I got you."

Instinctively, I want to jerk away from him, but I don't, and instead allow him to wrap his arms around my back, pulling me into his chest. His warm, woodsy scent invades my airways, calming my tight muscles.

I should hate how he silences the chaos. Hate how he feels good to fall into. Hate that when he takes over, I can finally breathe.

But I don't.

He's peace.

My peace.

A warm, heavy hand finds my face, his calloused fingers stroking the length of my jaw. The act makes both dread and lightness expand in my chest, the constant fight of what I secretly want and am terrified of having.

My lashes flutter open, finding the green-and-gold eyes that plague my thoughts. His face is covered in shadows, but immediately, I know something is wrong.

I grab his hand to use as leverage, but then he winces. It's the smallest twitch in the corner of his eyes but I see it. He's hurt.

My spine straightens, my finger finding the lamp string and yanking it on.

"What happened?" My eyes instantly snap to his injuries, taking them all in, one at a time.

Light bruises line the sides of his face. Small cuts near his lip, and by his jaw. His brow has the largest abrasion, blood still bright under his butterfly closures. And his knuckles... all of them are busted.

Unwarranted panic seizes my insides, twisting everything until I feel on the verge of sickness. This is precisely why I don't let myself care. It leads to worrying. To weakness.

A weakness that can be captured and exploited.

"We don't grow attachments to people, Onyx. They won't have your tolerance, nor your strength. You'll know that, and so will the enemy. They will make them suffer because they won't be able to handle the pain like you can. And after that, it never fails, the enemy will always win."

My uncle's words ring in my ear, the constant reminder as to why I never take a partner. Why I don't entertain the thought of ever becoming like my parents.

"Who did this?" I hold my breath, waiting for him to say the words.

That's all I need. One syllable of the name I've waited to destroy and they're dead. All of them. I'm exhausted with them mistaking my silence for submission. For them to think they can continue to take what's mine and not suffer the consequences.

Despite the obvious pain, he smirks, leaning in and pressing a soft kiss to my lips. I tense against him, but he ignores it, tucking a loose hair behind my ear. "It's nothing."

I clear my throat, arching a brow. "I asked you a question, Kane. Answer it."

His grin grows. "I knew you had a soft spot for me."

My brows furrow. "You say that as if it's an admirable thing."

"It is."

His voice is so flat, so sure. So utterly idiotic. "The only soft spot I have for you is between my thighs. Nothing more, Kane."

He nods, letting his hand trail slowly down my jaw, his thumb tracing over my bottom lip. "What were you dreaming about?"

"Tell me what happened."

Yesterday was his day off, and since I didn't get any reports from any of my establishments about a fight, I know it wasn't there. His eyes leave my mouth, his hand dropping into his lap. It's then I notice the red rim highlighting each one and the puffiness right under. His face interchanges between tightness and defeat.

He doesn't want to tell me. He's... embarrassed, perhaps. I should tell him not to worry, how it's not my business, but I can admit I'm curious as to what he does when he leaves. Where he goes, who he's with.

So instead, I wait, and just as I think he won't tell me, he sighs. "My mom has been doing well for a while now. Taking her walks with neighbors, eating all the food I make for her. Hell, even keeping the house clean."

Kane's shoulders fall, and he shakes his head. "I went home and found her face down, high out of her fucking mind. She'd found out some pretty fucked-up shit and relapsed. I found her dealer, but he was with three others, so they got a couple licks in."

"What was the news?"

His jaw clenches tight, the nerve running vertically, pulsing. "My sister. She, um..."

He clears his throat, shaking his head again as if it will rid him of the pain he's feeling. "She's always been good about getting into some trouble. Her heart's in the right place, she just has really horrible execution."

"Will she be alright?" I ask, watching his slight shifting, the many times he chews on the corner of his lip, and the way his chin keeps dropping toward his chest.

It's guilt. He's not sad; he feels guilty.

Why?

After a moment, he nods. "She will be soon."

Before I realize what's happening, Kane's firm lips are on mine, his tongue running along the seam in an almost effortless attempt to open them.

I let him claim my mouth, the foreign feeling both overwhelming and incredibly sensual, stroking my inner desire.

He shifts, slowly pressing me back into the bed, while his hands tug at the tie on my robe. When it falls open, the cool air makes my nipples draw tight, and I moan into his mouth, arching my back to put my chest flush against his.

"Hmm, my needy girl."

I bite into his lip, enough to taste the tangy copper, and have to suppress a smile when he groans, thrusting his extremely hard length into my thigh. There's something about both hurting and turning him on that drives my fire, spurring me to do it more.

But when both my hands reach for his hair, he captures them, holding them above my head.

"Naughty girl. Did I tell you to move?"

My eyes narrow, but the heaviness in my stomach is too much to ignore. I squirm beneath him, wrapping my legs around his waist and grinding against his cotton-covered dick. "Give me what I want, Kane."

He smiles into my neck before running his teeth along my collarbone and kissing down until his warm mouth is around one of my nipples. His teeth sink into my soft flesh, adding to the marks he's already decorated my body with. But the delicious pain fades quicker than it came, melting into intoxicating pleasure.

I draw in a sharp hiss, squeezing my legs tighter until one of my heels gets caught in his waistband. I'm able to hook myself underneath and slide his underwear down, freeing his erection that slaps right over my wetness.

"*Fuckkkk.*" His head falls back at the same time mine lolls to the side. "Fine. You want it? Take it."

His hands release my wrists and find my hips, turning us over in my next breath. I land on my knees, straddling either side of his legs, my pussy hovering mere inches over his cock.

Lifting myself, I glide along him, wetting the head and reveling in the way he tenses. "Don't lose focus now."

He smirks, shoving his hand under me and swiping a hand through my wet folds. When he pulls his hand back, he glides it over my swollen lips, smearing my wetness on them. My tongue peeks out to lick it off, but he grabs me by the nape of my neck and hauls my face to his, kissing me so deeply my mind stops.

The taste of copper and sweet musk overwhelms my senses, making me dizzy and needy, my hips rocking feverishly until I'm able to slide his tip inside me.

Our groans flow out in unison as I sink down, filling myself until I'm fully seated.

Once my body adjusts, I lift again and fall.

"Again," he commands, the deep rattle of his voice vibrating through my core.

And it's then I lose control, rising to my knees and slamming back down. The small sting of pain from his width is intoxicating. Addicting. My body begins moving of its own accord, my hand finding my throat while the other tugs on my barbells, pinching my nipples tight.

"That's it." He strokes my sides, spurring me on. "Take what you need from me."

It only takes a moment but one look into his soft gaze and I piece it together.

A small huff of frustration and admiration works its way from my nostrils as I realize what he's doing. He's giving me control. Control over him, over what I dreamed about, over what I *can't* control.

I work harder, move faster, take all that my body can handle until my lungs burn from the quick intakes of air and my knees quiver at his sides. Sweat beads across my brow, through the valley of my breasts and down my spine.

Tingles start to shoot up my cunt, my release beginning to build. But as soon as the moment starts, Kane takes back the reins.

He slips his index finger inside with his cock, this one curling while his thumb strokes my clit. My rhythm falters, the overwhelming tremors rolling down my spine in vicious waves.

He plays me like a harp, each time his finger moves, or his thumbs stroke me, I sing a different song, my moans coming out wilder and louder as he continues his assault. It doesn't take long before my orgasm comes.

"Look at me," he barks. "Look at who makes you come undone."

The second my eyes flash down, my release tears through my body so violently I stop moving, lost in the waves of immense pleasure. But Kane takes over, turning us around in one go, and fucking the rest of it out of me so it doesn't ebb too quickly.

He lets out a guttural groan as he follows behind.

When his shoulders stop shuddering, he collapses at my side, his pants of air blowing my strands of hair over my neck.

"You're breathing as if you put in some type of work."

Kane scoffs. "Letting you take over required more self-restraint than you can possibly fathom."

My eyes roll, a genuine soft laugh tickling my nose hairs. "I'm sure."

"Oh, you think that's funny? Do I entertain you, Boss?" He's up on his knees in a second, drawing his shirt over his head. My insides are girlishly giddy as I watch him.

"Let's see if I still make you laugh when my tongue is cleaning up our mess."

"Kane," I whisper-hiss, grabbing at his disheveled hair. But he's already between my legs and his mouth is on my pussy.

EZEKIEL

CHAPTER TWENTY EIGHT

The sun is hidden today, tucked behind thick dark clouds. Thunder rolls overhead as we ride through the city, the skyline of trees fading into houses, then turning into buildings.

Even though we've been out before, and even with everyone from the house coming, I'm still on the edge of my seat. And for more than one reason.

I lied to Onyx.

My mom is fine, staying with her neighbor friend for the foreseeable future. The house is currently... uninhabitable, and I refuse to pay for repairs when I already have everything set up to get her the hell out of the city.

The truth is more boring, and far less fucking noble.

When I got home and called my sister, she had news.

"You have one week, Zek. Seven days and I'm their property." Her voice cracks, severing the small string holding me together. *I've been so fucking caught up in my own shit... in Onyx, I... I thought I could figure out a way to spare them both.*

"I'm scared. I—"

"It's going to be okay. Just give me a couple more days and I'll figure it out."

"If they don't trust you enough by now to give you codes or

keys or whatever, what is a couple of days going to do?" She's trying not to yell, but she's failing, her voice muffled by tears. And when I don't answer fast enough, it's as if something's clicked in place she's been trying to put together.

"You already have the codes, don't you?"

"Fi, wait. Just wait. Let me explain. Things aren't what we thought. I can still fix this. Plea—"

"You have forty-eight hours, brother. Two days until I run out on the grass and let them shoot me like a dog because I refuse to give them my body."

Before I could respond, the line disconnected, and I was left standing in the middle of my living room like a fool. I *am* a fool.

The realization, or maybe the acceptance of it, caused me to lash out, tearing the home to shreds and hurting myself in the process. The worst of which was when the old metal chandelier fell and hit the side of my face. But the physical pain is almost nonexistent next to the war raging through my body.

I know what I have to do. I *know*. But it doesn't make things easier. Or right.

I'm trading one life for many, yet I *can't* not do it.

My eyes squeeze shut, the burning in my throat nearly unbearable. I have twelve hours.

Twelve fucking hours.

"Thinking about your mother?" Onyx's voice jolts me from my self-inflicted torment. "Do you need to go be with her?"

My chest caves in under the weight of her words. The theoretical hitting of the nail on the head, knocking me further into my shitstorm of guilt. "No. She's with someone I trust."

Onyx nods, leaning on the passenger door. "Despite what onlookers might think, my mother was a worrier. My father even more so."

I raise a brow, following Trick's car in front as it turns down a long road. "Oh yeah?"

"Yes. But only about family. It was the one thing they would do anything for. The one thing they would risk their lives to protect. My parents did the stupidest thing imaginable to save me."

She swallows, and it's one of the few times I see her tender walls threaten to curl in. But as always, she clears her throat and straightens her back. "Family makes us weak; makes us do stupid things. Try not to judge your mother too much."

The corner of my lips lift. "Yes, ma'am."

Pulling up to Embros Hearts, it's exactly what I saw from the pictures online when I first did research about Onyx. It's a two-story building, with an all-glass front and bright curb appeal. Wide green bushes line the front walkway, while a valet sits under the overhang in the roundabout. Onyx directs me to the man standing post at the booth, where I park and hand him my keys.

When we exit, we find the twins standing near Shi, engulfing her small body between them, while Maddy and Kilo have a wildly funny conversation, spoken at a pace only they can understand.

It's the first time since our first meeting that I've seen them all together and it's oddly familiar.

Onyx pats my shoulder, leaning close to my ear. "This is what started it all. I hope you see what I do here isn't half bad."

She brushes past me, and the rest follow behind, entering the center. Inside, the lobby is far less medical than I'd imagined. Instead, it's more like the entrance to a grandiose hotel. There's a fountain in the middle, ferns around the brown leather couches, lots of glass and chrome to match the massive chandelier, and a bustling café to the right of the entrance.

If I brought my mother here, she'd think it was some type of resort.

A woman with large brown eyes and an ear-length bob stands behind an elevated counter. When she sees all of us entering, her pupils widen like moons, sparking her to life as she bolts around her counter.

"Miss Embros, it's so lovely to have all of you with us today! Everyone will be so happy to see you." She juts a small, manicured hand out, gesturing toward an open hall surrounded by windows. "Please, follow me."

Onyx merely nods, and rather than trail behind her, she walks next to her, leading us down the wide hall.

On the left, the parking lot can be seen through the tall windows, but on the right, an incredible atrium. It's large— about forty feet wide— and bustling with women. A large tree rests in the middle, surrounded by benches. A small path made of wooden slats leads from one end to the other, and over a small bridge covering a koi pond. Some of the women are walking around, some feeding birds, while others tend to plants growing along the edges, and more are reading under the branches.

Although very serene and peaceful, I notice something that makes my stomach tight—they're all similar. They are all small and borderline malnourished. They also all bear faint scars that shine silver and pale tan that reflect off their skin.

"Survivor reminders," Shi says, catching me staring.

"I apologize. I—"

"Don't," she cuts me off, drawing up her own sleeve. Along the creases and near the wrists, she carries the same small marks. All different lengths, depths, and forms. "Not all, but many of them were tied down for long periods of time while drugs were forced in their bodies in timed intervals. They got them addicted to drugs so they would do anything for their next hit. If you already had no family and a shitty life, it was easy to give up. And a lot of them did. These are the women who were strong enough to not only go through the sewer of being with the Murphys, but to weather the storms of withdrawal. Then, try to live again. We celebrate their marks because they *made* it."

An understanding washes over me and I nod. "Thank you for sharing that with me."

She waves me off. "It's important to tell people your story. How else will word spread that people can survive?"

We exchange a solemn smile as our group reaches a new area. It reminds me of an upscale mall. Each opening is similar in color with its iron frame and glass exterior. There's a bookstore, a nail shop, a small grocery center, clothing store, and even a massage parlor. All together there are a dozen stores with a *Mico movie theater* at the end, and I can't help but gawk.

Onyx has us walk by each shop, inspecting each one silently. There are about thirty women in the area and all of them stop and talk to the members of the group briefly before moving on to whatever they were doing before. All of them have smiles on their face and are chatting as if they really are just Saturday shopping.

Maddy bounces next to me, her vibrant eyes glowing as she examines the confusion on my face. "It's awesome, right? Completely wild."

"What even is this place?"

She giggles her high-strung laugh and points to a table near the bookstore. I follow behind, joining her to sit, while keeping Onyx in my periphery. She's currently talking to the host about something she doesn't like in one of the stores. The woman nods frantically, tapping away at her phone for notes to call someone about flooring.

"This isn't just a rehab center. For some people, it's home. It's safe from the possibility of ever being taken again."

"So what is this?" I gesture to the mini mall around me.

"The women have to work. They pick a store and their hours, and they get paid a normal wage. In turn, it's how they shop. Nothing is taxed, of course, so the majority of the way we buy items is from corporate donations as well as profits we make legally through real estate."

"And you buy real estate?"

She shrugs. "Through not-so-legal means."

"Where do they live?"

She points back the way we came. "If we would have gone to the other side, it's similar to this except there are rows of one-bedroom apartments. There's only sixty, though, and Onyx is here to scout where we could have more added. In the back, there's a large pool and a workout center. And then all of our doctors' offices are just beyond that."

My interest in how everything is set up piques. "Why wouldn't the doctors be located *inside* the facility?

"It was long ago, but the idea of 'going to the doctor' and not living inside one was more appealing and the women liked the idea. It made them feel more independent."

"So the same reason their jobs and stores are on the opposite side of their home."

Maddy shoots a finger gun at me. "Precisely."

"And who thought of all this?"

"I did." Onyx slides up next to Maddy, replacing her at the table.

Maddy shoots me an overly elaborate wink before excusing herself and mingling with the others next to the massage parlor entrance.

"This is incredible," I tell her honestly.

"It is. All because of the hard work and consistency of everyone here." She tilts her head, her eyes trailing over the bruises still prominent across my face. "Your mother can stay here if you'd like."

"What?"

"You'd like me to really repeat myself or—"

I wave a hand, overwhelming emotions clogging my throat. "No, it's just, I..."

"I have some of the best rehabilitation doctors and emotional therapists in the state working here. She'd be in good hands."

My mouth opens and closes twice, words lost on me. *How the fuck am I supposed to...how?* My heart squeezes in my chest, my lungs pulling tight around an ache that's beginning to grow too big to hide.

But instead of saying anything more, Onyx stands, brushing her hand lightly down her pleated skirt. "Take some time and think about it. You won't insult me if you'd rather not, but the option is always on the table. Until then, though, let me show you around."

I nod and rise to my feet to rejoin the group.

Before the host moves us to the next area, a blonde-headed woman catches my attention. She's waiting by a bench, crouched down to scare another who's seemingly looking around for her. To most it would seem juvenile, but then Maddy's words ring in my ear.

"Perhaps it's because I don't remember even having a childhood and I wish to live it now."

The small woman jumps up, scaring the other girl, and it reminds me of when Fi and I would play a game in the woods with some of the neighborhood kids.

We would both hide in different trees, and I'd watch, high from my vantage point. When the child seeking us would pass by her with enough room for Fi to run to home base, I'd crack a thick branch to signal her.

    We won every time.

    ...Every time.

    And just like that, I figured it out.

Onyx

CHAPTER TWENTY-NINE

There was a saying my mother once told me when I asked why she went against my uncle's wishes and took in the boys. He saw them as frail lumps of muscle and flesh, incapable of doing anything for the family but becoming a liability.

They were already tainted.

Broken.

Unmalleable.

They had suffered at the hands of others, and folded, allowing their addictions to rule them.

But my mother merely sighed and smiled as my father kissed the tip of her nose. "You see, weakness is not a reason. It's an excuse. You think these boys can't find strength in themselves and want to use what they've been through as an excuse not to take them in and you're wrong. They will fight the hell coming their way, and when they make it out on the other side, they'll be stronger than you ever thought possible."

When I asked how she knew, she looked over at their door and wiped the lone tear sneaking out the corner of her eye. "Anyone can fight for redemption, baby love. But only those that deserve it will face any obstacle. Because they don't just want it.

They need it. Crave it, even. But most importantly, if they never lose sight of what they're fighting for, it's always worth giving them the chance."

I'm so glad she did give them a chance. Without them, Embros Hearts wouldn't have been possible. It's the foundation of everything we stand for. And sometimes, people need help finding their way. That's why I told Kane his mother could stay.

I can see the guilt he has over her wearing on his shoulders. It's tearing at his frayed edges and there's only a matter of time before she falls too far to be saved.

Too far down to be redeemed.

I don't want him to lose a parent. The pain is everlasting and changes us in ways no one can possibly begin to comprehend.

Especially when we could have saved them.

Shuffling by the front door garners my attention. I've been standing in the foyer discussing a lost shipment with Kilo, but we had to pause as he went through his files, trying to locate the runner.

"Maddy, I have to *goooo*. But I'll be back." The brown-haired waitress Maddy is currently dating tries to tug her hand away lamely. "Promise."

She must have to work as she's dressed in her waitress outfit, and her eyes keep looking at the phone in her hand.

"Pinkie?" Madeline whines, pulling the girl back into her arms.

The poor girl turns fuchsia, her gaze darting to me and Kilo. Her voice turns into something close to a whisper-yell. "Yes, but if I'm late again, I'm totally getting fired."

Madeline waves her away, smacking her lips together. "So what? You don't need to work! Stay here with me, my love!"

Love.

It's a word I haven't said in years. Haven't wanted to. My uncle erased it from my vocabulary long ago, and since then, I've not wasted time thinking about it.

It's not that I don't love anyone. I do—dearly. But to use the words out loud feels like placing yet another target on their backs. A bigger and brighter one, and I'd rather not evoke more danger.

Unnecessary danger over a word.

Over a weakness.

Weakness is not the reason, it's the excuse.

My mother's words have a way of always making me feel foolish. Like I've forgotten everything she's taught me and replaced it with my uncle's teachings. As if I've forsaken the softer parts of me and traded them out with armor. But that's what they would have wanted, right?

To never allow an enemy to see my vulnerabilities?

To harden everywhere so that I can avenge them?

I sigh, taking a card out of my pocket to twirl between my fingers as I turn back to my current problem. "Kilo. About the lost shipment. It must have been on the twelfth. You weren't feeling well, remember?"

Kilo nods harshly, his white strands of hair falling into his face. "Yes, yes, the lost shipment. I..."

His eyes are unfocused, his mind going down the rabbit hole as he sorts through his thoughts. I wait, letting him mutter to himself when a flash of black catches my eye.

My heart flutters when my eyes land on Kane. He's standing at the top of the step, his hand tucked into his hoodie pocket. He still looks so troubled. So heavy. As if the weight of his world is becoming too heavy for him to bear.

I want to help him.

I want him to know he doesn't have to go through what he's going through alone. I'm here. No, all of us are here for him should he need it. That's what we are—a family. And whether he's been told or not, he's becoming a vital part of our fam—

My thoughts are cut off by a loud crash and a door slamming into my face.

Kilo
CHAPTER THIRTY

The lost shipment. I remember now. There was a lost shipment, and the Murphys were hunting the pretty girl.

I remember thinking how I hoped they wouldn't find her. How I hoped they couldn't so they wouldn't tear her pretty eyes from her head. Her eyes are so pretty. Or maybe, *were* so pretty.

They found her.

I remember now.

They found her and her name was Fiona. Fiona Kane.

Kane.

Kane.

The name on the house. The house where I saw Ezekiel.

They have the same eyes. His are much lighter. Full of greens, and glitter and gold that sparkles. I like him.

We all like him.

He makes Boss happy. I've never seen her so happy. She even tends to the white roses now in the garden. Not for too long, but she wasn't even able to look at them before. He's healing her. Like she healed me.

Slowly. With time.

But I am out of time because I remember now.

The pretty girl is his sister.

I open my mouth to tell Onyx, who is watching me go through my thoughts. She's always so patient with me. I wonder if she'll be patient with him. I don't want her to kill him before we know the truth.

But when the first word comes out, all I hear is a loud bang.

All I see is white.

All I feel is pain.

EZEKIEL

CHAPTER THIRTY ONE

Am I about to die? More than likely. But it's not as if I planned to live and see this through to the end anyway.

Two hours ago, I made a deal with Sam. It's a sleight of hand, and if done right, no one ends up dead but me. Three months ago, I would have welcomed death with open arms—ready to pay that damn debt I owe the universe. But now... well, now I have Onyx.

Had.

I hope she's the one who pulls the trigger. It's only fair. I betrayed her no matter what the reason or how it started. In retrospect, maybe I could have explained it to Maddy at the bar. Told her I could feed the Murphys false info until we found a way to get my sister.

Or maybe I could have told Onyx. We had more than a few moments when I could have tried. But the chance of her killing me and leaving my sister to a worse fate was too much of a risk.

My heart was in the right place. But things changed. I... like Onyx. I like her a hell of a lot more than I want to admit, and it made me give the Murphys the bare minimum.

Does it make me a shitty brother? Fuck yes.

But also, there was something from the moment I stepped

into this house, I knew I couldn't send these people to their deaths. The entire estate felt like *home*.

I'm going to miss it. The banter with Russ and Cat in the morning. The guards trying to teach me how they bet on horses. Maddy's impossible riddles and Shi's random life lessons.

...Everything Onyx.

I'm going to miss them.

Miss her.

I pull my hoodie over my head, tossing the letter I wrote on the bed before exiting my room. Even if she kills me before I get the chance to fully explain, I hope she takes the time to read it. I need her to know the truth. To understand I was between a rock and a hard place and I tried like hell to figure it out.

Doing my best not to dwell, I round the hall but stop at the top of the stairs. Onyx and Kilo are in the foyer.

He's trying to explain something but can't quite get the words out. Onyx sees me in her periphery and glances up, a soft smirk curling her lips. Even if it's out of line and completely fucked up, I need to kiss her one last time.

I make it two steps.

Two.

Then everything happens at once.

The stairs shake under my feet, the inward explosion of the heavy double doors splitting and hitting the banister. Onyx, Kilo, and the doorman fly backward, blood and debris spraying out like confetti.

My back hits the wall, my head bouncing from the hard surface and sprinkling my vision with white spots. Searing pain ricochets through every limb, but somehow, I find my voice.

"ONYX!" It sounds more like a guttural roar than a real word. But I try again, scrambling to my feet.

"ONYX, ANSWER ME!"

Again, no answer.

Panic takes over, flushing all the pain away as I grab on to the banister, steadying myself as I stumble down the stairs.

Rushing over the glass and splintered wood, I find Onyx, and my heart fucking stops. The air evaporates from my lungs as I crouch down, gently cradling her while my eyes rake over any injuries. Nothing appears to be bleeding too badly, but there's no telling what was jostled on the inside.

What the fuck just happened?

Her eyes are closed, but the soft stirring of her head moving brings the air back into my body. I stroke her hair, doing my best to keep my voice calm. "Shh. I got you. I'm here."

"Where's Kilo?" I have to strain to hear her, but after a quick scan, I see all I need, and it's not good.

"He's alright. He's just unconscious."

"You're a terrible liar, Kane." She coughs, attempting to sit up, but I tighten my hold. The crunch of feet over the debris signal help is on the way.

"Please don't move. I can hear people coming. The guards are coming to hel—"

"Well, look how the mighty have fallen." A deep, husky voice fills the space, spreading to every corner of the room and sludging down my spine.

It's a voice that makes the white spots still decorating my vision disappear, replaced with red. My fists clench beneath Onyx, my body shaking from the violent tremors ripping through me.

At least a dozen steps crunch over the mess, stepping closer than needed, the metal of their guns clinking as they hold them at the ready.

When a shadow finally covers me, I gaze up, my jaw locked so tight, my molar cracks, sending jolts of muted pain across my mouth.

The man's robust belly is the first thing I see, his suit jacket barely held in place by the magical button. His round face is pale except for his pink cheeks, mostly hidden under his scruffy facial hair.

He always did look like an evil Santa Claus to me.

"Phineas Murphy." Onyx sits up, her eyes fixed on only the disgusting creature in front of her.

"That I am. And it is such a pleasure to meet you, Onyx." His dark eyes flash to me, a sneer curling his lips.

A guard comes behind me, but I'm too busy watching her to move fast enough. The blunt end of his gun hits me in the back of my already tender head, and I go down, the darkness immediately encroaching over my vision

But before the darkness takes me, I hear him. "I see you've met my son. He's such a good boy. I knew he'd come through."

Then, I see black.

CHAPTER THIRTY TWO

When I was a child, I always wondered how the Queen of Hearts became the way she was. I thought perhaps it was from not getting her way. Maybe a suppressed need for power from the loss of it, or a desire to prove herself after being constantly doubted.

An overcompensation.

Perhaps it was a deep loss of the only people that she ever loved, killed—slaughtered in front of her like nothing more than common cattle.

But I know now.

It's from betrayal. Betrayal from the one you let in, even though you *knew* it was a bad idea. It's from the one who made you feel that maybe, just maybe, you were going to be able to live again.

Yes, it's that type of betrayal that will take away every last piece of light you had. Once that happens, there is only darkness.

That and death.

Cat
CHAPTER THIRTY-THREE

Antonio stirs, his brows wiggling as sloppy groans fall from his thin lips. The insufferable man is such a dramatic thing, he can't even muster enough energy to wake quietly.

As if he can hear my thoughts, his eyes peel open to find me, a horrible wheeze escaping his throat.

This coerces a cackle from me, and I blow a long stream of smoke over his frail body. "You act as if anyone else would be here to feed your sick ass."

He coughs, a slow hand rising to wave off the plum of thick smog wafting over him. "I'd hope someone else would have for once. Maybe the reaper. Or I don't know. Maybe my *niece*."

I laugh harder at this, pointing the end of my hookah stick at him. "You are nothing but a detached weakness to her. A horrible replacement for a loving parent."

"I taught her everything she fought them to learn," he retorts.

"A fact. And so, I believe it is also you who taught her to let go of anything that may distract her from the end goal. Ain't that right?"

He coughs violently, his chest concaving with each stilted breath. I roll my eyes, standing to shove another pillow under his head and tapping the bed remote to elevate it a bit more. "I'm. Her-r-r." Another fit of coughs sputter out of him. "Uncle."

I nod, grabbing a glass of water in one hand while steadying the straw to his chapped lips with the other. He takes a few tentative sips, and I use the chance of peace to scold him. "You told her when she was sixteen that you would kill her if you ever found out she lost sight of your plan. If she ever let go of that anger corrupting her insides. You told her to bury it, let it fester, and grow until all she could see was death."

Taking the glass from him, I set it on the table. A heaviness moves over my heart, and I rub at the unbearable ache. "You drilled her into the ground and made her the perfect soldier. The perfect Boss. But what happens to her when the job is done? You're so worried about her coming to visit you but what will be left of her, Antonio?"

Antonio does the only thing he ever does when we have this same conversation and sighs. "If she is meant to lead the Embros family, she will survive. She will find peace in her vengeance and rule how it should have been all along."

As I said, he's insufferable.

But karma is retributive. His second bout of cancer is doing him in, and I think he's madder that it's his own body destroying him and not someone who can later be killed to avenge him.

The poor man is nothing more than a former shell of who once walked the halls. Of the man who held my heart in his strong hands.

After his first remission, he did what he was meant to do, and I mean it when I say he did right by Onyx's parents and made her the woman they always envisioned. But he also stripped her of her mother's compassion, and her father's inherent love.

He instilled fear of failure. Fear of passion and love.

But a part of me hopes the guard, Ezekiel, will be enough. He seems to balance her out—forcing those things I thought Antonio had buried too deep back to the surface. He takes some of her load while letting her remain in control.

He—

An explosion rings out downstairs, and my hookah falls to the floor as I cover Antonio with my body.

The room shakes, pictures swaying slightly before falling off the wall and crashing to the floor. Antonio's machines go haywire, the beeps become erratic and loud. I catch his IV stand, just before it tips.

In another time, he'd make the worst joke about us in such a position, but instead his eyes are wide with a fear I've never seen cross his face. "Onyx."

My head bobs up and down frantically, my body moving quickly to fix him up.

"I'm going. And please, for the love of everything, please don't move." I give him a brief look of warning before grabbing my old satchel from the corner and dashing through the door.

I run the long halls, my old joints screaming as I stretch them to their limits. But I keep pressing forward.

My veins pulsate through my body, the sheer speed of my blood flow burning as fear and apprehension take over, propelling me down the stairs. I force myself to ignore the debris.

To ignore the streaks of blood headed out the door.

To ignore that, despite the broken glass, dozens of red footprints, and the screams of the maid, there's only one body.

I rush to his side, my hands working fast to get out the tourniquet. "CALL 911 NOW!"

The foolish woman screaming her head off jolts, bounding away for what I hope is the damn phone.

I turn back to my dear boy, taking in the jagged cuts. All of them are superficial, only a few needing stitches, but his legs...

"I waastoote."

"Kilo, honey, listen to me. You're in shock." I tie the rubber band around the stub, just above his knee. "You're going to make it. Just stay with me."

I want to scream and ask him who was taken. Where everyone is and what the fuck happened. But he grabs me around the neck, pulling me close as I wind the tourniquet tight. "What is it, Kilo? Tell me."

His light-blue eyes fill with tears, his body convulsing as a seizure begins. But before he goes, I hear him clear as day.

"I was too late."

TO BE CONTINUED....
KING OF RUIN

Acknowledgments

AHHHHH! You made it here. You're not too mad right? I mean, I understand if you are, but listen, *listen*, it will be soooooo worth it. Promise.

Now, I'd like to thank you, my lavish readers, for taking the time and fill it with my words and the characters of Wonderland. They are a blast to write and I hope you enjoyed getting to know them!

There is so much more they can't wait to show you!

As always, I also want to thank my hubs who made this book possible with wrangling the kids and cooking me yummy meals. To my kids for always walking in when I'm writing the spiciest scenes. And to my incredible alphas and betas.

Tasha. TASHA! WE DID IT GIRL! I came to you with a crazy ass idea and said HELP ME MAKE IT HAPPEN! And you did! My first dark romance and I have to say, I'm pretty damn proud. You have unleashed a hungry beast in me that I can't wait to feed.

Garnet, M.L., Matti, Gab, Andrea, Sam, Sophia, Jodi, Lauren.
Ya'll are the offing bomb and I hope you never leave me!

Ya'll helped me shape and mold this story into perfection and I couldn't of done it without each and every one of you!

Thanks to my amazingggggg editor, proof readers, and cover designer. Ellie, Rosa, Cat, and Mackenzie, I don't know how I got so lucky but y'all are incredible. Please stay with me forever and ever and always. Y'all polish my art to a shine no one else can and without you, **sadness**. Thank you ladies!

Again, thank you to everyone! I can't wait for you to get your hands on Ezekiel, because I know you have a lot of words you want to say to him.

About the Author

Lee Jacquot is a wild-haired bibliophile who writes romances with strong heroines that deserve a happy ever after. When Lee isn't writing or drowning herself in a good book, she laughs or yells at one of her husband's practical jokes.

Lee is addicted to cozy pajamas, family games nights, and making tents with her kids. She currently lives in Texas with her husband, and three littles. She lives off coffee and Dean Winchester.

Visit her on Instagram or TikTok to find out about upcoming releases and other fun things! @authorleejacquot

Also by Lee Jacquot

I wrote a couple books before this one! Check them out here!

The Emerald Falls Series

The Masks We Wear

The Masks We Break

The Masks We Burn

Holinight Novellas

Christmas on the Thirteenth Floor